THE
BOOK OF
LEARNING

THE BOOK OF LEARNING

NINE LIVES TRILOGY 1

E.R. MURRAY

MERCIER PRESS
Irish Publisher – Irish Story

For Mick O'Callaghan
and the village of Schull

MERCIER PRESS
Cork
www.mercierpress.ie

ISBN: 978 1 78117 362 6

10 9 8 7 6 5 4 3 2 1

Printed and bound in the EU.

Prologue

The thick, black night hangs heavy with murder. Two figures in a hilltop field edged with woods are silhouetted against the bright moon: one chunky and slow-moving with a cap wedged on his head, the other slim and nimble, hair blowing free. Hands clenched on each other's arms they wrestle, their struggle silenced by the roar of the wind and the storm-tossed ocean.

No one should be in this desolate place at such a late hour.

A shadow comes alive as a creature slips between the gnarled trunks of the nearby trees, too big to be a fox. A crack of lightning splits the sky, revealing an angry, weather-worn face, unshaven and unloved. Why does he race so quickly through the woods? Is he a friend or an enemy?

A second lightning strike shows why the pair struggle: a small handgun. A third flash and one man is down – a desperate cry carried on the wind. 'Ebony!'

1

Most girls wake on their twelfth birthday to the sound of laughter and songs or the whiff of sizzling bacon. They tremble with the excitement of opening brightly wrapped gifts and being the centre of attention. Instead, Ebony Smart was shocked out of her sleep by a high-pitched bleep which droned long and loud, piercing her eardrums like needles. Its callous din signalled to the world that Grandpa Tobias was dead.

Despite the fact that Ebony had sat holding his hand for three whole days, telling him his favourite stories and mopping his sweaty forehead, he hadn't once opened his eyes. It broke her heart that now he would be silent forever. She didn't yet know what had caused his death, but one thing was certain: there was a motionless husk where Ebony's grandpa used to be.

The old man could no longer regale his granddaughter with tales of tugboats in America. He'd never again show her how to steer their little fishing boat around hidden rocks or when it was safe to push forward, harnessing the wind's power. He wouldn't fry sprats with wild garlic, or prune back the lavender bushes, and he'd never visit Swaziland as he'd always dreamed. Saddest of all, the world had lost his smile.

Ebony sat holding her grandpa's hand, her head bowed. It was 10.30 a.m. on April 13th. She was officially twelve years old and truly alone in the world. Her only birthday present was to be allowed to sit with the body of her grandpa and say her goodbyes.

The second hand on the clock in the hospital room hammered like a timpani drum. Her grandpa used to tell her that all over the world, timpani drums announced the most important arrival in any show, from ballet to bullfighting. Ebony's mouth tightened. She hoped that wherever her grandpa's soul had gone to, the drums would be beating for him.

She pressed her lips to his hand. It was as pale as her own, but coarse and cold. Despite her best efforts not to, she began to cry. Closing her eyes, Ebony was back on the sea with her grandpa, forcing their small boat home towards Oddley Cove harbour against a tough wind. As the vessel smashed into the angry waves, her face stung with sea water and her hair stuck flat to her head. She could hardly see through the grey sheets of rain, but she wasn't scared because her grandpa knew the seas.

'When I go from this life, love, I want my last breath to be here,' he'd said. 'I don't want to be dying in no hospital. If I have to bottle it up and carry it down myself as a ghost, I will. You mark my words.'

'I'll bring it for you, Grandpa, in my pocket,' she'd promised.

He'd laughed heartily. 'I'm sure ye will, love.' His craggy face crinkled until the flesh around his eyes hung in folds and his eyebrows jiggled underneath his cap as though trying to break free of his face.

'I don't ever want you to die, Grandpa,' she'd said, cuddling into him as the storm raged around them.

'We all have to go someday,' he'd replied, 'but we're not lost forever. You just have to look for the signs: the glint of sun on the water or wind rustling through the treetops – that's when you know that anyone you've ever lost is there.'

Pulling herself away from the painful memory, Ebony wiped her tear-filled eyes. She'd missed his final exhalation, sleeping at his side. Now she would never get the chance to complete her promise. Her tears slipped off his hand onto the stark white sheets.

'It's OK, Ebony. We'll meet again, you'll see.'

Feeling a tremble run through her grandpa's body, Ebony sat up abruptly. The lifeless face stared back at her. She had heard the words clearly, but his face was grey, his lips motionless, and yet they seemed to have shifted into a slight smile.

'Grandpa?'

Ebony bit her lip and shook his shoulder gently.

'Grandpa!'

A doctor entered the room, straightening the collar on his stiff white coat. He fiddled with the pens in his pocket, then coughed. He'd never handled a death like this before. It was an unusual case; the man's heart had stopped yet none of the hospital's tests had found anything wrong with him. The doctor placed his hand on Ebony's shoulder, trying to soak up some of her sadness.

'My g-grandpa, he's s-still alive,' she stammered, shaking the body again. 'Do something!'

Leaning over the body, the doctor felt the cold wrist and pressed his fingers against the dead man's leathery neck. Ebony waited, barely daring to breathe.

'I'm sorry, he's … gone.'

'But he spoke to me. I heard him. He told me we'd meet again …' Her voice faltered.

'Let him rest now. He's in a better place.'

'At least tell me how he died,' pleaded Ebony.

The doctor shook his head. 'We're not sure yet,' he said. 'It was probably just old age, his body shutting down.'

'But he was never sick!' cried Ebony.

The doctor sighed. The living always tried to cling on to their dead.

'We'll be able to tell you more after we've done further tests.'

As the doctor left the room, Ebony started to weep ferociously. Her grief ricocheted into the pristine corridors where it rattled like a ball-bearing. The hospital's few patients gathered outside the door to pay their respects through the window. An old man crossed his torso in blessing.

'Grandpa, don't go!' Ebony's words were barely audible, entangled in sobs, as the timpani drum continued to announce every second without him: tick, tick, tick.

'Ebony, I'm sorry to say this, but it's time for you to leave,' said a distant voice some time later.

Ignoring the doctor, Ebony slumped over Grandpa Tobias for the last time. Her hair flooded his face with thick black curls, like seaweed trapped at the shore. The doctor gulped. 'A man from the authorities has come to pick you up. He's in the waiting room.'

Ebony frowned and wiped her eyes. She kissed her grandpa's forehead and turned to the doctor, nodding her assent.

'I know this is difficult for you, love. But it'll be all right, I promise.'

'It's OK, Doctor. I'm going.'

There was so much more she wanted to say, like not to call her love – only her grandpa was allowed to call her that. And not to make promises, because how could anything ever be all right again? But the words caught in her throat like fog. Standing tall, as her grandpa had always taught her, she left the room without a backward glance. But not to go, as instructed, to the waiting room; Ebony Smart had other ideas.

2

Back at the cottage, Ebony ran straight to her pet rat, Winston, a gift from her grandpa on her eighth birthday. She took him out of his cage and balanced his fat stomach on her shoulder. Winston clung on with pinprick claws, nibbling at her hair. Ebony chuckled as his whiskers tickled her ear – but the laughter sounded wrong somehow.

Everything in the cottage was how she'd left it three days ago. The living room still shared its warm, homely space with the kitchen and led to two snug bedrooms. The ceilings remained too low and the floors overly rickety. The woody smell of cigar tobacco lingered in the air. The last time Ebony had been here she'd been planning the next fishing trip with her grandpa. Afterwards, he'd gone out for supplies but never came back. She'd received a telephone call from the hospital that night.

Ebony sighed. The suffocating Grandpa-shaped void loomed everywhere: in the wellies near the front door, in his favourite armchair, next to the radio in the kitchen, and, worst of all, on the garden bench where he used to sit and watch the sea. 'It's like learning to read,' he would say. 'You've got to practise every day until it's second nature. The sea tells you stories and secrets if you take the time to read its moods. Just like young girls!' When he wasn't worried about the weather conditions, he would ruffle her hair. When he could sense a storm coming, he'd keep his gaze fixed on the water.

Flicking on the radio to fill the silence, Ebony opened each window just an inch – exactly how her grandpa liked it. He reckoned that the sea air stopped you getting sick. Apart from in the hospital, she'd never seen her grandpa poorly; even over the last few days, he'd been unconscious but didn't seem that ill. She'd never expected to be returning home alone. As her broken promise rose in her stomach, tears threatened to fall, but Ebony forced them back.

She didn't have much time – people would come looking for her soon.

First: fresh water and food for the cats. At the first whiff of meat, all six of them appeared from their favourite lolling places, all fur and mews. As she stroked each one in turn they curled around her legs and purred. Next: the dogs. Ebony headed out to the yard overlooking the woodland and, with two fingers in her mouth, blew a loud whistle. Several dogs appeared, barking and yelping with delight. She herded them into the garden and tipped a whole bag of food into their makeshift trough. As they fed, she listened carefully to the rustling treetops – after all, her grandpa said that's where you'd hear people you'd lost – but the familiar sound only made her feel more lonesome.

'Good boys.' She sighed, bending down to stroke Mitzi, the one-eyed Shih Tzu that her grandpa had rescued as a pup. Mitzi whimpered and pawed Ebony's shin. 'He's gone, but he's in a good place,' she said.

Her eyes went out of focus as tears welled. Ebony blinked them away. Then, with Winston firmly in place, she marched down to the goat field. The goats looked at her dumbly, completely unaware of any change. She hosed water into their trough and left them grazing on the grass. Finally, the chickens. A few handfuls of seed and the late morning feed was complete.

If only she could run this place on her own and make her grandpa proud.

Ebony climbed over the fence and wandered down to the steps that led to the sea, careful to avoid going near their private quay; she couldn't bear to see their little fishing boat just yet. Winston's nose twitched, detecting the salty air. He scurried into the warmth of her jumper sleeve.

Standing on the huge grey rocks, looking out across the ocean, Ebony could sense how deeply the sea mourned the old man. She pictured him lying on the ocean floor, looking up to the surface of the water and smiling at the sun. Reaching into her left pocket, Ebony imagined her grandpa's last breath to be there. Waving her hand as though skipping stones, she released it out across the sea, to be carried on the milky-grey waves and gulped up by the tide. Under her breath she whispered a final farewell, hoping her words would fall to the deepest ocean bed and be buried like treasure.

At the front of the cottage, a midnight-blue car with the number plate 'N1NE L1VE5' inched into the driveway. Peering out from behind the wheel was a shiny-faced man, his grey-blond hair slicked into a V at the nape of his neck and his face as expressionless as a puppet's. Unable to get an answer by knocking on the front door, he sidled across the grass towards the back garden, barely acknowledging the mud that caked his gleaming shoes. As he reached the corner, the man was confronted by a cacophony of snarling mouths, loud barks and vicious teeth. One dog leaped up, pinning him against the side wall of the house with its heavy paws, its angry face just inches from the tip of his nose.

The man lifted his briefcase high above his head without a flicker of emotion. But before he could strike, he saw a small, bony figure with wild black curls hurtling in his direction. The figure turned out to be the girl he was looking for, her skin too pale and her eyes too big. She was dressed like a boy. Her mud-splattered jeans had a hole at the knee and she wore a thick, cherry-red jumper which was fraying at the cuffs. One sleeve bulged heavily.

'You must be Ebony,' said the man.

'They don't like intruders,' replied a young, husky voice, as the girl nodded towards the dogs, 'and neither do I.'

'I don't care what you do or don't like,' replied the man. 'I'm Judge Ambrose and you're coming with me.'

3

Judge Ambrose sat bolt upright on the sofa, directly across from Ebony, fixing her with a black stare. Ebony glared back, surveying the stranger's pinched face. It resembled a vole – all nose and teeth, with sharp, distrustful eyes. The man's hair was as slick as oil and his skin was taut and glossy, as though it had been stretched across a skull that was too large.

After what seemed like a very long time, Judge Ambrose cleared his throat, ready to speak. Ebony smiled inwardly; she'd won the first battle.

'I know this is a difficult day for you, but you can't go running off like that. Everyone was worried,' said the judge, sounding more inconvenienced than worried.

Irritated by the lie, Ebony couldn't help her outburst. 'Everyone knew exactly where to find me. The animals need feeding at the same time every day.' She folded her arms and waited.

'I don't mean these … *Oddley Cove* fools … I mean *us*, the Order of Nine Lives, your own kind.' His tight skin quivered slightly as he clenched his jaw. 'But I take it from the dumbstruck look on your face that you have no idea what I'm talking about.'

Ebony shrugged, feigning indifference, but inside, her mind raced. *Who is this rude man? And what does he have to do with me?*

'Let me enlighten you … I'm the High Court judge at the Order of Nine Lives headquarters.' A slight, proud smile played on the judge's lips, suggesting that she should be impressed. When she didn't react, he continued haughtily. 'Everything about you is answerable to me – where you live, with whom you speak, even what clothes you wear.' He threw a disapproving eye over Ebony's outfit. 'You are now in *my* charge and *I* must be obeyed.'

Ebony had heard about these official types from her grandpa, sticking their vole-shaped noses in where they weren't wanted. When her parents died in a boating accident – their bodies never recovered – the authorities had said Grandpa was too old to look after a baby. His wife had died many years earlier and they said it would be too difficult for him to raise a child on his own. But he'd proved them wrong, and now maybe she could prove them wrong too.

'You could be anybody,' she said coolly.

Judge Ambrose flashed an identification badge, which Ebony instantly dismissed.

'That could be fake. So, if you don't mind, I have things to be getting on with.'

As she stood up, Judge Ambrose fixed Ebony with an icy

stare. She felt a sudden sting in her wrist and cried out in pain. It was as though someone or something held her in a vice-like grip, but when she looked down, her wrist was completely untouched. She wriggled and twisted in an effort to get away, but the grip tightened.

'Stop struggling and it will stop hurting,' said Judge Ambrose matter-of-factly.

As Ebony continued to fight, the pain in her wrist became unbearable. Her breath quickened and sweat beaded on her forehead, but no matter what she did, she couldn't break free. When she grew too tired to struggle, the pain stopped, but her heart continued to pound. *How did he do that?* she thought, rubbing her wrist and trying to keep her nerve.

'As I said, I must be obeyed. You may not understand yet, but you will. Your aunt in Dublin will see to it. She's expecting you later today.'

Ebony felt her whole body tense. His words sounded like a threat, rather than encouragement.

'What aunt in Dublin? I've never heard of an aunt in Dublin.'

'Your father's sister.'

Ebony slumped a little. She didn't really know anything about her mum or dad because Grandpa had always been too grief-stricken to talk about them much. But why didn't he ever mention an aunt? She'd always thought he was her only family.

There was another long silence. It reminded Ebony of the

hospital corridors, the echo of her footsteps as she left her grandpa's body behind.

'I'm staying here. I have the animals to look after and no one can run this place like me. I can take care of myself.'

'That is not an option.' Judge Ambrose's words were so forceful, Ebony fell silent. 'You can't stay here alone. It's the law.'

'I won't be on my own, if that's what you are worried about. I know everyone in the village, and Grandpa's friend, Old Joe, comes to help out. He'll make sure I'm all right.'

'Out of the question.'

Ebony felt like screaming at the man, but she remained quiet and let the anger gnaw at her insides – at least it replaced some of the fear that he inspired in her.

'It's not safe for you to stay. Not without Tobias's protection. We've got to get you out of here. You need to make friends – and quick.'

'I have George. And Cassandra.'

'Are they reliable? Do they live nearby?'

Judge Ambrose clicked open his briefcase and started typing into a small notepad computer.

'Yep. Just there,' she replied, pointing.

Judge Ambrose glanced out of the window, then slammed his briefcase shut. 'They're goats!'

'Yep. But they're my friends and good friends too. Loyal and trustworthy; all the friends I need.'

Judge Ambrose's face darkened, but Ebony wasn't about to stop there.

'And I have my best friend, Winston.' As Ebony lifted her arm, Winston popped his ratty face out from her cuff and squeaked. Judge Ambrose paled. His body shifted and his eyes widened a few millimetres.

'It's OK. Look, he's friendly.'

Ebony shoved the rat under the judge's chin. Judge Ambrose took a sudden swipe at Winston and Ebony cried out in surprise, snatching her pet out of harm's way just in time. As she did, the front door burst open.

'Everything all right, missy?' It was Old Joe, holding a spade in his two hands like a staff.

'Kind of,' panted Ebony. 'Judge Ambrose here is scared of Winston, that's all.'

'Scared, never. Disgusted, yes. It's a rat and rats carry disease. They're vermin.' A vein in the judge's forehead pulsated ever so slightly.

Old Joe and Ebony exchanged glances.

'I'm sorry about your grandpa,' said Old Joe.

Ebony looked at the floor, unable to respond. It was like something hard and cold was lodged in her throat, preventing her from speaking. As though completely oblivious, the judge composed himself, straightened his tie and locked his eyes firmly on Winston.

'I'm sorry, Ebony,' he said, not sounding very sorry at all. 'You have exactly thirty minutes to pack your things and be ready to leave.'

Ebony sat down, fixing her eyes on the carpet until the

patterns danced. Old Joe scratched his chin. 'So it's true then, missy? You're leaving Oddley Cove?'

'I don't have any choice, do I?' she snapped, her hair swamping her face, covering the redness of her eyes and cheeks.

'Where are you off to then?'

'Dublin.' The word stung, wasp-like.

'Well, you'll be missed, that's for sure. Just as much as your old grandpa.'

She took comfort in those words and looked up at Joe's wrinkled, bristly face.

'It'll be all right, Ebony. Don't you worry yourself. I'll look after the animals and this place. Now, you'd better go and pack.'

Ebony hesitated.

'You can come back as often as you like. This'll always be home, ain't that right, Judge?'

Heading out through the door before she could hear the reply – she didn't care what the judge thought – Ebony went into her grandpa's bedroom and pulled his bruised suitcase from the top of his wardrobe. It was covered in faded stickers which showed the countries he had visited and was bound together by strong leather straps. Her grandpa had loved that suitcase and had taken it everywhere. Ebony vowed she would do the same.

Taking it to her own room, she loaded the suitcase with jeans, jumpers and T-shirts. Winston watched quizzically from the pillow. But when it came to fastening the straps, she found she'd packed it too tightly and the buckles and straps wouldn't join. As she tried forcing the top down, a small square lump appeared, sticking up under the leather. Ebony lifted the suitcase lid and slid her hand over the silk lining – there was something inside. Taking out her pocket knife, she sliced through the silk. Inside was a small black presentation box. She flipped its velveteen lid open to find a round mahogany disc gleaming like a polished conker. It had a small ribbon and pin attached to it, like a medal. On the top side, burned into the wood, was the image of a door surrounded by trees and a huge, round moon. Ebony turned the medal over in her hands; on the back she found the words *Presented by the Nine Lives High Court*. Ebony gasped. *What had Grandpa been hiding?*

'Are you ready yet?'

Ebony jumped as Judge Ambrose's voice floated from the doorway.

'Almost,' she replied, glancing over her shoulder at him but being sure to shield the medal from his view. 'I just need another minute or two.'

'Hurry up, we need to get going,' he said and turned back towards the main room.

Only when she was certain that he was gone did she quickly shove the medal back in its box and return it to the lining, before removing some of her clothes and buckling the case up tight. Then, grabbing her small rucksack, Ebony stuffed it with a bag of food for Winston, a framed photo of her grandpa and a carefully labelled scrapbook of every animal she'd ever owned. Finally she reached out of her bedroom window and sliced three cuttings from the rosebushes that grew beneath the ledge. The flowers were rare and special and almost as black as Ebony's hair. When they bloomed, the petals were frilled and unruly. Her grandpa had planted them especially for her and just looking at them reminded her of him, of his great big smile as he lumped manure around the main stem to help them grow. Taking the roses felt like she was taking a piece of her grandpa with her and she knew that, if she looked after the cuttings properly, she could grow several bushes in his memory.

Wrapping the stems in wet paper and sealing them up in a small plastic bag, she carefully hid them in the top of her rucksack. They were her roses, her memories, and she didn't want to share them. After checking several times to make sure the cuttings weren't getting squashed, Ebony scooped Winston onto her shoulder and marched out of the room to where Judge Ambrose was waiting, stiff and silent.

'Let's go,' she snapped, clutching her belongings.

Judge Ambrose flicked his head in the direction of the cage.

'Where is *it*?'

Ebony tilted her head towards her shoulder. Old Joe moved quickly, despite his years. 'Here, you'd best put Winston in his cage for now. Make sure he's safe on the journey. Don't want Judge what's-his-name to get distracted and crash into a ditch.'

Ebony thought she wouldn't mind the judge crashing into a ditch one bit, so long as Winston wasn't harmed, but there was no point arguing.

Old Joe took Winston and Ebony's case and followed the judge to the car. Ebony surveyed the cottage one last time before joining them. She sat in the back seat to avoid having to talk to the judge and hugged her rucksack. As they pulled away, she waved at Old Joe who tipped his cap in reply. With Winston relegated to the boot of the car, she faced a miserable journey all alone.

This was the worst birthday ever.

4

It was almost ten o'clock at night when Ebony Smart stepped out onto the rainy streets of Dublin without an umbrella. The judge was tutting angrily, annoyed by the city's one-way system and lack of available parking spaces.

'You go on inside while I find somewhere to park the car and report back to headquarters. Number 23,' said Judge Ambrose, pointing across the road. 'We can't have you catching a chill.'

Before the judge drove off, Ebony rescued Winston from the boot. Glancing into the night, it was almost impossible to see anything because of the heavy rain cutting through the air at a slant, cold and sharp. The moon was hidden behind chunky grey clouds and the street was aglow with dull orange street-lights. She watched sullenly as the 'N1NE L1VE5' number plate disappeared into the gloom. The drive had been silent and tense; there was so much she wanted to know but she had no desire to ask the judge anything. She had to make it clear that she wasn't going to answer to him. But he hadn't seemed to care and, instead, she was left feeling foolish and lonely.

Crossing the road in the thick rain with the rat cage

clutched to her chest, Ebony's stomach lurched. She walked quietly even though the sounds of the city were drowned out by the drum of raindrops on the pavement. It made Ebony feel even lonelier as she stared up at 23 Mercury Lane.

The imposing building resembled an angry face. Only two of the eight windows glowed with an amber light, flickering in the downpour like blinking eyes. Ebony had never seen a house so big. A willowy figure glided past one of the dimly lit windows. *Could it be my aunt?* she thought.

Wind and rain swirled around Ebony's heavy coat, sneaking up the hems of her jeans. Bells chimed somewhere nearby as a clock struck ten. She sighed. Even the judge would be a welcome companion right now.

'I know, at least I have you,' said Ebony, as Winston shuffled in his cage.

Winston puffed out his fur and settled down contentedly. As Ebony looked back towards the building, she spotted a shadow creeping along the railings. She glanced around but she was alone in the street. Still, the shadow grew and Ebony stared at it, mesmerised. Her breath quickened.

'It's OK, Winston,' she said, 'it's just our imagination.'

Frozen to the spot in his cage, Winston stayed silent. His whiskers quivered and his tail pointed straight. The shadow grew until it became human-shaped and covered Ebony's own. She turned around.

A rough-looking man stared down at her from inside a black hood. He looked like he hadn't washed or shaved for weeks. His eyes bulged, red raw and bloodshot, and his coat was covered in stains. Under the streetlights his skin had a bluish tinge.

'You've returned,' he said, reaching for Ebony's coat sleeve. She took a step back, avoiding his hand. Winston rushed from one end of the cage to the other. Ebony tightened her grasp so she wouldn't drop it.

'I'm sorry, do I know you?' Her voice quivered.

'It's me, Icarus. Icarus Bean.'

'I'm sorry, you must have made a mistake,' she said, her voice firmer and louder this time. She glanced into the night; how long did it take someone to park a car? She could moor their fishing boat quicker.

'No mistake. I've been waiting for you.'

The man called Icarus pulled down his hood. His hair was matted, sticking out like twigs. His eyes gleamed and his thin lips looked pale and mean in the black night. Ebony took another step back and tried to hide the fact that she was trembling.

'I-Icarus Bean,' she stammered. As soon as she said his name, a shudder prickled her bones. 'I'm certain we've never met. This is my first time in Dublin.'

'But you do know me,' he insisted, desperation tinging his voice.

Winston ran to the back of his cage and burrowed into the straw, leaving only his tail poking out. Ebony fought back tears for the umpteenth time that day.

'Stay back. You're scaring me.'

She immediately regretted her words. She knew that animals attacked when they sensed you were scared and weren't people just animals, after all?

Icarus Bean looked into Ebony's eyes. 'You must try to remember!'

The man was clearly insane. As he stepped towards her, Ebony backed up until she was wedged between him and a lamp post. There was no escape. He leaned in and Ebony closed her eyes.

Somewhere nearby, a car door slammed. Ebony's eyes shot open and Icarus jumped. He looked towards the sound with nervous eyes and quickly backed off.

'This won't be the last you see of me,' he said, taking slow, retreating steps. 'I can promise you that.'

Hearing footsteps approach, Ebony shouted 'Judge Ambrose! Over here!' By the time the judge arrived, Icarus had melted into the shadows.

'Why are you still outside?' He looked at her closely, squinting. 'You look like you've seen a ghost.'

'Did you see that man?'

'What man?'

'The scruffy man, with a hood and red eyes; he was just here …'

'I didn't see any man.'

'He was right here. He said he knew me.'

Judge Ambrose fixed his gaze on Ebony. 'It's just your imagination.'

Ebony seethed. *How dare he speak to me like that?*

'You're tired and you've had a shock. Grief can play strange tricks on the mind. I suggest you don't go troubling your aunt with your wild imaginings – now is not the time for stories.'

'But–'

'No buts. I don't want any mention of this to your aunt. She's a sensible lady. She'll not take kindly to storytelling.'

Unable to listen to any more orders, her bones throbbing with anger, Ebony grabbed her case and marched up the stone steps. It seemed heavier than when she'd set out from home that afternoon. At the top, the door was bright yellow and glossy. It had a heavy knocker made out of tarnished brass, adorned with a gargoyle's face – and on the wall there was an old-fashioned letter box showing a snarling lion. Judge Ambrose sauntered after Ebony and bashed the knocker against the door with a resounding boom. The noise made Winston poke his nose out of his warm straw.

'Don't go in yet,' a voice grunted from the shadows.

Ebony looked around and saw two pinpricks of red in the darkness. *Were they his eyes?* She drew closer to the judge, who was staring intently at the door, completely unaware. Ebony willed the door to open. Thunder rolled across the sky, dying in the distance with a low groan. Judge Ambrose banged again. Shivers rippled along Ebony's spine and into her numb toes. Winston sneaked back into the safety of his straw.

'You're not safe,' Icarus Bean called, a little louder this time.

With a thumping heart, Ebony looked at the judge pleadingly, but there was no reaction – it was like only she could hear Icarus's voice. She stared back towards the red pinpricks. A flash of lightning split the sky open, illuminating the street. The red dots were nothing more than reflections of bicycle lights. The rusty old frame chained to the railings looked as though it had been abandoned for some time.

As another bolt of lightning sparked across the sky, turning it white then violet, Ebony leaped up onto the top step. Winston's cage banged off the door, sending a loud twang of metal out into the night.

'You're in terrible danger,' shouted Icarus Bean at the top of his voice.

Ebony couldn't see him, but his words seemed to come from all directions. The hairs on her neck bristled as the door of the monstrous house creaked open.

'Judge Ambrose. Miss Smart. Do come in,' said an invisible, gravelly voice from the gaping hallway.

Ebony didn't need telling twice: she was already inside, panting and clinging to Winston's cage.

5

The hallway was dimly lit and dingy. Its high ceilings made the air chilly and damp. A gilt-framed mirror ran the length of the wall, reflecting the gloom. Ebony could just make out the outline of a tall, bony woman lurking near the door.

'I'd like to thank you for taking charge of Ebony, Mrs Von Blanc,' said Judge Ambrose, extending his hand.

'We all have to do our duty. Isn't that right?' answered the voice from the shadows, ignoring the gesture.

A long, thin face emerged from the darkness. Mrs Von Blanc had a small pointed nose and an angular chin. She wore a stiff black dress, which went right up to her neck and down to her ankles. The long sleeves tapered to her wrists, giving her the appearance of a wintery tree. She wore a grey scarf tied around her head which hid every scrap of hair. Everything about her aunt looked grim, Ebony thought. And sensible, as the judge had described.

Ebony felt a single raindrop drip from her collar and trickle down her neck into the crease of her back. She stiffened but didn't dare move. Goosebumps prickled on her arms. Winston peeped out from his straw but quickly hid again.

'Is she always this sullen?' asked her aunt, nodding in the girl's direction.

'She's rough around the edges, madam, but that's to be expected.' Judge Ambrose lowered his voice. 'She reminds me of you in your wilder days, only she's completely ignorant.'

Ebony straightened her back despite the rainwater running down it and clenched her jaw. There was no way she was like this stiff, spiky woman. And she was not used to being talked about as though she wasn't there.

'I see. Then we shall have to make sure that she's educated quickly.' Aunt Ruby turned towards her niece. 'Well, turn around. Let me look at you.'

Fury rose inside Ebony; perhaps being ignored was better after all. Back home, people spoke to their chickens more politely than she was being addressed now. But she forced the anger down and turned around as requested.

Like her aunt said, she would have to learn quickly.

As she turned, Ebony caught a reflection of herself in the mirror. A sorry, rain-soaked girl stared back at her. Her black hair was flattened to her head in coils and her cheeks were luminous with cold. Her skin looked transparent.

'You look a fright, don't you?' barked her aunt.

Ebony looked at the floor. This was a miserable city and a miserable house belonging to miserable people. She wanted to go home. But there was no one there for her now that her grandpa was gone. She hugged Winston's cage closer to her chest.

'I can see that this one is going to need plenty of discipline. Stand up straight, girl. Did your grandpa not teach you anything?'

Judge Ambrose smirked. 'Right, well, I see that everything is in order. You have a duty to protect and care for the girl. Make sure she is educated in our ways – but don't go spoiling her. And keep her out of trouble. If you could just sign here, Mrs Von–'

In a split second, the papers were wrenched from the judge's grasp and signed. Before he knew what was happening, Judge Ambrose found himself out on the street, the door closed firmly behind him.

After securing several locks, Aunt Ruby attached her eye to the spy hole and waited. Satisfied that the judge had gone, she spun around and whipped off her headscarf, revealing the most luscious shock of red hair that Ebony had ever seen.

'Right, let's try that again without any snoopers around.' She extended her long, gracious hand. 'Ruby Von Blanc, at your service.' Her voice was like corn popping in a tin pan.

Ebony stared, completely stunned. Her aunt's hair flowed down to her waist, as straight as newly ironed sheets. It burned the colour of fire, making her violet eyes sparkle like jewels. Instinctively, Ebony recoiled from the outstretched hand.

Aunt Ruby let her hand drop.

'I'm sorry about being rude and for that comment about your grandpa,' she said, sounding so genuinely regretful that Ebony felt a little guilty for rejecting the handshake.

'You knew my grandpa?'

'Of course. He was my father! And a very good one.'

'He was a good grandpa too,' said Ebony, trying not to let too much emotion show and wondering why Aunt Ruby seemed so unaffected by her father's death.

'Honestly, I didn't mean a word of what I said, but it's the only way to get the High Court off the scent. They look after us, create our laws and uphold them, but they really are far too nosey and I like my privacy. Power can be a terrible thing, and when someone gets as powerful as the judge you can never be quite sure whose side they're on.' Aunt Ruby peeped through the spy hole again, for good measure. 'Here, can you help me out of this horrible dress? I have to wear it to hide the fact I'm still in action. Wild days, indeed … if only he knew!' She spun around, clunking and clattering as she went, revealing a long zip.

Placing Winston on the ground and moving forward tentatively, Ebony pulled the zip down as far as it would go. Her aunt struggled out. Underneath she was wearing a green camouflage-patterned jumpsuit complete with what looked like an enormous tool belt. Ebony stared dumbstruck as the belt jangled with pliers, compasses, stacks of keys and other odd-looking instruments. *Who is this strange woman?* she thought.

'How come my grandpa never mentioned you?'

'He didn't?' Aunt Ruby looked into Ebony's distrustful eyes. 'No, I guess he couldn't. Oh, you poor girl!' She rushed at her niece and gave her a tight squeeze. Ebony didn't know how to respond. She patted her aunt's back in a polite gesture as a wave of longing flooded her heart.

'Now, let me take a proper look at you,' said Aunt Ruby, eventually letting go and pulling Ebony into the living room. As she switched on the light, Ruby Von Blanc let out a sharp gasp and ran to the window, slamming the heavy wooden shutters closed with a frightened look. 'You can't be too cautious, dear. You never know who is watching or when danger is near.'

The words of Icarus Bean rang in Ebony's ears and she wondered what dangers lurked in 23 Mercury Lane. But she didn't have much time to think. As soon as her aunt calmed down, she grabbed Ebony and held her at arm's length under the light.

'Hmm, not bad. A bit paler now, but then you've got your mother's skin.'

Before Ebony could react, Aunt Ruby spun the girl round slowly on the spot, poking and prodding her like a prize cow at market.

'Thin but definitely stronger than before. Not bad at all.'

Paler now? Stronger than before? Why does everyone here seem to think they know me? wondered Ebony.

As her aunt continued checking her over, Ebony tried to make sense of her surroundings. There was a real fire, with flames lapping up the chimney flue. Their bright flickers made the golden leaf pattern on the shutters glimmer and dance.

There was no sofa. Instead, the floor was littered with bean-bags and cushions made from thick, lush materials. Many were decorated with flowers; Ebony recognised pansies, roses, daffodils and irises. A huge urn next to the fire was decorated with lilies; her aunt obviously loved plants. At least they had something in common. Ebony thought of her own garden back in the village and hoped that Old Joe would water the leeks.

Remembering her roses, she opened her rucksack to take them out so she could put them in water. But the roses weren't there. Frantic, she yanked everything out of her bag. Still no roses.

'No!' she cried.

'What's wrong?' asked her aunt.

But Ebony was too distracted to reply. Running out into the hall, she stuck her eye to the peephole to see if she could see the bag of roses on the steps or in the road, but there was no sign of them. Frustrated, she tore at the locks on the front door. Her aunt followed after her.

'Stop!' she said, grasping Ebony by the shoulder and pulling her round to face her. 'Whatever is the matter, girl?'

'My roses!' gasped Ebony. 'They must have dropped out of my bag in the car. They'll die.'

Aunt Ruby narrowed her dazzling eyes. 'Roses?'

'We have to stop the judge and get them back.'

'Roses?' repeated Aunt Ruby, wrapping one arm around Ebony's shoulder and guiding her gently from the door.

'Black roses. Grandpa planted them for me …'

Aunt Ruby took a turn at the peephole. 'He's gone,' she said. 'But tell me more about these roses. Are they frilled, black like your hair?'

Ebony nodded, her blood boiling with frustration. How could she have been so stupid, leaving them behind like that?

Aunt Ruby clamped her hand over her mouth. She pulled Ebony back into the living room, giving her just enough time to scoop up Winston's cage and set him on one of the beanbags as she closed the door.

'*Ebonius Tobinius*? You have some?' asked Aunt Ruby in a low whisper.

'I don't know what they're called. But they're black – they're special.'

'Of course they're special! The crafty old devil kept them a secret from me all this time … How many do you have?'

'A whole bush outside my window at home; I brought some with me to help me remember.'

'Did Judge Ambrose see them?'

'I don't think so. No.'

'This is great news. I thought … we all thought they were gone. Destroyed.'

Ebony wasn't sure how any of this was good news. She stuffed her hands into her pockets. 'Are you sure you know them?' Her face twisted in confusion. 'My grandpa said they were very rare.'

'Of course I know them. Who doesn't?'

Ebony pulled a face but Aunt Ruby looked her straight

in the eye. 'Did you leave all of them in the car? Did any fall deeper into your bag?'

Ebony checked her bag again, then carefully repacked it one item at a time.

'I've lost all of them.' Ebony stared at the ground.

'Oh, dear, that is very disappointing,' Aunt Ruby whispered to herself, as though forgetting Ebony was there. She paced in front of the fire, her long thin shadow flitting across the walls.

A grave feeling welled up in the pit of Ebony's stomach. From somewhere in the hallway a floorboard creaked. A draught sneaked under the door and around her ankles, making her quiver. After a momentary glance towards the sound, Aunt Ruby took Ebony by the hand and led her to a beanbag in front of the roaring fire.

'Why don't you sit down? I'll get you some hot chocolate. It's been a long and terrible day.'

6

Ebony sipped on the warm mug of chocolate and felt a little better. As its welcome sweetness slipped down her throat like velvet, Aunt Ruby whipped a pipe out of her utility belt and lit it with a slim, silver lighter. She chugged on the pipe stem until the tobacco crackled. It didn't smell as nice as the tobacco Ebony's grandpa had used; it lacked the hint of sea air. Aunt Ruby suddenly stopped chugging and pointed her pipe towards Winston's cage. Winston was snoozing peacefully.

'Is that a rat?'

Worried that Winston might be taken from her, Ebony picked her words carefully. 'He's a friendly rat.'

'Good. I like rats. Clever creatures. But make sure you watch him around here. Your Uncle Cornelius is even fonder of rats than I am.'

Uncle Cornelius? No one had mentioned an uncle. Ebony's head swam. Her seemingly simple life was suddenly full of secrets.

'Aunt Ruby, why haven't I ever met you – or Uncle Cornelius – before?'

There was a long pause as her aunt examined the stem of her pipe, before staring into the fire.

'My father, your grandpa, thought it was for the best.'

'To keep me isolated? I thought I had no one …'

'He was trying to keep you safe.'

'Safe?'

'From the city. From your destiny. Who knows what dangers lurk? He was trying to safeguard your future.'

'The city I understand but … my destiny? What does that even mean?'

Sucking on her pipe, Aunt Ruby stared into space, her fingers tapping the pipe stem restlessly. Brows knitted, she seemed to be searching for the right words. Just as Ebony was convinced her aunt was never going to answer, Ruby began to speak.

'Did your grandpa ever mention anything about the Order of Nine Lives?'

'No.'

'Not even once? A passing comment, perhaps?'

'Not that I can remember.'

'So he didn't tell you about our beliefs? Didn't share any thoughts on certain matters that you might find unusual? Reincarnation, for instance? Mystical worlds?'

Ebony searched her memory. Her grandpa had shared many thoughts but none that stuck out as odd. And he'd certainly never mentioned life after death.

'No. Nothing.'

'Then this is not going to be easy,' said Aunt Ruby. 'You'll think I'm mad if I tell you who you really are. Promise me you'll at least hear me out with an open mind?'

Ebony thought hard for a moment, trying to imagine what her aunt could possibly have to say. 'I promise,' she said, intrigued.

'OK, here goes ...' Aunt Ruby cleared her throat, then began. 'You are part of a special, ancient tribe called the Order of Nine Lives. According to our beliefs and customs, we are reincarnated. After we die, our souls go to a wondrous after-land called the Reflectory until we are ready to be reborn. This place holds the secrets of our past as well as our future.'

'So, this Order of Nine Lives is some kind of secret society – like the Freemasons or Druids?'

'Something like that.'

Ebony liked the idea. Ancient things had always intrigued her. Once, she'd hauled in an old, round-bottomed jug in one of her lobster pots. The fact that it was broken didn't matter; she'd spent months searching through encyclopedias looking for a likeness. She was so convinced it was an ancient am-phora that her grandpa had finally taken her to a historian to get it evaluated. It turned out to be a novelty honey jar from Spain, but the initial excitement of the discovery had never left her.

Aunt Ruby smiled, sensing her niece's interest.

'As part of the Order of Nine Lives we each have one body and one soul, which returns to the earth over and over –

until our destiny is fulfilled or we've died nine times without achieving it. Some families, like ours, have always been here – we've been reincarnating time after time since the Order of Nine Lives came into existence; others were chosen to join as replacements for the families who succeeded in achieving their destiny.'

'Chosen how?'

'That, we do not know. The choice lies with higher powers. Either way, we each get only nine chances to succeed at our purpose. Otherwise …' Aunt Ruby drew a finger across her throat.

'So after the ninth time we're not reincarnated but we actually die?'

'Even worse. We are simply wiped out – and every memory of our existence is erased. It's like we never even existed. It's called Obliteration.'

Ebony shuddered. 'So what happens if we do achieve our destiny?'

'Oh, then we reach Ultimation.' Aunt Ruby's eyes grew round and bright as a full moon. She stared at Ebony as though expecting a response.

Ebony shrugged, clueless. 'Ulti-what?'

'Ultimation. Our people are on this earth for a very special purpose; we are part of the fabric of the universe. Our actions affect the equilibrium of everything in existence. We all have a specific destiny to achieve – which is always for the greater good – and once we achieve this destiny, the part of our soul that makes us who we are gets to live as one with the universe. We shed the need for earthly bodies and mingle with every breath of wind, ebb of tide and chip of stone. Our positive energy helps to keep the balance of goodness in the world. Even better, when we reach Ultimation, we get to spend eternity this way with the other members of our family. The other part of our soul, that causes our reincarnation, goes to a new chosen one.'

Ebony's eyes lit up.

'Does that mean, according to your beliefs, Grandpa could come back again?'

'Or he could already be in Ultimation,' said Aunt Ruby, smiling.

Ebony tried to imagine what living forever with her grandpa and never having to lose him again would be like. Her heart fluttered.

'And you really believe all this stuff?' asked Ebony.

'Oh, yes. We all do. Your grandpa was a staunch believer.'

Ebony didn't like her grandpa being spoken about in the past tense. 'If he was, why didn't he ever say anything?'

'Like I said, he obviously thought he was protecting you.'

Ebony scuffed her shoe on the floor.

'So if it's true, and I'm reincarnated, why don't I remember anything from my past lives? Like what my supposed destiny is.'

'Each time we come back, the amount we remember depends upon what happened in our previous life. Certain things happen that we want to forget, other things just aren't worth remembering. Some people remember lots, others forget completely.'

'Can we come back as other people or animals? Like when people say if you're good you come back as another person, but if you've been bad, you come back as a rat?' She glanced at Winston.

Aunt Ruby chuckled. 'No, not quite. You've got the general idea, but we're always reincarnated as the same person. We're reborn as babies, to our natural parents, so the time we return is decided organically. Sometimes it can be many centuries until we're reincarnated; we have to wait for our parents to be reborn and reach child-bearing age first. It's encoded in our DNA.'

'And you say we have nine lives?'

'Yes, unless of course our parents reach Ultimation before their ninth life and we can't be reborn. In this instance, we automatically follow their fate. It's like a Get Out of Jail Free card in Monopoly.'

'And the people who are chosen when the others go to Ulti-whatsit?'

'Ultimation. The chosen people undergo a transformation when they join. Nine Lives souls are implanted into their bodies and the soul fuses with its new body to give it the power to reincarnate. The soul inevitably takes on a little of the previous personality – although our bodies are vessels, you can't completely separate the two – so that's why the people are carefully chosen. They really are quite lucky. We all are.'

Ebony considered her aunt's words. The idea of reincarnation was outlandish, but what about the bizarre incident at the hospital – hadn't she been sure she'd heard her grandpa speak?

'Go on.'

'I think that's enough to be getting on with. For now,' said Aunt Ruby.

'There's more?'

'There's always more. No one can ever know everything, even if they think they do.'

'But Judge Ambrose – where does he fit into all this?'

'He's the head of the High Court. It's an elected position. He's been chosen to lead the Order and we have to obey his rule.'

'Elected by who?'

'That's a good question. Historically, there were one hundred Nine Lives families, and we all voted. But now there are only sixteen that we know of. The others are somehow lost. We don't know if their souls stopped returning to the earth or stopped being replaced for some reason, or if they have just forgotten who they are. Both myself and my brother held positions within the High Court when Ambrose was elected – but we certainly didn't vote in his favour, and very few that we spoke to did either.'

'So you answer to him, but you don't trust him.'

'Other than your grandpa and Uncle Cornelius, I don't trust anyone.'

'Even me?' asked Ebony, wearing her most innocent face – the one she used to get out of trouble.

Aunt Ruby chugged on her pipe and shrugged. 'Trust is something that has to be earned.'

That works both ways, thought Ebony.

Aunt Ruby's face settled into a serious expression.

'The High Court is in charge of us, Ebony, and Judge Ambrose is in charge of them. When it comes to the time when we pass to Ultimation or Obliteration, they sign the final decree. They say whether we can pass through to our eternal realm.'

'So they have the power to prevent it from happening?'

'Exactly.'

'But what happens then?'

'We become suspended for eternity in excruciating pain. As far as we know, the High Court have never gone against the natural order of things – but it's always a possibility. So it's important to at least make them think you are doing what they say. That's all you need to know for now to keep out of trouble. Keep your head down and don't attract their attention.'

'Is that why you pretend to be something you're not? To keep out of trouble?'

Taken aback by the perceptive reply, Aunt Ruby coughed, sending a huge puff of tobacco smoke into the centre of the room. It swirled and danced, forming a crescent moon shape in the air before disappearing.

'I'm involved in certain research they wouldn't necessarily approve of because I'm not authorised for such work.'

'Such as?'

'Such as searching out more of our kind. It used to come under my jurisdiction, but just as I felt like I was getting close to discovering what had happened to the missing families, I was taken off the case.'

'So why do you keep searching?'

'There's an imbalance that needs correcting – there must have been one hundred families originally for a reason, and the others have to be out there somewhere. I refuse to believe that that many reincarnated souls could just die out without being replaced. It messes up the whole infrastructure! But if the Order found out I was meddling, I'd have certain privileges removed.'

'Like what?'

'Like taking care of you. I promised my father that if anything happened, I'd make sure you were looked after and I intend to keep that promise.'

Fully aware of the importance of promises, Ebony didn't question her aunt any further.

'No matter what happens, just make sure the judge thinks you are obedient to him and the High Court.' Aunt Ruby raised an eyebrow and fixed her niece with a piercing stare. 'Do you trust me enough to do that?'

Ebony squirmed in her seat – what choice did she have? 'OK. But is the Order of Nine Lives anything to do with Icarus Bean?' she asked.

The fire flared suddenly at the mention of that name, making eerie shapes flicker and swoon on the shutters. Ebony suddenly wished she'd listened to the judge and kept her mouth shut.

'How do you know that name?' asked her aunt quietly.

'I … I overheard the judge say it to someone on the phone, that's all,' Ebony lied, her heart racing.

'And what *exactly* did he say?'

'I dunno … That's all I heard.'

Her aunt's shadow grew sharp and spiky against the walls as she towered over Ebony. Taking the mug out of her niece's hand, she lowered her voice to a whisper. 'Please, never mention that name, especially when we might be overheard.' Aunt Ruby looked around her as though she feared the place might be bugged. 'You'll get us all into big trouble with the High Court.'

Straightening her jumpsuit and composing herself, Aunt Ruby continued in a friendly voice. 'It's late. You must be exhausted so I'll show you to your room. We'll do the full tour tomorrow.'

Without further explanation, Aunt Ruby picked up Ebony's case and headed out the door. Ebony had no choice but to gather up Winston and follow.

Aunt Ruby was already bounding up the stairs two at a

time, her hair gleaming like a beacon. Ebony raced to catch up. The floorboards creaked as she climbed. Above her, the ceilings seemed to reach to the sky, making the hallway draughty. There were no windows and every door they passed was closed tight.

Ebony decided that she'd be watching *everything* closely around here, not just her rat.

After several flights of stairs, they reached the top of the house and Ebony found herself staring at two adjacent rooms, both with closed doors. Aunt Ruby flung open the door on the left, plonked the case down beside the bed with a loud thump and beckoned for her niece to enter.

'You have your own bathroom,' she said, opening a small door and turning on a light to reveal a surprisingly modern en suite. The edginess in her voice had passed. 'But worry about cleaning yourself up tomorrow.' When Ebony showed no sign of moving, Aunt Ruby flung her arms open wide. 'Come in, come in. This is home now. I hope you like it.'

Stepping into the bedroom tentatively, Ebony placed Winston's cage on the bedside cabinet and looked around.

The room was horrible. It was almost four times the size of her bedroom back home and contained just a few pieces of huge, clumpy furniture. The mahogany wardrobe was so big she could have slept in it and just one of the drawers below it would hold the entire contents of her suitcase. The bed looked too big and too hard. A high sash window took up the left half of the outside wall, the shutters closed and secured with a lily-shaped bolt. To the right of the window, opposite the foot of the bed, was a mirrored dressing table littered with brightly coloured bottles filled with liquids and lotions.

'It's … nice,' said Ebony.

'Does anything feel familiar?' asked her aunt, looking hopeful.

Deep down, Ebony felt an overwhelming urge to try to belong. She took a slow, optimistic breath and eyed every corner carefully but was quickly forced to admit, 'No. Nothing's familiar.'

'What about these?' Aunt Ruby gestured to the colourful bottles.

Frowning, Ebony screwed up her nose. Grandpa Tobias had never been a fan of what he called fancy things. He'd always used scratchy gardeners' soap, which cleaned the dirt from her hands just fine. Still, Ebony couldn't help crossing the room to take a sniff. As she uncorked a garnet-coloured bottle, there was a gentle pop and mist spilled from the neck. The aroma from the hazy vapour was somehow comforting. Ebony's heart lightened as she took another lungful, trying to recall the scent.

'I know this smell,' she said, looking up quizzically. 'It's my roses.'

Aunt Ruby smiled. 'It always was your favourite. I hoped it would make you feel more at home.'

How could her aunt know what her favourite scent was? They'd only just met. *Anyway, it'll take a lot more than rose-scented lotion to make me feel at home*, thought Ebony, *especially since I've just lost the real thing.* She took the photograph of her grandpa out of her bag and placed it next to Winston's cage.

'Will we get my roses back?' asked Ebony.

Her aunt nodded. 'We'll certainly try. We can't chance them falling into the wrong hands. When you have something that important in your care, letting anyone know of it – including the judge and the High Court – should be approached with caution.'

'I don't understand. What's so important about my roses? They're just flowers aren't they?'

'Oh, dear girl, you do have a lot to learn. There are many seeking those roses – the High Court included. And if the wrong person comes into possession of them, it could mean trouble, real trouble. But we'll worry about that tomorrow. Get some sleep now. You're no good to anyone exhausted.'

Staring into her aunt's face, Ebony's eyelids felt heavy. Her aunt's violet irises seemed to swirl invitingly. Unsure whether it was tiredness or the strain of the day, Ebony suddenly found it difficult to keep her own eyes open. She quickly used the bathroom to change into her pyjamas, then kissed Winston goodnight and climbed under the warm duvet. Aunt Ruby tucked the covers around her niece and sat next to her, gently stroking her hair. Ebony suddenly realised it would be the first night of many without her grandpa. She pulled the covers up around her face.

'I know it hurts,' said Aunt Ruby, 'but try to rest.' She rose and moved to the door. Switching off the bedroom light, she hovered in the mild glow from the hallway for a moment. Before closing the door behind her, she whispered, 'We're counting on you, Ebony.'

Too tired to hear, Ebony sank into the huge, squishy bed. The house came alive with noise in the dark: the walls, bricks and wood talked to each other in groans and creaks. Ebony found herself wishing for her own lumpy bed and the whisper of the sea outside her window. In the room next door, footsteps padded on the floor and a window slid open.

Ebony imagined it was her grandpa and snuggled deeper into the covers, yearning for sleep. Then she realised that not one person had wished her a happy birthday. Feeling rather selfish, she pushed the thought away and let herself drift off. There would be other birthdays but there had only been one Grandpa.

7

'Good morning, rise and shine.'

Aunt Ruby held a small pile of clothes and a glass of juice. Morning had arrived too quickly. Ebony's bones ached as she sat up, stretched and rubbed her eyes. There was nothing shiny about the day as far as she could see. Her aunt had pulled the curtains open to let the light in, but the sky was dull and listless. You could hardly tell it was daytime at all.

'I thought you'd like this.'

Aunt Ruby walked over to the bed and handed Ebony a camouflage jumpsuit identical to her own. Opening her eyes and mouth wide with horror, Ebony looked from the bundle to her aunt. *She can't be serious*, thought Ebony. *Nobody in their right mind would like this!* But the proud look on her aunt's face showed otherwise.

Trying to hide her dismay, Ebony climbed out of bed and held the suit up against her.

'Well, what do you think?' asked Aunt Ruby.

Ebony fixed her gaze slightly to the right of her aunt, onto the dressing table's mirror. It was a trick her grandpa had shown her. He said that people would think you were still looking straight at them and it would help in uncomfortable situations. Ebony forced a smile, trying to think how to get out of having to accept the awful, outdated clothes. Meanwhile, she noticed that, despite her uncomfortable sleep, her hair had regained its bounce and colour had returned to her cheeks.

'Maybe I'll try it on later?' she tried.

But Aunt Ruby was having none of it. 'No time like the present, dear. I'll wait outside while you make sure it still fits – it's been a while.'

Ebony opened her mouth to protest, but a blur of movement in the mirror caught her eye. It was as though something was travelling at high speed, like a comet. Checking behind her, there was only the flat white wall above her bed. Yet Winston was poking his nose out of his straw, also staring at the mirror intently.

'O–OK Aunt Ruby,' Ebony stammered, distracted by the mirror. 'I'll try it now.'

She waited until her aunt had left the room before lifting Winston out of his cage. Hoisting him onto her shoulder, she crept over to the mirror. Her reflection moved with her, like normal, but then she noticed: where was Winston? She could feel him shivering on his perch, but there was no sign of him in the mirror.

'It's OK,' whispered Ebony, feeling compelled to move closer. Although fear convulsed her body, she couldn't fight the urge.

The image in the mirror swirled. When it settled, Ebony's

reflection was wearing different clothes. The girl in the mirror was dressed in a long black gown and a strange hood; it was black with long white wings flicking out to the side, like something from pictures she'd seen of old-fashioned nuns. A bloodied bandage was wrapped around one hand.

'My mind's playing tricks on me, Winston,' said Ebony shakily.

Hardly believing her eyes, she stretched her arm towards the mirror to see what would happen, breathing a loud sigh of relief when her oddly dressed reflection did the same. But when her fingers touched the cool, smooth glass, her reflection suddenly jumped back.

Frozen to the spot, her fingers still pressing against the mirror, Ebony watched as her reflection lifted a finger to its lips in a quietening gesture. *Sshh!*

Unable to speak, Ebony's jaw dropped open. She felt the colour drain out of her face but, for some reason, she couldn't look away. Her reflection smiled from behind its finger, and a small, tinkling giggle rang out.

Covering her mouth with a hand to stifle the giggles, the girl in the mirror checked behind her. Her happy smile faltered, quickly replaced with something that looked like fear. A strange droning noise rang out from behind the glass and shadows began to form. They reminded Ebony of Icarus Bean and the hairs on her arms stood on end. The reflection took one last glance at Ebony, waved and then ran away so fast that she soon became just a speck of light. Her comet-shaped blur whizzed around the inside of the mirror then disappeared.

The spell broken, Ebony gasped, automatically shoving her hand over her mouth to staunch the noise, and staggered back. Winston leaped off her shoulder and onto the bed in fright.

'Are you OK in there?' called Aunt Ruby from outside the door. 'Do you need some help?'

'I'm OK. It's just a little tricky,' replied Ebony, quickly hurrying away from the mirror and swapping her pyjamas for the jumpsuit, her back turned and heart racing. 'I'll just be a moment.'

As soon as she had composed herself she called out for Aunt Ruby to enter.

'Well, do you like it?' asked Ruby.

Ebony shrugged.

'Take a look in the mirror!' insisted her aunt.

Ebony pressed her hands into her pockets to hide their trembling. Turning slowly towards the mirror, eyes to the floor, she counted to ten under her breath. When she finally dared to look into the mirror, she was relieved to find that her normal reflection had returned. But she still didn't like what she saw.

The jumpsuit looked ridiculous. The pattern was faded. The sleeves were too short and nipped her when she moved. Just when she thought things couldn't get any worse, her aunt thrust a helmet and stupid-looking goggles in her direction.

'You'll need these too,' she said, placing the helmet on the girl's head with a thwack. 'Now, what have I forgotten? Ha! Of course!'

Ebony stared down at her outfit, avoiding her reflection. There was no way she could wear these awful clothes. When her aunt returned with a thick utility belt, it was too much.

'Aunt Ruby, stop!'

'Wait till you see the finishing touches …' said her aunt as she fixed the belt in place, stepping back to view her handiwork. 'Hmm. It's not too bad.'

'Not too bad? It's too small!' cried Ebony, hardly able to move with the added weight of the belt.

'Maybe you've returned ganglier this time? Perhaps in your last life you were–'

Exasperated, Ebony's voice grew shrill. 'Aunt Ruby – I don't know what madness you're talking, but I wouldn't be seen dead in this.'

Stopping in her tracks, Aunt Ruby's face fell. Ebony was as shocked by her outburst as her aunt.

Taking out her pipe and taking a long, deep pull on the stem, Aunt Ruby heaved a huge sigh, temporarily hidden behind clouds of smoke. 'Madness, hey?'

Mad as a bag of frogs, thought Ebony, but she stayed quiet. Her grandpa had always told her if you don't have anything kind or helpful to say, don't say anything at all.

'You think I'm crazy?'

'No. It's just …'

Her aunt's face was so serious, Ebony felt the urge to laugh. She probably would have if she wasn't so terrified of attracting another weird apparition – if that's what it was – from inside the dressing table mirror.

'Don't you believe anything I told you last night? What happened to keeping an open mind?'

'Reincarnation? A special ancient order and living forever as part of the fabric of the universe? You have to admit, it all sounds like a fairy story.'

'The history of the world is built on stories.'

'And most of them are just myths, legends people believed before science proved them wrong.'

There was an uncomfortable pause. Aunt Ruby scratched at her head. She looked to the window, the floor and finally in Ebony's direction, but she couldn't look into the girl's eyes. Her voice shrank to a throaty whisper.

'Maybe your grandpa was right not to tell you anything after all,' she said, shaking her head.

At the mention of her grandpa, Ebony felt a stab of pain, as though a knife had been plunged into her heart. A bolt of emptiness and sadness shot through her bones.

Don't be sad, said a voice. Instinctively, Ebony looked at the mirror but all she could see was her own solemn face staring back. *Don't be sad*, said the voice again, more firmly – it seemed to be coming from deep within her.

The jumpsuit collar suddenly felt like it was knotted tightly around her throat. She tugged at it, gasping for breath. Her aunt moved to help but Ebony waved her away and calmed her breathing.

'I guess you'd better wear your own clothes for now,' said Aunt Ruby, seizing the moment to escape the awkward atmosphere. 'Keep the utility belt. You'll need that, though it will take a little time to get familiar with it again I'm sure.'

The room swam in front of Ebony's eyes. All she could think of was getting out of the stupid outfit.

Aunt Ruby left the room. 'Come down when you're ready,' she called behind her, 'breakfast is on its way.'

As soon as the door was closed, Ebony tore off the jumpsuit and lay down on the bed, her heart pounding. If only she could be back home with her grandpa, preparing for a day's fishing. Tears spilled down her face. When she was too exhausted to cry any more, she pulled on her red jumper and holey jeans. They smelled of soil, sea and dog fur. After a few gulps of the scent of home, she felt a little better.

'What's going on, Winston?' she said, cuddling him close. 'Aunt Ruby's a freak. I hate this place. I want to go home.'

But as she spoke the words, she knew they were only partly true. After all, Grandpa always said home is where the heart is – and Ebony's heart was broken without him. She had no home.

As though trying to cheer her up, Winston flopped onto his back, legs in the air. Ebony smiled and tickled his belly in his favourite spot. But just as she was starting to feel a little better, he squealed and jumped off her lap.

'What is it?'

The rat twitched his nose and stared at the dressing table. Smoky shadows swirled inside the mirror, growing thick and dark.

'Let's get out of here!' cried Ebony, shuddering.

Planting Winston firmly on her shoulder, she quickly threw a towel over the mirror before racing downstairs two steps at a time.

8

When Ebony opened the kitchen door, there was a huge explosion and two flaming pieces of toast zoomed past her, smashing into the wall and landing on the carpet, cinders trailing behind them. As Ebony stepped into the kitchen, her aunt rushed past and stamped on the slices of toast to put out the flames.

'Pesky toast; it never was my forte.'

Gaping open-mouthed, Ebony couldn't believe how different the house seemed from the night before. It was alive with sizzles and crackles, steam and smoke. Around the ceiling was a rail filled with remote-control toys zipping around at top speed. Low-slung cable cars hung from the rail, dropping bread into the toaster, while helicopters attached by tiny wires flew above it, propelling eggs into the frying pan. In between the two, mini dump trucks carried rashers of bacon to the end of the track where they unloaded it onto a grill pan. Everywhere, wires sparked. Winston scurried behind Ebony's neck, one eye peering out from amongst her curls.

Seated at the table was a small, podgy man with a moon-round face covered in a soft ginger down – he was the hairiest man Ebony had ever seen. He was dressed in a white shirt and black waistcoat with a bronze pocket watch dangling from the chest pocket. His shoulder-length hair was golden and silky, streaked with black. Fluffy auburn sideburns grew on his cheeks like an old sailor's and bright ginger eyebrows exploded from his forehead. His eyes were amber, with long, thin pupils, like a cat's.

'Sit, sit,' urged Aunt Ruby. 'I'll get you some nice tasty breakfast in just a moment. It'll keep your strength up and put some colour back in your cheeks.' Ebony sat down in front of a huge, empty plate. 'Uncle Cornelius, this is the girl we've been waiting for. Meet your niece, Miss Ebony Smart.'

Uncle Cornelius rubbed his chin with a big hairy hand. His sharp nails glistened. He cocked his head to one side and stared at her, without blinking. Ebony stared back. An egg whizzed past her head and, although she ducked, she could feel small blobs of yolk on her curls. Luckily, Winston was fond of egg yolk. She heard his teeth gnash together as he lapped it up.

'Uncle Cornelius, say hello.'

Leaning over with a sulky look, Uncle Cornelius held out a limp hand. Ebony took it, shaking it gently. He made a strange, whimpering sound.

'Hello, Uncle Cornelius,' she said. His grip tightened and Ebony felt the points of his nails pricking the back of her hand. She tried to let go but his nails gripped harder. Ebony yanked her hand away and her uncle's hand dropped to the table with a thump. He threw an angry glance in her direction.

'That's nice; I see you two are getting acquainted,' said Aunt Ruby, slapping two fried eggs and several hot rashers onto Ebony's plate.

The smoky scent wafted up, making Ebony's stomach rumble. Uncle Cornelius smiled a wide, slow grin. There seemed to be too many teeth in his mouth. As soon as Aunt Ruby's back was turned, he reached over and speared a rasher on one of his nails. He chewed it with his mouth open, keeping his eyes fixed on Ebony. She quickly grabbed a rasher and gobbled it up.

'Uncle Cornelius has been very excited about your coming – haven't you, dear?' said Aunt Ruby over her shoulder. As if in reply, Uncle Cornelius speared more bacon from Ebony's plate, wolfing it down and licking his fingers. Ebony cringed as his big tongue rasped against his hairy thumbs. Grease dripped down the front of his shirt.

Aunt Ruby returned to the table with bacon for Uncle Cornelius. He smiled as she plopped it onto his plate. He picked up a slice and nibbled on it daintily as Aunt Ruby stroked his hair. 'You're so good, aren't you?' she cooed. He leaned against her hip, still chewing, and pulled a face at Ebony.

'How about some toast?' asked Aunt Ruby, as another fiery piece flew above Ebony's head.

'No thanks,' said Ebony, chomping on another rasher, much to her uncle's dismay. He looked up at Aunt Ruby and across at Ebony's plate. As the pile of bacon diminished, he began to fidget. He slid his chair around the table a little, then a bit more and a bit more until he was almost sitting on Ebony's lap.

'Isn't it nice that you're getting to be friends already?' said Aunt Ruby. She leaned in to Ebony and lowered her voice. 'He's not usually this welcoming to guests. He must like you a lot!'

Ebony stared in disbelief. Her uncle drew closer still, smiling a toothy grin. When her aunt turned back to load the helicopters with more eggs, Uncle Cornelius lifted his huge hand and slowly reached for Ebony's final rasher. She gave his hand a sharp slap. Leaping up with a howl, Uncle Cornelius collided with one of the cable cars. A shower of sparks exploded across the room as one of them became entangled with a dump truck. A small section of her uncle's hair caught fire. He patted it out instantly, turning on Ebony with a loud hiss.

'Don't mind your uncle,' said Aunt Ruby. 'He got a fright, that's all. His bark is worse than his bite.'

Looking at the sharp, gleaming nails on his hands, Ebony wasn't so sure. She quickly ate the eggs and the last rasher of bacon and swallowed a whole glass of milk. Her uncle paced up and down the room, rubbing his hands over his face. The air smelled of sizzling fur. The wires fizzed and crackled.

'Is there anything else I can get you, dear?' asked Aunt Ruby.

'No, thanks, I'm full.'

Her aunt surveyed the disaster around her. 'We'll order in for dinner. Come, I'll show you around. It'll be a flash tour, mind. I've got to get to work hunting down those roses.'

As Ebony rose from her chair, she decided to try to quiz her aunt once again about Icarus Bean.

'Aunt Ruby, I *know* you said not to mention his name but–'

Her words were cut short as Winston darted out from his hiding place and leaped onto the table, searching for crumbs. Before Ebony could react, Uncle Cornelius had flung himself onto the middle of the table, belly first, see-sawing back and forth on his huge, round gut as he tried to grab the rat. Winston froze. Uncle Cornelius seized his chance and snatched the creature up with both hands, squeezing his claws around the little body. The rat's eyes bulged.

'Uncle Cornelius!' shouted Ebony.

In a flash, Aunt Ruby was at his side. She prised Winston out of Uncle Cornelius's fingers and placed him in Ebony's shaking hands. He ran for cover up Ebony's sleeve.

'It's definitely time for that tour; it'll let things calm down around here.' Her gaze shifted to a snarling Uncle Cornelius, who was rubbing his hands with his bottom lip stuck out. 'Like I say, you'd best keep your eye on Mr Friendly Rat; your uncle can be rather friendly himself!' She turned on her heel and bounded out through the door.

Unable to contain her anger, Ebony glared at Uncle Cornelius. His bronze pocket watch swayed from side to side, casting shadows on his grease-splattered shirt. Ebony stuck out her tongue, but Uncle Cornelius didn't even notice; he was slouched back in his chair with his legs dangling, busy picking his teeth with a fingernail, his eyes half closed.

9

'We'll start at the bottom and work upwards,' said Aunt Ruby.

As she mounted the stairs, Ebony's heart raced. She wondered what she would encounter next. She felt a million miles from Oddley Cove, where everyone knew each other's business and nothing exciting ever really happened. In the last twelve hours, Ebony had witnessed more weirdness than she'd ever seen at home. Strangely enough, there was something magnetic about it. She felt drawn to it like a moth to a bare bulb, and she had a feeling that there was a lot more to come.

On the first floor, there were two very plain bedrooms and a bathroom. There was nothing special about them. Disappointed, Ebony followed her aunt up to the next floor. When she realised the door they were approaching was locked, she hovered expectantly.

'This is your uncle's study,' whispered Aunt Ruby, pulling a key from a bunch on her utility belt. She put her finger to her lips and Ebony nodded. She didn't want to be anywhere near Uncle Cornelius but felt a twinge of triumph as she crept inside.

A large sash window overlooking rooftops and back streets gave the room a dark, austere air. A reading desk filled with maps and globes dominated the room. New and old documents were strewn everywhere, each marked with handwritten notes and colourful stickers. The walls were lined with cases of sailing memorabilia: fisherman's knots, old photographs of sailing voyages and stuffed puffer fish. The head of a marlin stared at her with glassy eyes from above the door.

'Your uncle's famed for his fishing,' said her aunt. 'He loves the sea. That's how I knew you'd get on.'

Fighting the desire to snort with disdain, Ebony moved in for a closer look. Each specimen was labelled and dated, but the dates spanned several hundred years.

'Personally, I hate the water. I have it on good authority that I drowned in a previous life.' She eyed her niece quizzically, but Ebony chose to ignore her. Being in her uncle's study was too exciting an opportunity to waste by listening to her aunt's fanciful ramblings – especially as she only spoke in half sentences and riddles. Sounding disappointed, Aunt Ruby continued. 'I prefer to stay on dry land with books. These have been collected from all over the world.' Aunt Ruby paused near a wall covered in book cabinets, her arms wide open like a game-show hostess demonstrating the prizes on offer.

Each shelf resembled a row of crooked teeth. Ornate metallic lettering on leather-bound spines glinted from behind the glass. Aunt Ruby turned her back and rustled around in a pouch on her utility belt. Ebony moved closer, trying to peer over her shoulder to see what she was doing, but Aunt Ruby was far too tall. Ebony heard the sound of a key going into a lock and, as Aunt Ruby stepped back, the cabinet door squealed open. Winston popped his head out to see what was going on.

'These are very important books and have to be guarded carefully,' Aunt Ruby said, counting them one by one. Ebony found herself drawn to a small, slim volume that was wedged between the larger tomes. The spine read *The Book of Learning.*

She slid it from the shelf. The cover was made from silver metal. Examining the book closely, she found a small design engraved in the top right-hand corner: a key with a crescent moon for a handle and a rose at the end of the blade. Ebony flipped the book over, enjoying its weight. On the back cover, neatly engraved, were the words: *Property of Ebony Smart.*

Almost dropping the book in surprise, Ebony tightened her grip and looked round to see if her aunt had noticed. Thankfully, Aunt Ruby had her nose buried in a thick, dusty tome. Delighted, Ebony tried to peep inside *The Book of Learning* but it seemed to be glued together. No matter how hard she tugged, the book remained closed. Forgetting herself, Ebony growled with frustration. Aunt Ruby, suddenly alerted, slammed her own book shut, replaced it on the shelf and snatched Ebony's book out of her hands.

'I said they need to be guarded, not pried into.'

'It has my name on it! On the back!' cried Ebony.

Narrowing her eyes, Aunt Ruby turned the book over in her hands and raised one eyebrow.

'I think you'll find it has *my* name on it,' she said matter-of-factly. Grinning fiendishly, she stuffed the book onto the top shelf of the cabinet and slammed the door so hurriedly that the glass shuddered. 'Don't go looking for trouble that doesn't concern you. Your grandpa did a good job of keeping you safe and it's up to me to do the same.'

This safety thing is getting annoying, thought Ebony as Aunt Ruby shooed her away, forgetting to lock the cabinet in her haste. *I've survived storms at sea and managed twelve whole years without her stupid help. What does she think will happen?* But the mirror-shadows and the words of Icarus Bean – *you're in terrible danger* – crept into her mind and she let her aunt usher her from the room. With her finger on her lips, Aunt Ruby locked the study door and tugged on the handle. Satisfied, she hooked the key back onto the bunch hanging from her belt. Ebony noticed that an ivy design twisted around the key's handle. As her aunt looked up, Ebony averted her eyes.

'And next door is my room.'

As the door swung open, Ebony gasped. There was a hammock suspended from two huge hooks in the ceiling and a dangling egg-shaped chair filled with cushions. The walls were plastered with sheets of carefully annotated designs, plans and diagrams. It took a moment for Ebony to catch her breath.

'Are you an inventor?' she asked.

'Yes, dear.' Aunt Ruby puffed out her chest. 'I'm a transport and travel specialist. It's a very important position.'

Sounds boring to me, thought Ebony, even though she was drawn to the walls for a closer look. Submarines, motorised unicycles and jet packs were amongst the repertoire, as well as a gun – even though a gun couldn't possibly have anything to do with transport. Another oddity was a strange diagram of a rose made out of some sort of metal. It seemed to have a complicated locking mechanism made up of several layers.

'There it is: my greatest invention yet. I knew you'd recognise it!'

Ebony looked from her aunt to the diagram. It was labelled *Ebonius Tobinius*.

'I'm not sure I do. It can't be the same as my grandpa's roses,' said Ebony.

'Nonsense, child … Look, here is the security system – its code is not revealed, of course. It's most complex – and I'm not sure it matches the original exactly – but …' Her voice trailed off.

There was no point in arguing. *Security system? For a rose?* Ebony concentrated on trying to make sense of the rose diagram. Each layer splintered off into another diagram, but the annotations were so small she couldn't read them – except for one. It read: *Gateway to the Reflectory*.

'Is this why you're so interested in my roses?' she asked. 'Have they something to do with this gateway?'

Busying herself with calculations, Aunt Ruby seemed not to hear.

'Does this gateway have anything to do with my roses?' insisted Ebony.

Stopping in her tracks, Aunt Ruby sighed. 'Yes, dear.'

Ebony waited for her aunt to explain some more, but Aunt Ruby remained silent.

'Do you have a mechanical one somewhere? A prototype?'

Aunt Ruby looked aghast. 'Your roses *are* the prototype,' she said. 'That's why they're so important. They're a copy of an ancient rose that became extinct. I had to recreate the *Ebonius Tobinius* from a fossil. I used the DNA and tried to match the mechanics as best I could with the few records we still have.' A wistful look flitted over Aunt Ruby's face, darkening her eyes to a deep indigo. 'I had to see if the legends were true.'

'*Legends?*'

On long winter evenings, Ebony's grandpa would light a blazing fire and over steaming mugs of cocoa he'd share ancient tales of murder and bravery, love and revenge. Ebony would sit wide-eyed, soaking in the details, imagining herself part of the story. Sometimes her grandpa would make her one of the characters.

'Please tell me them, Aunt Ruby!' cried Ebony, hitching herself up into the suspended egg, legs swinging.

Closing her eyes, Aunt Ruby breathed in and out slowly, each breath growing heavier and thicker until she began to rasp. Ebony began to wonder whether her aunt was ever going to open her eyes and join the real world again. When she did, Aunt Ruby had a faraway look. She clambered into the egg next to her niece.

Ebony closed her eyes and listened like she used to with her grandpa.

'You remember I told you about the Reflectory? Well, it is meant to be a magical place and indescribably beautiful. It's where all souls go when they're waiting to be reincarnated. It's where each soul recovers, storing the good memories and releasing the bad, ready to reconnect with its body for another life.'

Ebony's heart fluttered. She remembered her grandpa sharing a similar story with her once, but the memory was a faint glimmer, almost extinguished. She hoped her aunt's words would reignite it.

'It is believed that, in ancient times, nine guardians could enter the Reflectory at will, to safeguard the souls and make sure that order was kept,' continued her aunt. 'But, sadly, greed set in, and others tried to break into the Reflectory and steal the secret powers of reincarnation for themselves. They hoped to appoint whomever they wanted to the Order, not just those born into it or chosen ones. Can you imagine, with the effect that could have on the world, how dangerous that would be? After much conflict and civil unrest, the Reflectory closed the gateway and hid it from all but one specially chosen guardian. Since then, everyone alive except for that guardian has been barred. The gateway remains hidden until the guardian is reincarnated and chooses to enter. All we know is that the gateway was linked to the ancient *Ebonius Tobinius* rose and an amulet. The roses reveal the entrance, and the amulet somehow unlocks it.'

Ebony let the final words linger, washing over her like sea spray. She could almost imagine her grandpa in front of her, eyes wide with glee.

'What about when the guardian is in between lives?' asked Ebony.

'Things just continue as normal. The cycle of birth and rebirth is out of our control. The High Court have certain powers and responsibilities to keep order, but the Reflectory controls our nine lives.'

'So why have a guardian at all?'

'She is the link between the two worlds,' replied Aunt Ruby.

'It's a girl?'

'Yes, and it is her role to maintain the peace and make sure our past mistakes aren't repeated.'

'And when her nine lives are up?'

'The Reflectory will choose another to replace her.'

'Aunt Ruby?'

'Hmmm?'

'You honestly *believe* this Nine Lives stuff, don't you?'

'Of course – it's part of my genetic makeup, my very existence. I can't imagine what it would be like to not believe! The evidence is all there – even if the records are a bit old and obscure. If only I could find some more of our kind, restore the Order to what it should be. Without access to the Reflectory, we're like magicians who read books about magic instead of performing tricks.'

'The roses … did you ever use them to try to get into this Reflectory place? Find out if it was real?' Ebony's face brightened for a moment, a flash of hope lighting her eyes.

'Yes. Many times, but without success. Then our rose supply ran out. Judge Ambrose was very disappointed with my work and took me off the project. The High Court were talking about revoking my invention licence, so that's when I decided to hide my research.'

'Wouldn't it be lovely if this Reflectory stuff was true?' said Ebony softly.

'Why do you say that?'

'Then my grandpa's soul could be there, preparing for his next life. And he wouldn't be gone forever.'

Putting her arm around Ebony and pulling her close, Aunt Ruby sighed. 'But it *is* true. That's why we keep searching for a way in to the Reflectory and for others of our kind. Hope and perseverance – that's my motto.'

'Is the guardian thought to be alive now?' asked Ebony – it would be nice to think someone could be looking after her grandpa's soul.

'Yes, we think so. But she seems to have forgotten her role.' Aunt Ruby looked at her niece quizzically.

'Can't you help her to remember?'

'We are trying,' said Aunt Ruby. 'But it's not easy when we don't know the answers ourselves.'

Aunt Ruby felt her niece's shoulders slump. She tightened her grip a little to keep her from sliding out of the suspended chair.

'When do you think we'll find out what happened to Grandpa? The doctor said they were doing more tests.'

Aunt Ruby shrugged. 'Hopefully, it won't be long. As soon as I hear anything, I'll let you know. Don't worry, Ebony, we'll get to the bottom of his death.'

The firmness of her aunt's voice gave Ebony hope. Placated for the moment, and emboldened by what they'd shared, Ebony had one final question. 'Do you use that room upstairs? The one next to mine?'

'No, dear, I sleep in here. One room is quite enough for anyone to sleep in.'

Aunt Ruby whipped a pencil out of her pocket and leaped from her seat to scribble on one of her diagrams. The pencil lead scratched against the paper like trees scraping a window in the wind.

'Is it Uncle Cornelius's room then?'

'Uncle Cornelius sleeps in the basement,' said Aunt Ruby. She caught the puzzled expression on Ebony's face. 'It's not somewhere you'd want to visit, believe me. In fact, consider it out of bounds. Why do you ask?'

'I thought I heard someone moving around in there last night. I heard the window being opened.'

The pencil lead snapped with a loud crunch. 'You must be mistaken. That room hasn't been used for a long time.'

'I definitely heard someone walking around and then the window slide up.'

'It's been locked for years,' said Aunt Ruby. 'And anyway, all the windows are nailed shut in this house. They have been for as long as I can remember.' Her eyes grew distant for a moment, but then she jumped, as though suddenly yanked back to the present. She pulled herself up tall, lengthening her back and neck with her head cocked to one side. 'You didn't try to go in, did you?'

'I was too tired,' replied Ebony.

Aunt Ruby's shoulders relaxed. 'I'd say it's probably just the tricks of the night, my dear. Always happens in an unfamiliar house, particularly in one as old as this. They've seen a lot of things, these walls. I often wish they could talk.' Aunt Ruby showed Ebony out into the corridor. 'But I'd suggest you keep away from that room, nonetheless. Now, tour over! I'd better get to work. I'm sorry to do this so soon, but I have to go out for a while on important business. I won't be long.'

'Uncle Cornelius won't be looking after me will he?'

'I'm afraid not; he has to come with me.' Aunt Ruby lowered her voice to a whisper. 'I might be the travel and transport specialist but I can't drive.' She looked at the floor.

Her cheeks flushed so badly, they almost matched her flaming red hair. 'I'll lock the house up – don't worry, you'll be quite safe.'

Delighted to have the chance to explore on her own, Ebony tried to look innocent while her mind raced – where would she look first?

'It's OK. I'll play with Winston.'

'Are you sure you'll be all right? We'll be an hour, max.'

'I'll be fine.'

Her aunt paused, then reached out and stroked Ebony's hair. 'You're a good girl. Right then, it's time for that awful dress again. Give me a hand will you?' As soon as she was covered up and Ebony had zipped her in, Aunt Ruby leaned over the banister and hollered, 'Cornelius! Fire her up!' As an afterthought, she pulled a tarnished silver whistle out of her pocket and added, 'And I've arranged for someone to look in on you – they won't bother you unless they're called. So if you need anything, blow on this.' She handed the whistle to Ebony and headed off down the stairs before Ebony could ask any questions.

Ebony pretended to go to her room, pocketing the whistle, even though she was certain she wouldn't need it. But as soon as the willowy form of Aunt Ruby disappeared down the stairs and she heard the click of the locks on the front door, she rushed to the room next to her own.

Her heart quickened as her hand grasped the cold metal doorknob and twisted it round.

The door was locked.

Never mind, thought Ebony, *this room can wait. I know exactly where to start.*

10

Peering from behind the curtains in her bedroom, Ebony watched as her aunt climbed clumsily into the sidecar of a khaki-coloured motorbike, her long dress catching and snagging. Uncle Cornelius was perched on the bike, revving the engine impatiently, looking like he was going to take off at any moment. When Aunt Ruby was safely wedged in, complete with tight-fitting helmet and goggles, she cried out, 'Hit the gas, Cornelius!' He responded at once and they zoomed into action. Ebony chuckled as she watched them ride away. For someone trying to keep a low profile, her aunt certainly made enough noise.

Within moments, Ebony was at the door of her uncle's study. She'd forgotten that it was locked. Grunting, she kicked the door.

Hurriedly, she returned to her bedroom and pulled out the old utility belt her aunt had given her. It jingled and clunked noisily as she strained to lift it. How or why her aunt expected her to wear it, she had no idea. Placing the belt on the floor as carefully as she could, Ebony pulled out the contents from one of the pouches with fumbling fingers – it was all junk! There was a rusty spanner, several small brass picks, a compass, an empty tin and some strange tools of a type that she hadn't seen before. Then her luck changed as the next pouch revealed a bunch of keys. About twenty were jammed onto the keyring, leaving hardly any spare ring at all. She thumbed through the keys one by one. They came in all shapes and sizes, covered in varying degrees of rust. After several rejects, she spotted the ivy pattern she'd been looking for and ran her finger along the leaves. Bingo!

Putting Winston in her sleeve, Ebony raced down the stairs. With a little jigging, the lock on the study door clicked open. Thief-like, she crept into the musty room, hoping her aunt hadn't been back inside to lock the book cabinet. A mild shiver tickled her neck and she checked behind her. The room was empty but she felt as though someone was watching. As she tugged at the cabinet door, a small spider fell onto her arm, making her jump.

'Me, scared of a spider?' Ebony laughed nervously. 'Who'd have thought it, eh, Winston?'

Winston wiggled inside her sleeve as though he understood, making Ebony laugh harder. The sound lightened the atmosphere and gave her the confidence she needed to keep going.

The silver book glinted on the top shelf. Coaxing Winston out onto her uncle's desk, Ebony wheeled the big leather chair over to the cabinet. She climbed up and pulled the book from where her aunt had tried to place it out of reach. Jumping down, she sat at the desk, tracing the engraved lettering with her finger.

'See, Winston? Property of Ebony Smart. I knew it! Didn't the judge and my aunt say I needed educating? *The Book of Learning* sounds just the place to start.'

Winston sank down and hid his face in his paws. Then his nose twitched and he started to scurry round the desk, sniffing the various items. Finding a small crust of bread on a plate, he settled himself down for a feast.

'It's a good job I'm not relying on you to help me figure out how to open this,' said Ebony, stroking her rat's head before returning to the book.

Despite its small size, the book was weighty. She tried to open it but, even though she pulled with all her might, it wouldn't budge. Ebony turned the book over and over in her hands. Around the edges, a slight seam and a long, fine hinge were visible. *It's definitely meant to open*, she thought. But digging her nails in didn't work either.

As she poked around the desk, looking for something that might help, all Ebony could find was an endless stream of papers, maps and manuals. Exasperated, she tried banging *The Book of Learning* on the table. Still nothing. Winston, having finished his bread crust, waddled over to see what the fuss was about. He pitter-pattered over an open atlas and nibbled on the corner of a map.

'Winston, don't eat that. We're not meant to be in here!'

Again, Ebony felt as though eyes were upon her and her

skin prickled. She checked over her shoulder. Everything was still in place and, other than Winston, she was completely alone. But she couldn't shake the feeling of being watched. Undeterred, Winston continued chomping on the map. His teeth had just begun to take chunks out of the coast of Africa when Ebony snatched him up.

'Let's see if you can help after all. You've got just as much chance of figuring this out as I have.'

She set Winston down on the book. As soon as his paws touched the metal, his fur bristled. He let out a high-pitched yowl and bared his teeth. Ebony jumped up from the chair, the hairs on her own arms standing on end. Winston leaped from the table, his legs spread wide as he glided through the air, landing on Ebony's open hand. He clawed his way up her forearm and hid in her hair.

'It's OK, Winston,' said Ebony, looking around her. 'It's just a book – a silly book. There's nothing to worry about.'

Feeling Winston's heart pounding hard and fast against the back of her neck, Ebony reached around to try to stroke him. Winston flinched.

'Come on, let's give you a cuddle. It'll be all right in a – Ouch! Winston!'

As Winston bit down hard on Ebony's finger, a sharp pain ran through her knuckle. She pulled her hand away. A drop of blood oozed its way out of the cut. She sucked on her finger. Still more blood. Winston's claws were digging in her hair. D-dung, d-dung, d-dung beat his heart. Ebony inspected the wound. It was pretty deep and would take a while to stop bleeding. She rummaged around on the desk and found a scrap of blank paper which she wrapped around the cut like a bandage. Then Ebony returned to the book – but no matter how many times she flipped it over or turned it around, there was no sign of how it unlocked.

'Just open,' Ebony growled, placing her lips close to the seam. Then she shook it.

Frustrated, she slammed the book down, her hands spread on the cover. Her finger was really sore now. Blood seeped into the makeshift plaster, spreading into red butterfly wings. A blob of crimson gathered on the paper and dripped off onto the book cover.

As the blood continued to drip, Ebony realised that she'd better clean her finger properly; although Winston was her friend, he was still a rat and rats carried germs. As she stood up to head for the bathroom, a loud springing noise stopped her in her tracks. She turned and froze to the spot.

The book lay open on the desk.

Lying flat on the table, the inside cover showed her name at the top in an elegant script:

Ebony Smart

Below it was a list of numbers:

857	869
1057	1069
1514	1526
1654	1666
1745	1757
1826	1838
1859	1871
1929	1941
2003	2015

The title page to the right was blank.

'What does this mean, Winston?' she said aloud, taking comfort in the sound.

Winston stayed hidden in her curls, well away from the book.

Using the hand that wasn't bleeding, Ebony flicked through the pages but found that they were all blank.

'What are you meant to learn from an empty book?' She sighed, frustrated.

Turning back to the inside cover, Ebony blinked, then leaned in. In the centre of the right-hand page there was now a drawing of a closed eye.

'That wasn't there before!' she said, voice trembling.

The eye opened.

Ebony recoiled, but when nothing happened she cautiously leaned closer again.

Suddenly the eye blinked. Then its pupil began to glow and a bright beam shot out.

Ebony jumped, but quickly recovered. The beam began to expand and move, like a spotlight, searching her out. Rooted to the floor, she couldn't tear her eyes away from the light, which was growing, illuminating the ceiling. A vicious wind burst from the book, carrying with it a hundred unhappy voices.

'Who dares to disturb us?' wailed the wind, brushing against Ebony's skin and whipping her hair out behind her. Terrified, Ebony covered her ears. Winston dug his nails deeper into Ebony's neck, his heart almost bursting out of his fur. Very soon, the whole room was engulfed in light, and the glare was so powerful she had to close her eyes.

'Stop, please,' Ebony called out.

'Ebony, is that you?'

The voices began to sing her name over and over, and the wind continued to blow, tangling her hair. Ebony felt herself being shoved backwards, away from the book. Instinct told her to grab on to its cover. As the wind fought against her, the voices screeched in her ears, calling her name and begging her not to let go. She clung on, but her fingers started slipping; the book was getting away.

A loud bang from downstairs made Ebony jump; her aunt and uncle must be back! The light, wind and voices disappeared instantly – but the book remained.

Instinctively, Ebony slammed the cover shut and shoved the book into the back of her jeans. Pulling her jumper down to hide it, she climbed up on the chair and straightened the books on the shelf to try to disguise the gap. Quickly returning the chair to its original spot, Ebony fled the room as quietly as she could. A quiet skulking sound shuffled up the stairs and a shadow climbed along the walls. It had a long body and a bulbous head – like the shadow of Icarus Bean. Ebony flattened herself against the wall in fear, trying to quieten her breathing as much as she could. The blood pumped in her ears as the figure drew closer.

Ebony waited …

Out leaped her aunt, holding the flowery urn from the living room high above her head.

'Goodness, Ebony, you gave me a fright. I thought you were …' Her voice trailed off, mingling with the silence of the stairwell.

'Sorry, Aunt Ruby. I–I was just heading to the kitchen to look for some antiseptic.'

Her aunt looked at her niece quizzically. She spotted the bloody finger.

'What happened?'

'Winston,' said Ebony miserably.

Her aunt took a closer look. The makeshift bandage dropped to the floor.

'It looks pretty deep. I'll get you a plaster.'

Ebony's cheeks burned a deep damson. 'Don't bother, it's not as bad as it looks. I'll just give it a wash. I've survived worse.'

She edged her way to the stairs, careful not to move too fast in case the stolen book became dislodged, and headed up to her room. Her breathing was fast and shallow.

Aunt Ruby watched her go. She picked up the scrap of bloody paper. In the corner, the letter C was lightly printed in an elegant curlicue script. It was Cornelius's headed paper. She crept over to the door and, as soon as Ebony disappeared up the stairs, tried the handle. The door was unlocked. Aunt Ruby closed her eyes and smiled.

'That's my girl,' she whispered. 'Maybe this time the legends are right about you, after all.'

11

No matter what she tried, Ebony could not coax Winston from his straw bedding. As soon as they'd reached their bedroom, he'd scurried straight up the bedpost, along the bed to the bedside table and into his cage, his bright eyes peeping out of gaps in his straw.

'It's OK, Winston,' said Ebony. 'There's really nothing to worry about.'

But Winston hung his head and stayed cocooned in the fluffy warmth. Ebony stroked him, but he cowered when he saw the wound on her finger. His whole body shook.

'You're worried about that? Don't be – I forgive you,' said Ebony, holding up the cleaned finger to show him it was OK.

Winston relaxed a little. Ebony kissed her finger and laid it on his head before returning to the stolen book. The engraved words *Property of Ebony Smart* glinted at her as she turned the strange item over in her hands.

'The voices – they were calling my name. It sounded like they wanted me to help them.'

As she set the book down, she admired the engraving of

the ornate key. Could the rose on the detail be linked to her own? The thought, as silly as it seemed, drove her on.

'I have to try to open it again – just one more time – in case I'm right. It may be gruesome, Winston, but I think this is what made it open.'

As she spoke the words, Ebony squeezed the cut on her finger. A tiny drop of blood formed on the surface. She wiped it on the cover but there was no response. She squeezed harder, until a sizable red droplet formed and plopped onto its target. Her blood sat on the silver case but still nothing. Winston popped his head out of the straw.

'This is ridiculous! It's not working. But I was certain …'

Winston sat up on his hind legs. Then he jumped up and hung from the roof of his cage with his front paws. He swung his body until he could grasp the top of the cage with all four legs and then climbed along to the opening and hauled himself out. As he sat panting, Ebony stared at the silver cover, willing it to open.

'Why isn't it working? Stupid contraption!' Ebony growled.

Winston ran over to Ebony and nuzzled her hand before slipping underneath it and onto the book. His body quivered as he touched the cold, hard metal. He dipped his paw in a bit of blood that wasn't yet dry and stumbled on three legs to the edge of the silver binding. He wiped his bloodied paw on the corner engraving. The book sprang open and Winston squealed as he was catapulted through the air, smashing into the wall. His flattened body slid down it and he landed with a soft thump.

'Winston!' Ebony cried, snatching him up at once and stroking his head. 'Are you OK? Oh, Winston!'

Winston opened his dazed eyes and seemed to wink. Relieved, Ebony placed him on her lap and returned to the unlocked book.

'So the blood needs to touch the engraving – the key unlocks the pages? Aunt Ruby was right; rats *are* terribly clever.'

Winston blinked and moved closer, limping slightly on his front paws. Ebony frowned as she studied the change in the pages.

The information on the inside cover was the same, her name at the top and the numbers below, but the page with the eye had turned dry and the colour of tea. She could still see the eye, but it was clear the page had nothing more to offer. It crackled like tree bark and smelled of damp autumn leaves as Ebony held it up to her nose. In the centre of the page, the static open eye stared back at her. Below it were new words:

The Order of Nine Lives bids you welcome. You may enter.

Hands trembling, Ebony turned the page.

At first, it was blank, like before. But then the page shimmered, as delicately as meadow grass in a breeze, and letters began to form. The writing was curled and beautiful. The fluid words danced across the page, mesmerising Ebony so she couldn't look away:

Once upon a time, in ancient lands, when the secrets of creation were honoured without question …

Knowing that an ellipsis meant there was more to come, Ebony waited. But she was not prepared for what happened next. Before her eyes, the three dots multiplied to twenty and each grew a head, arms and legs and climbed down from the sentence. Ebony gasped as they started to dress in costumes like actors, most with long white robes and nine in shimmering grey. A lush, green meadow appeared below a swirling, silver-grey mist and, as soon as the figures joined the scene, the story continued:

… our people lived side by side with ordinary humans, in harmony with the universe.

The little robed figures settled in the meadow underneath the swirling, glittering mist, playing happily. Winston stared at the image before him. Ebony couldn't break her gaze either and she gripped the book more tightly as she watched the scene unfold.

The tiny figures multiplied, but every now and again one would fall. Ebony watched as the ones in white were buried, but when any wearing grey fell, a shimmering silver thread would drop from the sky, wrap itself around the fallen figure and haul it up above the mist into a sky world, where it would remain suspended for a time. Not long after, it would abseil back down and rejoin the meadow.

'I think that's meant to be the Reflectory my aunt was talking about. The place where souls go. The figures in grey must belong to the Order,' said Ebony, so caught up in the story that she'd stopped wondering how it could come alive on the page.

Winston patted the book, as though eager to see more, and Ebony quietened.

There were always one hundred Nine Lives families, and from nine of these families came a guardian who could enter the Reflectory at will, to make sure that order and balance was maintained, honouring the pact that has existed from the beginning of time between our people and everything else in creation.

Nine of the figures in grey sprouted ivy headdresses, marking them as the guardians.

But over time, as centuries passed, our people grew more inquisitive. They all wanted the knowledge of how to get into the sky world; they all wanted to see what was in store, where their souls would recuperate. Our people grew envious. They turned angry and tried to force their way into the sky world.

On the page, the grey figures began to stare upwards. One constructed a ladder from rope. It climbed up, trying to break into the silver-grey sky world, but the mist swirled and shook, repulsing the attempted intruder.

'This doesn't look good, Winston.'

Failing to break through, the rejected figure turned amber, then flame-red with rage. In turn, some of the souls in the Reflectory began to turn red too, furious at the threat of invasion, at the threat of changing the order of things, the very nature of existence. Ebony could feel the heat coming off the page.

In turn the souls grew angry. To protect the ancient ways, the sky world let these angered souls keep their memories when they returned to the earth. With their memories intact they sought to punish those who threatened the order of things and, as a result, fighting broke out, resulting in many casualties. But while the fighting was in full force, one of our tribe who was not a guardian finally managed to break into the sky world.

Together, Ebony and Winston watched as fighting broke out and an intruder sneaked into the Reflectory. Instantly the silver-grey sky shattered into millions of particles, expelling the intruder.

As our ancestors turned on each other, a young female guardian tried to restore peace. But she was murdered and the sky world wept and turned away from us all. For decades, the universe plagued the earth with floods and storms, disease and famine, as the sky world mourned her loss. The only thing that could save us was her precious soul; in return for trying to restore peace, the Reflectory honoured its duty to nurture and prepare her soul for her next life. Meanwhile, on earth, our people were punished and they suffered, but the humans suffered also. They knew it was our fault the universe had turned against us, and this created a rift. Our people had to go into hiding. We could no longer live openly as part of the Order. The soul of the murdered guardian became our only hope.

Ebony spotted a robed figure with a golden ivy crown lying on the floor of the Reflectory. Winston crept closer and squealed. Leaning in, Ebony froze, eyes bulging. The face – tiny though it was – looked like her own! Sitting back, short of breath, Ebony kept her distance as she watched the rest of the story unfold.

As the girl's soul recovered, the anger in the sky world healed. Before she returned to the earth, the girl pleaded with the sky world to honour the ancient pacts, and they struck a bargain: if she safeguarded the security of the Reflectory, the sky world would keep its ancient promises and honour the old ways, keeping equilibrium in the universe. The sky world would only agree if she – in each of her nine lives – acted as the sole guardian, her position to be replaced by a chosen one when she reached Ultimation. The deal was sealed with the presentation of an amulet to the girl, the only thing that would allow access to the Reflectory – but the sky world warned that if any part of the pact was broken, it would bring terrible calamity. The world as we know it would end, all happiness would be forgotten and life would be shrouded in pain, misery and darkness for all. The girl agreed and became the guardian of the Order, maintaining the equilibrium between our people, humanity and the sky world – safeguarding not just our ancient ways but the future of everything in existence.

On the page, the shattered mist particles returned, forming bricks which began to overlap, one by one, until a huge wall was built. Ivy threaded its way in and around the brickwork, and trees sprang up, forming a dense forest. The sky world could no longer be seen. The figures in the meadow – all wearing completely different clothes now, in an array of colours – returned to a state of calm and went about their business happily. Sometimes, a figure would die and the silver thread would drop from the sky then pull them up behind the sky wall, but you could no longer tell who was part of the Order and who was human. And, noticed Ebony, something else changed: some of the souls stopped returning to the earth. She assumed they had reached Ultimation.

Once again, some amongst the chosen families grow restless. We must learn from our ancestors: we must trust in our guardian. If we break our pact and infiltrate the sky world, then the world as we know it will end. It will become a desolate place and the human race will die out. That is why you must use this book to keep our people safe. The Order of Nine Lives must be protected.

'Winston, this must be one of the rare records that Aunt Ruby was talking about. If only Grandpa was here; he'd have loved to see the legend of the Reflectory in action!'

Winston nuzzled Ebony's hand with his nose. She picked him up and cuddled him tightly, her eyes closed to quell the tears welling in her eyes. When she opened them again, she watched as the two worlds faded away. The little figures scrambled together and took a bow. Then they ran towards each other, forming letters on the page. By the time they were all in place, the words read:

TO LIVE, FIND THE MURDERER AND REVEAL THE TRUTH.

Ebony let *The Book of Learning* fall to her lap and rubbed her eyes. *What murderer? Reveal what truth and how?*

Ebony had been brought up to believe that through hard work she could achieve anything. She was used to taking control of a situation and seeing it through. But things were different here. She'd been in Dublin for less than twenty-four hours and she had no idea where to turn. Her head ached. 'I wonder what the person who wrote this book looked like,' she said quietly to herself.

A warm wisp of air brushed her skin, making it pucker. A faint smell of roses wafted in the room and the book's pages flapped. Suddenly, the book began to shimmer and a tiny sketch of a fire appeared on the page. The orange-yellow flames intensified and she could hear the kindling splutter and crackle. She poked the drawing just to make sure the fire wasn't real. As soon as she touched it, flames leaped off the page, almost reaching the ceiling and lighting up the whole room. Eyes narrowed against the searing heat, Ebony stared into its white hot centre.

In the middle of the flames was an image of herself, wide-eyed, open-mouthed and dreadfully pale; only she wasn't in her own clothes, nor was she in a long white gown or ivy headdress. This time, she wore a short brown tunic fastened with a round wooden clasp. An animal fur hung in loose folds around her shoulders and a gold band crowned her head. Ebony looked down at her own clothing and gasped: over her own clothes, she appeared to be shrouded in a translucent brown fur. As she slammed the book shut, everything went black.

12

'Here, drink this.'

The voice was familiar but it sounded distant. When Ebony came to and could finally focus, she found her aunt standing over her.

'Are you OK, dear?'

Aunt Ruby sounded terribly concerned. Ebony nodded.

'What happened?' she asked.

'We heard a thud. By the time I got here, you were out cold.' Aunt Ruby placed a hand on her forehead. 'You've got a slight temperature.'

Remembering the image in the fire, Ebony searched around her. There was no sign of the book.

'If you're looking for Winston, he's in his cage. He had a bit of a fright, so I put him in there to recover,' said Aunt Ruby.

Ebony felt hot and weak; but she was pleased *The Book of Learning* had remained undetected. Realising that she hadn't been outside at all since arriving, she stuck out her bottom lip and blew upwards, trying to cool her face.

'Can we open the windows?'

'I'm afraid not, dear. Remember, all the windows are nailed shut in this house. See?'

Aunt Ruby crossed to the window and pushed on the frame to demonstrate. It was stuck fast.

'But I heard the windows in that room open last night,' said Ebony, pointing to the adjoining wall. 'I'm certain I did.'

'Like I said, that room's not been used for a very long time,' replied Aunt Ruby, shaking her head. Noticing the covered mirror, she took a step towards it. 'What a strange place to leave a towel,' she said, reaching out.

'No! Leave it!' cried Ebony in alarm. Registering her aunt's shocked expression, she softened her voice. 'I mean, please leave it. You've done enough for me already. Right now, I just need some air.'

'OK,' said Aunt Ruby, stepping away. Despite sounding calm, she twitched and quivered, glancing between the mirror and the window. 'I suppose you're not used to being cooped up indoors like this. There's a park just around the corner.'

'Sounds perfect.'

'Get ready then, dear. We'll leave in five minutes.'

Ebony nodded. As her aunt left the room, Winston climbed out of his cage and down the leg of the bedside cabinet, under the bed. He squeaked loudly. Ebony peeked underneath. Winston was sitting on the strange book – she had no idea how it had got there but she was pleased to have found it.

'You're the best friend a girl could have, Winston,' said Ebony.

She reached for the book, dust from underneath the bed covering her sleeves. She wiped it away hurriedly before stuffing the book into her rucksack. Winston peered up at Ebony from amidst the dust balls.

'You wait here, Winston,' she said, picking him up and placing him on her pillow. Winston licked his fur clean, coughing and spluttering in between licks, before sinking happily into the pillow's folds. 'I'm going to see if I can figure these numbers out.'

Winston twitched his nose and flicked his tail. Slinging the rucksack on her back, Ebony raced down the stairs. Aunt Ruby was waiting in the living room in her long black dress.

'Aunt Ruby, would you mind if … if I went alone?'

'Alone? But what if you have another turn?'

'I'm feeling much better, I promise. I just need some air. I'll go see the flowers and trees in the park. That'll perk me up, I'm sure. Anyway, I should start finding my way around if this is going to be home.'

She pulled her sweetest, most innocent face. Aunt Ruby smiled.

'Well, I guess the park *is* just around the corner. Promise me that you won't go too far and that if you feel ill you'll return straight home.'

Ebony rolled her eyes, but secretly, it was nice to have someone care. Back home she could roam the fields and woods to her heart's content; she would often stay out all day, enchanted by the beautiful cornfields and views over the Atlantic. But her grandpa would still worry when she was going to new places. Having her aunt looking out for her made it feel as though perhaps her grandpa was still there in their cottage and this was just a holiday. He'd be reading the shipping forecast and chugging on his pipe with a steaming cup of tea, waiting for her. The thought made her both happy and sad at the same time.

'I promise.'

'Wait! I have something you'll need.'

Her aunt rushed off and returned with a city map with the park marked. The map was also covered with various hand-drawn Xs.

'This one shows home,' she said, pointing at the smallest X. She traced the route from the house to the park with her finger. 'The other Xs are decoys in case the map falls into enemy hands. So make sure you remember which one is the real one. I don't want you getting lost.'

Ebony surveyed the map: it was a tourist edition with pictorial representations for key monuments and museums. One in particular stood out – the National Library on Kildare Street – the perfect place to study her book undetected. Ebony smiled; it was nearby and she could take a shortcut through the park.

Aunt Ruby handed Ebony a set of five sparkling house keys: one for each lock.

'These are yours to keep. Come and go as you please, but be careful, dear. The city's very different to Oddley Cove. Trust no one and keep to the busy streets.'

Ebony raised her eyebrows; she didn't need telling twice. The only person she really trusted was Old Joe and he was several hours' drive away.

The slam and bang of several locks being opened interrupted Ebony's thoughts. After surveying the street through the peephole and unbolting the door, Aunt Ruby pointed Ebony in the right direction and watched from the top step of 23 Mercury Lane until she reached the corner.

In the dim spring daylight, everything looked completely different. With nowhere for shadows to lurk, the street was spacious and welcoming. The house looked just like all the other Georgian buildings beside it – tall, flat and beige-bricked – only most of those seemed to have been turned into offices. The only thing Ebony recognised was the bike secured to the railings; she shuddered, remembering Icarus Bean, the way his shadow had come from nowhere. She looked back and waved to her aunt, pleased that she was still watching.

As soon as she turned the corner, Ebony spotted the tall iron gates of the park. The blossom on the trees looked so inviting that Ebony's heart leaped and she quickened her pace. As she reached the entrance, rain began to drizzle. A small round fountain with three lady statues in the middle guarded the main path into the park. A tall, wiry figure in a grey overcoat and pulled-down trilby came up close behind her. Ebony stopped at the fountain to let the stranger pass, but his movement seemed familiar. *I'm letting my imagination run away with me*, she thought, but she lingered anyway. By the time Ebony read the inscription on the fountain, the figure had disappeared. Drizzle had become huge droplets of rain, turning the park into a wonderland of smells and colours.

Walking along the pathway, sheltered by trees, Ebony gulped in huge mouthfuls of sweet, rain-soaked air. Robins, sparrows and magpies picked at the undergrowth for juicy worms. There was no one around but Ebony still checked behind her every time she heard a rustle in the undergrowth.

'I'm turning as paranoid as my aunt,' she said out loud, to make herself feel less alone. The sky turned darker still, but Ebony didn't want to go back to the house. The rain made her feel alive.

Following the path round, she found a circular, copper-topped bandstand to take shelter in. The uprights were made of metal, newly painted a dark green, which matched the tendrils of ivy that climbed halfway up. Ebony trailed her finger along the cool metal. Despite its pristine appearance, the lumps and bumps of rust underneath betrayed the bandstand's age. In the centre was a set of blue wooden benches which formed a hexagon; Ebony sat down and surveyed the park. It was beautiful. The bandstand overlooked another fountain: this one was larger, with multiple jets of water spraying out of fake reeds. A lone duck swam around the fountain in circles, quacking noisily, even though there was a pond just ahead. Ebony chuckled; it was a strange place for a duck to swim. The rain pelted down around her but she was dry under the dark-green eaves.

Looking up, she saw that the ceiling was a stunning midnight blue, decorated with bronze moons. The painting showed the full cycle, from crescent moon to full moon. She stared up at the images, lost in the melody of raindrops bouncing off the floor. The moons seemed to dance before her eyes.

'Perfect, isn't it?' said a voice.

Startled, Ebony spun round. A boy, who looked a little older than her, was slouched against the bandstand; his blue hoodie was pulled up over his head and a rucksack dangled casually over one shoulder.

'I didn't think anyone else would be out in this,' he said, gesturing to the rain. He pulled down his hood, revealing a pallid face. His narrow green eyes were thickly fringed with lashes and he wore his long, chestnut hair tied back in a ponytail.

'I got caught in the rain. I'm just waiting for it to pass,' explained Ebony. It felt nice to have some company – especially someone near her own age.

'The only people I ever seem to meet here are those who got lost or caught in the rain. Maybe you're both?' He laughed. Joining Ebony in the bandstand, the boy set his bag down a few seats away from her. 'Do you mind if I wait too?'

Ebony shook her head. Even though she'd been there first, she felt like an intruder. The boy opened his bag and pulled out a tinfoil package, a bag of crisps and a banana.

'It's the best time for a picnic, don't you think?' he said. 'I wasn't expecting company or I'd have brought more. But you can join me if you like. Here …'

He patted the bench beside him. Ebony stayed put.

'Please yourself,' he muttered, offering her the banana. Ebony found her hand accepting it. 'It's peaceful when it's raining like this. No interruptions; no adults, no children. Even the pigeons stay roosting in the trees and buildings. Some people love to eat in groups, talking and waving their hands around. So much noise. Like wolves fighting over a carcass.'

Ebony swallowed her banana as quietly as she could.

'Of course, it's nice to have company every now and again.' He offered her his sandwich. Ebony shook her head. 'You don't say much, do you?'

Ebony continued eating quietly. The boy turned away, disgruntled.

Together, they watched the rain in silence.

As she stared out into the torrent, Ebony desperately tried to think of something to say. She wondered whether it would be rude to ask his name; it would have been expected back home but, apart from her aunt and uncle, this was the first city person she had met.

City or no city, Ebony was pleased to be back amongst

trees and flowers; she'd always loved the way the world grew animated in the rain. Wondering whether her companion was thinking the same, she inhaled deeply and stole a quick glance at his face. The boy sat motionless. His eyes were as liquid as puddles and his skin was virtually transparent. His expression was relaxed and peaceful, reminding Ebony of one of the old sailors who'd passed through her village. He had sworn by meditating every morning before going out on a catch, said it helped him to stay alert. The boy wore the same expression as that sailor. Was he meditating?

'I don't like meditation,' said the boy suddenly, still staring into the distance.

Ebony started; it was as if he was reading her mind.

'It might seem like I'm staring into space, but really I'm staring into the bits between spaces.' He turned to face her. His eyes burned an intense jade. 'I like the bits in between, like when you drift off to sleep and you can still sense stuff around you but it takes a loud bang to shake you out of it. You know what I mean?'

'I think so,' Ebony replied slowly, locked in his gaze.

By the time she had finished her reply, he was beside her. Yet Ebony hadn't sensed his approach. His movement was too fluid. The air suddenly felt thin and Ebony jumped to her feet.

'I'd better go,' she cried, despite the downpour.

'But it's still raining. You'll get soaked!'

Ignoring his words, Ebony stepped out into the wet. She

could see a family feeding ducks at the pond under the shelter of the trees and headed in their direction at a quick pace, hoping she was also heading towards the library. The boy called after her.

'Are you OK? I didn't mean to scare you.'

Her steps quickened. The wind and rain rushed in her ears. She could feel the boy's eyes fixed on her. Behind her she could hear him calling: 'There's no point running, Ebony. Whatever is looking for you will always find you, one way or another.'

She hadn't said her name. How did he know it? Worried in case he was following her, Ebony battled to stay calm. She kept her walk composed and refused to look back. But as soon as the path curved round and over a small arched bridge, she checked over her shoulder to make sure the boy wasn't in sight and then broke into a run.

Ebony's feet pounded the wet path, flicking water up her legs. Her hair stuck to her face. On she ran, suddenly realising that she didn't know where she was. Spying two high stone pillars and a wrought-iron gate between the bushes, she ran towards the exit. She could see a mixture of old and modern buildings on the other side, as well as cars and horse-and-carriages for rent to tourists. Ebony ran faster, not caring that it was a different entrance to where she'd come in. She just wanted to be around people.

As Ebony dashed out through the gate and towards the street on the other side, looking back to make sure the boy wasn't following, she ran straight in front of a horse and carriage that was just pulling away, loaded with sightseers. The muscular black horse reared up, its hooves pedalling in the air. The carriage rumbled, almost toppling onto a passing taxi which sounded its horn furiously. The fold-up roof slipped from its fastening and fell back like a concertina. Rain poured down on the tourists; they glared at Ebony as they struggled to pull up their hoods or shelter their heads with opened newspapers.

'Watch where you're going,' the driver bellowed at her, trying to stay seated on the carriage. His flat cap wobbled as he fought to get the horse back under control.

'I'm sorry. Can you tell me where Kildare Street is?' asked Ebony.

'Down there,' replied the man, pointing across the road and to Ebony's right. 'Now, move outta the way.'

Heart racing, Ebony crossed the road and headed to where the man had pointed, conscious of the park railings on the other side. What if the boy had followed her? Frantically trying to get her bearings – the library must be somewhere to her left if she remembered the map correctly – she felt out of place and confused. Everything was big and imposing and it felt like the buildings were falling on top of her. Thankfully, Kildare Street was only two streets down. As she turned the corner, she broke into a run, racing past a bronze statue of a man and a building that was clearly the National Museum from the posters in the window, willing the library to be close. Halfway down the street, Ebony slipped on the wet pavement and landed in a heap on the stone flags. The street was busy and bustling; umbrellas bobbed up and down in lime green, iridescent pink and canary yellow, bright against the dull sky. But no one stopped to help; everyone kept going at their quickened pace. Someone even stepped over her, but by the time she looked up they were gone. Cold, wet and humiliated, Ebony picked herself up. Then she grinned. In front of her was a sign. It read: *National Library of Ireland. Visitors Welcome.*

13

Suddenly aware that she was completely drenched, Ebony darted through the spiky gate and along the path to the entrance, desperate to get out of the rain. The library's façade was made up of huge stone slabs which made it look even older than her aunt's house. Beastly lion heads peered down over the eaves as if they were watching her every move. This austere building contrasted sharply with her local library in Oddley Cove, which was a few boxes of books lumped into a van that parked in the village square every fortnight.

Ebony knew she must be a sorry sight, dripping with rainwater. The disapproving glare of a librarian confirmed her fears. She was a huge woman, over six feet tall – if she hadn't been wearing a bright yellow dress, Ebony would have guessed she was a man. She had extremely short blue hair and a massive toady face.

'Can I help you?' she croaked.

'I'm researching an assignment for school,' Ebony lied.

'Sign in here, please. Now, what information do you need, dear?'

Ebony hadn't expected all this fuss so she wasn't prepared.

She said the first thing that came into her head.

'Local history.'

'Any particular era?'

'Erm, no,' said Ebony, fidgeting. She felt too exposed in the huge entrance area and wanted to be hidden among the shelves on her own.

'I'd recommend the Georgian era: very smelly times but interesting. Did you know they had to keep their food up high on boards to stop rats getting at it? Imagine rats everywhere …'

Wondering what everyone had against rats, Ebony tried to picture it. It didn't seem so bad to her. Rats were proving more attractive than people right now, especially in this murky city.

'Follow me and we'll get you started,' said the librarian, leading Ebony through metal detectors to a room filled with lockers. Ebony was expecting her book to trigger the alarm, but the detectors stayed silent. Perhaps they were faulty? 'Bags and coats in here, please,' said the librarian, pointing to a small locker. 'Safety precautions. This is a very special library, filled with some of the most rare and most precious books in Ireland, if not the world.'

Ebony placed her wet coat in the locker and took her own precious book out of her rucksack, keeping the cover hidden.

The librarian sighed, like she'd been through this too many times before. She pointed at a sign on the wall: NO PERSONAL ITEMS.

'But if it gets wet from being in my bag, it'll get ruined ... And I need to write down my findings,' said Ebony.

The librarian thrust some blank paper into the girl's hands. 'Paper to record your studies. Pencils are available inside.'

Scowling, Ebony turned back to the locker and pretended to shove her book inside. Instead, she slipped it between the sheets of paper and hugged them to her chest.

'Don't worry, it'll be safe,' said the librarian. 'No one can get in. You make up a secret four-digit number and then enter that number again to open it up when you're done. It couldn't be safer or simpler.'

When the librarian turned away, Ebony quickly entered her birthday as the code – 1304. Then the librarian led Ebony into a vast octagonal room filled with desks, shelving, files and computers. It was deathly silent and her footsteps echoed noisily.

The librarian showed Ebony to a chair at a computer and motioned for her to sit down. As Ebony lowered herself into the seat, she surveyed the people in the room. There was a young man with a squint who looked like a professor and an old, olive-skinned lady snoozing over a foreign newspaper. Between them sat a girl around her own age, her hair tucked up into a cowboy hat and her downturned face hidden by the wide brim.

'Here's a computer terminal. It's linked to our archives. Type what you're looking for in that box,' said the librarian impatiently, checking her watch.

Ebony typed in 'Dublin history'. The search returned thousands of records.

The huge woman leaned into the screen so that her nose was almost touching the monitor. She pointed out the serial number on the first record with a pencil and then showed Ebony how to locate the matching shelves.

'The code is in numerical order, going up in that direction. But try refining your search. Use some important keywords to locate what you need.'

Then the librarian scurried off into the maze of shelves, as if she had something much more important to do. Ebony heaved a sigh of relief. She seated herself at the most private desk she could find – the end of the row, overshadowed by a tall shelf – and sneaked open her book, running her finger over the numbers on the inside cover.

857	869
1057	1069
1514	1526
1654	1666
1745	1757
1826	1838
1859	1871
1929	1941
2003	2015

Knowing there must be a link between them, Ebony reached for a pencil and began her investigations. She tried adding the numbers up in pairs. Then she swapped each number for a letter of the alphabet to see if there was a secret written code. Subtraction led her into complicated negative numbers, so she tried multiplication instead. But that was even worse: the numbers were too big and she wasn't sure her answers were right. Sighing, Ebony weaved the pencil in and out of her fingers, staring at the inside cover. The numbers jiggled in front of her eyes, as though mocking her.

There must be a link! What was it?

Without thinking about it, she began to subtract the numbers backwards. 1069 minus 1057: 12. 1757 minus 1745: 12. And 2015 minus 2003: 12! That was it!

Excited, Ebony finished and then double-checked all of her calculations. Each equalled 12. But 12 what? People? Months? Years?

The numbers glowed bright for an instant.

Years! The numbers were dates! But what did they mean? The first was right back in the ninth century and the last was 2015, the current year – a long timeframe to play with.

Feeling pleased with herself, Ebony sat back and tapped her pencil on the desk absentmindedly.

'Ssshh!' said a voice.

Looking up apologetically, Ebony couldn't see who the voice belonged to, but she stopped tapping anyway and laid the pencil flat on the desk. What now? She'd figured out the dates but what use was the information?

In front of her, *The Book of Learning* began to tremble, rattling its silver cover against the desk. The pencil bounced up and down on the mahogany surface beside it. Together, they sounded like an approaching train.

'Ssshh!' came the voice again.

This time, as Ebony scanned the room, she was surprised to find everyone going about their own business, as though they couldn't hear the racket. But as her eyes fell on the girl in the cowboy hat, the girl looked up from underneath the wide brim – finger to her lips – and Ebony recognised her own face staring back.

Giving a startled cry, Ebony instinctively slammed her hand on top of the book, but no matter how hard she pushed, she couldn't stop it from rattling. The shushing noise grew louder and echoed around the room – but only she seemed to be able to hear it.

'Ssshh! Ssshh!'

As Ebony let go of *The Book of Learning*, the pencil leaped from the table to the floor, rolling to the feet of the cowgirl. Taking a deep breath, Ebony pushed back her chair and slowly rose, tucking her book into her trouser pocket where it vibrated quietly against her leg. In an instant, the cowgirl leaped to her feet, spun a lasso in the air and snared Ebony, dragging her towards her. Ebony tried digging her heels in and calling for help, but nothing worked; in fact, no one moved. Not even a blink. It was as though time had frozen.

The cowgirl laughed as she reeled Ebony in. Ebony struggled with all her might, but she tumbled to the ground and was dragged along the floor. As she reached the cowgirl's spurred boots, Ebony braced herself for the worst. The girl leaned over her menacingly. But then, to Ebony's surprise, she loosened the lasso and helped Ebony to her feet.

'So, it's all true,' said the girl. Ebony saw a stray black curl fall from under the hat. It was exactly the same as her own. She stared into the mirror image of her own face, startled.

'What's true?'

The girl laughed. 'You said you'd say that.'

'Say what? I don't understand!'

The girl laughed again, louder this time, before reaching into her pocket. Ebony flinched.

'You said to give you this,' said the cowgirl, holding out her hand.

In it was a newspaper cutting, dated 19 April 1757. Ebony had never laid eyes on the cutting or the cowgirl before. What was going on? Baffled, she read the headline: *Mysterious Murder in Mercury Lane.*

As Ebony reached out and took the article, she couldn't help asking, 'What's your name?'

The cowgirl lifted up her other hand, smiling. It held a ragged old poster showing a sketch of their mutual face. It read: WANTED: EBONY SMART.

A queer sensation shot through Ebony's body, like she was falling and spinning at great speed. Closing her eyes, hands gripping the newspaper cutting, she waited for the feeling to pass. When she opened her eyes again, she was back in her seat, article in hand. People were once again fetching books and scratching their heads, reading. From beneath her hat, the cowgirl winked.

The book had stopped vibrating in Ebony's pocket, but now it was jammed uncomfortably against her leg. Pulling her gaze away from the cowgirl, Ebony set *The Book of Learning* on the table, quickly opening it to check the dates in the grid against that of the newspaper report – they matched. Nervously, she smoothed her hands over the news report and began reading: *Last night, city police uncovered a shocking crime at 23 Mercury Lane. The body of twelve-year-old Ebony Smart was discovered outside her home.*

Yet another girl called Ebony Smart had lived in the same house as herself in the 1700s? An image of the girl in the mirror with the bloodied bandage flickered through her mind and Ebony shuddered. Hastily, she read on: *Police suspect that at approximately midnight yesterday she was pushed from the top left bedroom window. Her body was found wearing a white nightdress. Police are calling for witnesses who may have been in the area or seen anything suspicious. They are particularly interested in speaking to a tall, unkempt gentleman who was spotted in the vicinity around the suspected time of death.*

Was that why all the windows in the house were nailed shut in Mercury Lane? If the cutting was right, the room where the previous Ebony's murder had been committed was the one next door to hers. No wonder her aunt kept that room locked.

At the end of the story, there was a list entitled *Victim's Details*. Ebony had to know more.

Name: Miss Ebony Smart

Born 13 April 1745, died 18 April 1757. Cause of death: Murder.

The twelve-year span – that was how long the girl had lived! Feeling queasy, Ebony read on hurriedly.

Parents: Rufus Smart, professor in Ancient Civilisations and Necromancy; Ivy Smart, professor's assistant.

Ebony gulped; those were the same names as her own parents. This was too weird.

Status: Missing. Lost during expedition. Bodies never found.

As she noted the details, Ebony could hardly believe what she was reading. She paused, forced to think about her own parents. She had no recollection of them at all and had never been told much about them, except for their names and that they had died at sea, their bodies lost to the ocean. When she was younger, Ebony had tried to talk about her parents many times but it made her grandpa too upset. After a while, she'd stopped trying. After all, they'd gone. Only her grandpa mattered – now he had gone too.

A strange sickness welled in Ebony's stomach. Many things in this Ebony Smart's life were the same as her own – and it didn't feel right. She remembered her aunt's claims about being reincarnated and sank back in her chair, stunned.

It had to be more than just a coincidence. With sweat beading her brow and stickying her palms, she felt a sudden urge to get back to Mercury Lane as quickly as she could. But as she stood up to leave, the pages of *The Book of Learning* flapped, as though wafted by a strong breeze, before settling on a new message: LOOK BEHIND YOU.

Breath short and heart pumping, Ebony slowly turned her head, terrified of what she might find. At first she couldn't see anything except for the dozing lady and the downturned cowboy hat. Then she noticed a shadow creeping along the back wall. A long, raggedy shadow that she recognised.

It was Icarus Bean.

She held her breath as he rounded the corner, wearing a new grey overcoat. In his hand, he held a trilby. So she wasn't turning paranoid; she *had* recognised him in the park!

Hoping he was too busy combing the shelves for books to notice she was there, Ebony quietly closed *The Book of Learning*. Hands and legs shaking with fear, she began to creep back towards the locker room. As the exit loomed closer, she sped up, bumping into the young professor-type and sending his pile of books crashing to the floor. The sound echoed around the library. More faces appeared and a dozen sets of eyes turned to see what the commotion was about.

The girl in the cowboy hat was gone.

'Shhh!' said the old lady, who now had a very grumpy face, having been awoken from her slumber. 'This is a library, not a coffee shop!'

Before Ebony could apologise, she felt a burning sensation prickle her cheekbone. Icarus Bean had his gaze locked on her. He gave a low, dramatic bow.

Seeing her chance, Ebony dashed straight out of the huge wooden doors to the locker room, only to find her locker door hanging open with a note taped to it.

In spiky letters, it read:

TO LIVE, FIND THE MURDERER AND REVEAL THE TRUTH.

14

As soon as Ebony found her way back to Mercury Lane, she let herself in and slammed the front door shut. Pressing her back against the door with eyes firmly closed, she paused to catch her breath. What an awful place this city was turning out to be – even worse than she had expected.

'Aunt Ruby? Uncle Cornelius?'

No answer.

The house was empty. It creaked and groaned.

Fearing the noises, Ebony peeped out of the spy hole, secured every lock and headed straight for the familiarity of her room. When she got there, she found Winston sleeping on the pillow where she'd left him. Thankfully, the towel was still slung over the dressing-table mirror.

'It's a fine life being a rat,' said Ebony, prodding him.

Winston opened a bleary eye and rubbed his nose with a back paw. Then he rolled on his back and stuck his front paws into the air in greeting. Ebony gently tugged on his paws, pleased to have his company.

'I'll not leave you behind again,' she said.

He scurried over to her rucksack and tried to climb inside.

Ebony chuckled, then went to the window and looked out. The street below was empty.

'Come on, Winston, we have to keep investigating. There's too much odd stuff going on – and I'm going to get to the bottom of things,' she said, pulling her rucksack towards her and taking out the book.

Laying it on the bed, she wiped the corner with blood from her old wound and then smoothed the next blank page flat. Winston climbed up the bedpost and sat in front of the creamy paper, as though reading it.

'You're a clever rat, Winston, but not clever enough to read just yet!' said Ebony.

Winston peered around at his friend and then turned back to the book as if waiting for it to reveal its secrets. When the book began to shimmer, Ebony smiled. 'OK, here we go.'

Winston leaped up onto his hind legs, his tongue hanging out with excitement. Ebony took a deep breath as five dashes appeared.

– – – – –

Then a drawing of a gallows and a clue: *If you want to be cleverer, I'm the place to go. I'm also what you do there. What word am I?*

'I know this game, it's hangman!' said Ebony, and Winston shuffled closer. 'I'm good at this. I have a method. I go through the vowels first, then my name. It always works. Watch!'

She took the library pencil out of her bag and tried to write the letter A onto the page, but as the pencil touched the paper, it was catapulted backwards at such a speed that it stuck into the wall. Winston covered his eyes with his paws.

'OK, I guess I can't write in here,' said Ebony. 'I'll try calling out instead. A.'

The letter A appeared at the side of the dashes and a rope swung down from the gallows.

'E.'

As a head appeared in the rope, Ebony felt a tightening sensation around her throat. *It's just my imagination*, she thought. *It'll pass.*

'I.'

A body next and the choking sensation worsened. Winston trembled, looking from the page to his friend.

'O.'

The body grew an arm. Ebony tried to stay calm and breathe normally as her throat burned. She started to wonder if she was playing for her life.

'U.'

The U sat in the middle of the dashes.

_ _ U _ _

Feeling a little relieved, Ebony took a deep breath.

'Now we go through my name,' she said, as calmly as she could. 'We've already said E, so B.' Another arm and more pain.

'N.'

Now, the hangman had a leg and Ebony felt like she was being lifted from the ground by her neck, with her tiptoes barely touching the floor. *If you want to be cleverer, I'm the place to go. I'm also what you do there … What does it mean? Think, Ebony think!* she willed herself.

Her voice trembled as she choked out next letter.

'Y.'

Thankfully, it appeared at the end of the word. But she had three more letters to find and only one more try. The pain in her neck was so sore, she started to cough.

_ _ U _ Y

If you want to be cleverer, I'm the place to go. I'm also what you do there … So it's the name of a place and also an action? Come on, you can solve this! But she could only draw blanks.

Trembling, tears filling her eyes, she tried another letter.

'S.'

The sound was barely audible, but the letter formed at the start of the word.

Winston jumped up on his hind legs and raised his two front legs up like a monster. Then he lay on his back, pushing his belly out, poking a claw at his teeth.

Exhausted, Ebony tried to make sense of Winston's actions. It looked like he was mimicking Uncle Cornelius at breakfast. Usually, it would have had her in fits of laughter, but now wasn't the time. She could hardly breathe, never mind laugh! Then an idea struck.

'I've got it! Study! You go to a study to learn. And what's another name for learning, but study?'

Instantly, the pressure around her throat stopped. Gasping

for breath, Ebony leaned forward and let the coughing subside. When she looked up, the word STUDY glowed on the page.

Winston ran around in circles, chasing his own tail with excitement. Then he stopped and perched up on his hind legs again, waiting for Ebony's reaction.

'That was a close one!' she said, scooping Winston up and sneakily wiping her tears on him. 'I won't be in a hurry to play that again. And I think my foolproof method needs revising!'

Winston scurried up her arm and buried his head in her curls. Ebony turned back to the book.

'I'm sure that every time this book shows me something, it's meant to help. So it must have chosen the word "study" for a reason, Winston. I think it wants us to go downstairs.'

She felt her pet rat's body go limp.

'I know you don't want to go near him, but Uncle Cornelius isn't here. You'll be safe, I promise.'

Winston began to tremble.

'Please don't be scared. I need you to come with me. I can't do this on my own.'

Her entreaty worked. Standing tall and puffing out his chest, Winston gave one of Ebony's curls a gentle tug and then clung on as, grabbing the ivy-handled key and *The Book of Learning*, she raced out the door and down the stairs, listening out for any signs of movement in the house. Silence. Within moments they were in the study.

But the room was not in the same orderly arrangement

as before. Cabinet doors hung open, books were scattered like domino tiles, papers screwed into balls littered the floor and drawers had been pulled out and abandoned. Even the stuffed marlin head was crooked. It looked as though the place had been ransacked – but the door had been locked, showing no visible damage.

'Looks like Uncle Cornelius lost something and had to leave in a hurry,' said Ebony, surveying the mess. Her stomach lurched. What if he'd been looking for the book she'd stolen? Maybe she should put it back? But as soon as she glanced at the words on the back – *Property of Ebony Smart* – the idea seemed ridiculous. 'At least the mess will cover our tracks,' she said. 'Let's have a nosey, see what we can find.'

Leaping from Ebony's shoulder onto the desk, Winston scurried over and under envelopes, documents and files.

'I'll try over here,' said Ebony, moving to some discarded drawers near the window. There were endless reams of documents and notes, but most seemed to be financial records or household receipts. She tried to read each one closely, but searching without knowing what she was looking for – especially when everything she found was boring – soon became frustrating. Disheartened, Ebony sank back against the wall, listening to the eager rustling of Winston buried deep below the desk's debris. Opening the book, she waited for some inspiration to appear. The hangman page had turned brown and crackly like the other used pages, but there was no new information on the fresh ones.

'I don't get it, Winston,' she said, staring at the open book on her lap.

Drawing a deep breath in, Ebony blew up towards her fringe in a huff. A soft thump interrupted her sulk. Winston had fallen off the desk, landing on his back atop a pile of envelopes. He quickly flipped himself over and snapped his teeth around the corner of the envelope on top. Seeing that he was OK, Ebony returned to sulking. But while she'd been distracted, a message had appeared:

WHY DON'T YOU LOOK THROUGH THE BINOCULARS?

'Binoculars, Winston, we're looking for binoculars.'

Standing up and frantically searching the upturned room, almost stepping on Winston, Ebony found a pair of binoculars mounted on a stand, facing the wall.

'You're not going to see much like that!' she said, reaching for them.

But they were stuck fast.

Standing on her tiptoes, she peered inside.

At first, she could only see blackness, but after a moment her eyes adjusted and a bright moon became visible. Treetops swayed around an exposed field, and she could hear them rustling and howling as the breeze whipped their branches. Below, the crunch and snap of disturbed scrub rang out, as though wild animals were fighting. A crack of lightning split the sky.

Ebony was too used to bizarre events by now to be scared.

Show me what I need to see, she willed, trying to see what was going on below.

A second flash of lightning struck and the sound of struggling magnified: something was wrong. A third flash lit up the scene and a loud shot rang out. The angle shifted, showing the ground. Lit by the moon, a limp body was half hidden by a man leaning over it. The image zoomed in, showing a slack old face, twisted with pain.

Grandpa Tobias!

The other man looked around him cautiously, then stood, dragging Grandpa's body up with him. With Grandpa slung over his shoulder, he staggered towards the trees. Stumbling in the long grasses and briars, the man paused and turned his face towards the moon, his matted hair and unshaven face full of shadows.

Icarus Bean!

Somehow, his eyes connected with Ebony's and widened.

Wrenching herself backwards, Ebony's foot tangled with a rogue drawer and she landed with a thwack on the floor. Groaning, she tried to push herself up, but her left arm gave way and she found herself eyeball to eyeball with Winston. Panting and head hung low, he gripped an envelope between his teeth.

'What do you have there?'

Carefully removing the envelope and pulling out the contents, Ebony read quickly.

Coroner's report concerning Mr Tobias Smart

13 April 2015
After close examination, it has been concluded that Mr Tobias Smart of Oddley Cove, aged sixty-four, died of natural causes. At approximately 22.00 on 10 April he suffered a severe heart attack, which eventually resulted in his death at 10.28 on 13 April 2015. The overseeing officer has ruled that there were no unusual circumstances. The case is now officially closed.

Coroner: Mr M. J. Black
Overseeing Officer: Judge Ambrose

'It wasn't a heart attack, Winston. I know I couldn't see any wounds on my grandpa, and the report doesn't mention any either, but I heard a shot just now – it was murder. Icarus Bean murdered my grandpa! *He's* the murderer we've been seeking. But why didn't Aunt Ruby mention the report? She must have seen it, yet she told me it would be a while before we heard anything.' Ebony screwed the report up in her fist. 'Somehow, the judge has been tricked, and I bet Icarus had something to do with it – but if that murderer thinks this case is closed, he's mistaken.'

As she stomped upstairs, book wedged firmly in her back pocket, Ebony got a frightening surprise. The door to the room next to hers was ajar.

It had definitely been firmly locked before.

Taking one look, Winston squealed, leaped off Ebony's shoulder and disappeared into her bedroom. This time, Ebony would have to go alone.

Trembling, her nerves shaken by what she had just seen through the binoculars, Ebony pushed the door open gently and crept into the forbidden room. A musty smell hit her immediately. The air was chilly and thick with dust. Sheets hung in folds on the furniture; where the material had slipped, cobwebs took over in thick white clumps.

There was a fireplace on the wall that adjoined her bedroom; the tiles surrounding it were filthy, but a splash of sky blue peeped through which looked vaguely familiar. Ebony rubbed the muck with the cuff of her sleeve, revealing blue tiles covered in white clouds and skylarks – exactly the same as those on her fireplace at home. Her chest thumped. She crossed the room to open the shutters and try to make it less spooky, leaving footprints in the dust as she went. The shutters were stiff and heavy; it took a good yank to get them to open. When she pulled them back, the dirt was so thick on the windows that the room stayed almost as dim as before; it was as though the panes of glass swallowed up any light from the world outside.

In the corner, to the right of the window, was a door. It had a round brass knob on the side nearest to her and thick, rusty hinges on the other side. Ebony guessed that there would be stairs behind it – but leading to where? As she headed towards it, it creaked open a little, as if it had caught a breeze. A waft of warm air brushed against Ebony's ankles, but it wasn't strong enough to have opened the door. As she looked down, watching dust swirl around her feet, the door slammed shut. Ebony jumped, letting out an involuntary squeal. Then she called out, 'Aunt Ruby? Uncle Cornelius?'

Saying their names made her feel a little braver, even though she knew it couldn't possibly be them. She'd have heard them return. Hesitating, uncertain whether she should go any further, she considered going back to convince Winston to come along. But as Ebony glanced back towards the door where she'd come in, she had to cover her mouth to stifle a scream.

There was a second set of footprints in the dust, leading to the centre of the room.

Other than the dust, nothing else had been disturbed. Where had the footprints come from? Ebony shuddered;

part of her wanted to run, but her legs were rooted to the spot, as though something was keeping her there. She really wished that Winston was with her, but she pushed her fear away. Now that she had finally got into the secret room, now that she finally knew the truth about her grandpa, she wasn't going to stop until she found out what was really going on.

Feeling sweat dribble down her back, Ebony yanked the door open. On the other side she could see a set of old stairs, which smelled of damp and bat droppings. Quietly, she started to climb. At the top she was greeted by an attic room full of heavy wooden crates. The walls at either end were freshly plastered; the others were made out of dull beige brick. Ebony walked over to the nearest of the plastered walls and tapped it: it was hollow. She remembered Old Joe telling her once about old houses with adjoining attics. Ebony guessed that the new walls separated Mercury Lane from the rest of the houses on that street; her aunt clearly wanted her privacy.

Ebony took a closer look at the crates. They had unusual destinations stamped on the side in big, bold lettering. Some matched those on her grandpa's suitcase: Peru, Venezuela, Uganda, Borneo. Documents, maps, files, photographs, tools and old toys spewed out of the gaping boxes. Ebony lifted out an old brown teddy; it had one eye missing and goose feathers were sticking out of the shoulder where the cotton was threadbare. She considered keeping it for Winston to snuggle up to in his cage – he'd have a great time pulling the stuffing out. But the sound of footsteps on the roof interrupted Ebony's thoughts.

Dropping the bear, she looked up: above her was a skylight with filthy glass which made the grey sky outside look even darker. The footsteps continued in slow and heavy thuds; whoever it was, they were right overhead.

Suddenly, a shadowy figure appeared through the dirt – someone was standing on the top of the roof and leaning over to look through the skylight!

Ebony shrank back behind a crate and waited until the shadow disappeared. However, as it left, a familiar smell filled the air. It was her grandpa's tobacco.

'Wait!' she cried, looking round for a way to get up to the skylight.

In the corner an iron ladder was propped against the wall. Ebony grabbed it and quickly fixed it into place on two rusty hooks secured into the ceiling next to the skylight. She raced up the rungs and fiddled with the skylight's bolt. It was jammed. Panic began to envelop her as the footsteps overhead grew quieter.

'Come on, please open,' she pleaded, rattling the bolt. She had to see if it was her grandpa!

Her hands were shaking, but after a moment she managed to release the bolt and quickly shoved the skylight open with a rough thwack of her hand.

Freezing cold air rushed at her face as Ebony pulled herself up and out onto the tiles, halfway up the roof. The tiles glistened with the residue of the earlier rain. Searching the sweeping skyline for signs of her grandpa, or puffs of smoke, all Ebony could see was a mass of grey slate and chimney pots. Where could he have gone?

The roof ran the length of the buildings on that side of Mercury Lane. In the middle, at the highest point, was a path which was just wide enough to walk along, and down below was the guttering. Suddenly, Ebony heard a loud clatter, like a tile falling from a height. She spun in the direction of the noise; it seemed to come from just beyond the roof's edge. Frantically, she clawed her way up the tiles towards the path. There was hardly any grip and her feet slid back again and again, but Ebony was determined. She reached the path in no time and stood up slowly, steadying herself. A second clatter made her jump, almost knocking her off balance.

The sound was definitely coming from the roof's edge. Taking a deep breath, Ebony shuffled along the path as quickly as she could. At the end there was a winding black staircase. Its heavy iron steps circled their way down to the street below, but there was no one in sight.

Suddenly, as if the clouds had cracked open, rain began to pour all around her, sneaking down the back of her neck. Thunder rumbled. Thinking back to the scene in the binoculars, Ebony carefully shuffled her way back to the skylight. Something told her she wasn't safe.

Having climbed back through the opening, she slammed the window shut. As her breath caught the cold glass and frosted it up, a mark appeared that was too straight to be an accident. Ebony breathed again on the window and this time the letter H appeared. She continued to breathe on the skylight, covering its surface with condensation. The same words that had been on the note in her locker appeared:

TO LIVE, FIND THE MURDERER AND REVEAL THE TRUTH.

Who is writing these messages? And how can they manage to be in both the library and Aunt Ruby's attic? Letting out a sharp breath, Ebony scrubbed the message away with her hand as though it would make the person who'd written it disappear as well. She sniffed the air one last time, but all trace of tobacco smoke had faded.

With a heavy heart, Ebony descended the ladder, snatching one last look at the skylight. Then she ran past the bulging boxes and down the stairs. Bursting back through the door, she let out a gasp. The footprints on the floor had changed. They now continued on to the window – the window where the Ebony Smart she had read about had been pushed to her death. Ebony raced out onto the landing and pulled the door hard behind her, not stopping to see whether it was properly shut. Inside her own room, she slammed the door and rested against it, eyes closed.

The sound of Winston's faint scratching in the wardrobe – how he'd got in there, she hadn't a clue – was nicely familiar.

Then a cold gust of wind fluffed her hair, making her open her eyes in surprise. Her bedroom window was open.

That's impossible, she thought, *the windows are all nailed shut*. The wind had picked up outside so huge drops of rain were pitter-pattering onto the floor. She ran to the window and tried to close it, but it wouldn't budge.

Giving up, she turned and walked to the wardrobe door to retrieve Winston – he always made her feel better. But then a movement at the side of her eye caught her notice and she realised that Winston was actually fast asleep on her bed, his fat tummy rising and falling peacefully. Ebony paused, her hand touching the handle of the wardrobe door.

As a barely audible cough sounded from the wardrobe, a chill crept through Ebony's bones and her blood ran cold – but it was too late to hide.

16

As the door burst open, kicked from the inside, Ebony jumped back, narrowly avoiding the impact. Icarus Bean was inside the wardrobe, wide-eyed, looking as surprised as she was. Ebony screamed at the top of her voice.

'Stop screaming,' said Icarus, climbing out.

But Ebony couldn't help it. A shrill cry continued to pour from her mouth. Icarus's eyes flashed murderously. He lunged at Ebony, who turned to run, and grabbed her, wrapping one arm around her shoulders and pulling her against him, and clamping his other hand over her mouth. Despite his new coat, he smelled putrid – a mixture of sage and dirt, stale sweat and old whiskey. Ebony felt nausea flooding her stomach and bubbling up into her throat. Close to being sick, she had to get away.

Struggling hard, Ebony grabbed his arms and tried to pull them away, but Icarus was too strong. When she tried kicking and hitting him, he managed to evade every attempt she made to hurt him. She tried wriggling free, but Icarus held her fast. Exhausted, Ebony forced herself to calm down. She decided to conserve some energy and look for a better opportunity to escape. When she was quieter for a while, Icarus loosened his grip slightly.

'You stupid girl,' he growled. 'You'll attract attention.'

Icarus dragged her towards the window. Ebony's whole body shook. She tried to make herself as heavy as possible and scuffed her feet along the ground so that he couldn't throw her out. But he simply peered out the window. When he was satisfied that no one was watching, he lugged her over to the bed and pushed her down onto it, keeping one hand clamped on her mouth. Winston's cage rattled noisily as he fled inside to hide.

'I'm here to help you, Ebony. I'll let go if you promise not to scream any more.'

Ebony remembered something her grandpa had once told her: when animals sensed fear, they would attack. She steadied her breathing, even though her heart was thumping rapidly, and nodded.

'You promise?'

She nodded again. Icarus let go and stepped backwards, and Ebony immediately ran towards the window while letting out the loudest blood-curdling roar she could muster.

'Idiotic girl,' yelled Icarus, right behind her, and before she could draw breath, he threw himself on her and they fell roughly to the floor. His whole weight was on top of her and this time Ebony was face down with his trench coat covering her head. She could hardly breathe, suffocating in his stench. She tried wriggling away but, despite his wiry frame, Icarus

Bean was far too heavy. She couldn't scream. All she could do was lie still. She could hear Icarus saying something on the other side of his coat. His voice was so muffled she couldn't understand a word, but it was clear that he was angry.

All of a sudden, Icarus's weight lifted from her. Ebony felt hands grip her tightly and then she was flung across the room like an unwanted teddy. Her head banged against the corner of the bed. The spot on her skull that she hit turned icy cold and she felt a lump forming straight away. Her vision clouded and it seemed to take a lifetime for her eyes to clear. When they did, Ebony saw the boy from the park struggling with Icarus Bean.

Although the boy was smaller, he was faster and unexpectedly strong. As they wrestled, the boy kept slipping out of Icarus's grasp like an eel. Each time he escaped, he would grab Icarus and shove him, wearing the older man down but making him angrier too. Icarus retaliated with wild blows, but the young lad was too fast and managed to duck them. As Icarus became tired, the boy took his chance and pushed the older man over to the window. Then he gave him an almighty shove, so Icarus's torso was thrust backwards through the window, and Icarus was left clutching the window frame and hovering precariously above the city street three storeys below. Using all his strength, the boy slammed the sash window down onto the man's chest and arms.

Icarus coughed, then snarled like a demon. Kicking the boy backwards, he grabbed the window with one hand and thrust it back up, high enough to allow him to slip inside to safety. The boy hit out again but this time Icarus dodged his fist. The momentum of the blow forced the boy past Icarus, who grabbed him from behind and wrapped his arm around the boy's throat in a headlock. The boy leaned back and jerked, managing to reach Icarus's ear. He bit down hard. The old man howled with pain, twisting and squirming in the boy's locked jaw, blood oozing from his wound. Icarus slammed the boy against the wall, forcing him to release his ear, then he threw him across the room. The boy landed with a thump but sprang quickly to his feet, pulling a gun out of his pocket.

'Zachariah, no!' cried Icarus.

Ebony's head was still spinning, but she was not too confused to notice that Icarus seemed to know the boy's name. However, she figured that this was her chance to escape and decided that that was the most important thing now. Although she was woozy and her head felt like it was full of hammers, she forced herself to stand and ran past the startled pair, out through the door.

When she was halfway down the first flight of stairs, there was a bang and a flash of blinding white light lit up the stairwell. The flash made her head hurt even more and she stumbled to a stop. Her eyes felt heavy; she longed to lie down and rest. The stairwell began to spin. Ebony touched the bump on her head: it was getting bigger. She reached out to steady herself, but no matter how tightly she clung to the banister, she couldn't shake the dizziness.

Footsteps started down the stairs and fear raced through Ebony's veins, but she was too woozy to move. Then a voice called out: 'It's OK. He's gone. It's just me.'

It was the boy.

He reached Ebony in a matter of seconds and put his arm around her waist. She leaned on him and he guided her back towards her room and sat her on the bed.

'Don't fall asleep. You have a concussion. I'll be right back. Promise me that you'll stay awake.'

Ebony nodded. The boy ran into the bathroom, returning after a moment with the plastic beaker that she stored her toothbrush in filled with water. He crouched in front of her and Ebony reached for the beaker but lost her balance.

'Whoa. Careful,' said the boy, grabbing her and righting her with one arm. When Ebony had regained her balance, the boy put the beaker to her lips. 'Try to drink.'

Gulping the water down, Ebony felt a little revived. The water tasted good and it seemed to reach every part of her body. She drank as much as she could, spilling it in cascades down her chin. The room began to spin less, but her vision was still foggy. She blinked rapidly.

'You'll be able to focus in a minute, I think,' said the boy.

Ebony sat still. A thundering pain rumbled in her head. With clenched teeth, she waited for the pain to lessen. She wanted to thank the boy for saving her. But first, she had to make doubly sure that Icarus Bean had gone.

'Like I said, he's gone,' said the boy, before she could ask.

'Do you mean … is he dead?' asked Ebony.

The boy laughed. 'Whatever gave you that idea? He escaped out the window.'

Ebony wondered how he'd managed that – it was too high up for Icarus to jump. Was there some way to climb to the roof? She thought about the footsteps that she had heard in the attic earlier: it must have been Icarus Bean. But that didn't account for the tobacco smoke. And how had he got down from the roof and into her room so quickly?

'The flash … just after he called your name.' Ebony leaned away slightly. 'Wait – do you know him?'

'Unfortunately, I do.' The boy spat out the words through gritted teeth, rising and turning away from her towards the door, as if he did not want her to see the hatred on his face.

Ebony rubbed her head and looked towards the window. Suddenly, she realised that they were no longer alone. In the corner of the room stood a girl with long black hair flowing over her floor-length nightgown – like the newspaper cutting had described. Her skin was transparent, so the window pane was visible through the contours of her nightie. Ebony could see right through her.

The girl was looking towards the door patiently, as though waiting for someone to arrive. After a moment, the ghostly figure became animated and reached out as though to take something – but Ebony couldn't see anyone else in the room. As the apparition pulled her hand back, she fainted, dropping something on the floor. Ebony narrowed her eyes, searching for the object. A shadow moved in the corner: someone was hiding there. As the shadow grew, covering the limp body on the floor, Ebony gasped.

'What is it, Ebony?' asked the boy. 'Do you see something?' He followed Ebony's gaze, his eyes squinting and widening with an effort to focus. The vision disappeared.

'Are you OK?' he asked, turning back to her.

'The girl … did you see her?'

'No. But I'd have liked to.'

Ebony could see something twinkling on the floor near the window – it looked like a crescent-shaped locket. Because he had his back to the window, Zachariah couldn't see it. A faint whisper from deep inside Ebony's brain told her to keep it secret, so she averted her eyes.

'Is something wrong?' asked the boy, looking at her quizzically.

'No,' said Ebony.

Her brain felt heavy. *Blank your mind*, said the whisper in her head, *rescue the treasure*. Ebony tried to make her mind go blank as the boy stared at her. She felt lost in his gaze. A dull thud pulsed and throbbed in her forehead, making it feel like her head was going to crack open. She got up, swaying with the effort. As she took the first few steps, her brain felt lighter and freer.

'I need some air,' she said.

A smile played on the boy's lips. 'Go to the window,' he said. His voice was sweet and gentle.

Don't look in his eyes, said the voice, but she couldn't resist. As Ebony stared at him, her brain throbbed even more. With a real effort she pulled her gaze away and the pain faded. The item on the floor glinted again.

Ebony could only think of one way to reach the locket without Zachariah seeing it. She staggered in the direction of the window, between him and the locket, then feigned a swoon. As she landed on the floor, she sneaked the piece of jewellery into her hand. The boy rushed to her aid. *Don't look at him*, the internal voice whispered, *not yet*. Ebony slipped the locket into her pocket as the boy helped her to her feet.

'Come, you need more rest.'

She was unsteady, but the warmth of his hands and strength of his grip encouraged her. She sat on the bed again, pretending to recover.

'I guess I should introduce myself properly,' said the boy, sitting next to her. 'I'm Zachariah Stone. Zach for short.'

He held out his hand. As Ebony took it, a shiver ran down her spine. But before she could ask how he knew Icarus Bean, a mighty crash came from the kitchen below.

'Stay here, I'll go look,' said Zach.

Ebony shook her head. 'I don't want to be on my own. What if it's him?'

'Trust me – we've seen the last of Icarus for now. It's probably just your aunt and uncle. But come with me if you're worried.'

Ebony really hoped it was her aunt and uncle. *Where were*

they anyway? What if they never came back, like her grandpa?
Then she wondered how Zach knew who she lived with. She
didn't have time to ask: Zach was already through the door
and heading down the stairs. She checked that *The Book of
Learning* was still safe in her pocket, then followed him.

As they reached the hallway, Zach put his finger to his
lips, signalling for Ebony to be quiet. A scuffling sound came
from the kitchen.

'Icarus?' mouthed Ebony.

Zach shrugged. His face was stern as he took the gun out
of his pocket again.

'We need as much protection as possible,' he whispered.
'Stick with me.'

Ebony winced. That flash – had he killed Icarus Bean? But
she didn't think guns usually created that sort of light. And
where was the body? They crept in to the kitchen and there,
crouched on the floor like a wild animal, was what Ebony
thought was Uncle Cornelius, although it was hard to tell
as his face was shoved into a heap of raw meat, tearing at it
with his teeth. Blood was smeared all over his face and he was
making a low whimpering sound.

Zach raised the gun and Ebony stepped back nervously. As
she did so, she knocked into the kitchen door and it banged
loudly against the wall. Ebony and Zach stood stock still,
afraid to move. Remembering the whistle her aunt had given
her earlier, Ebony slipped it out of her pocket and gave it a
hard blow. No sound came out, but the creature jumped and

looked in their direction. He could obviously hear something she couldn't – Ebony guessed she was holding a dog whistle.

Looking into the creature's face, Ebony was suddenly unsure whether it was Uncle Cornelius. He had almost identical features but his hair was silver, not golden, and wildly matted – and he had a tail! He looked more like a beast than a man and his eyes glared ferociously. But Ebony didn't have long to decide: as she lifted the whistle to her mouth to give it another try, the creature turned around on all fours, carrying the remainder of the meat in his mouth, and fled at top speed towards the cupboard under the sink. Instead of crashing into it, the door swung inwards like a giant cat flap as he pushed against it. It was a fake cupboard concealing a secret entrance, and the creature hurtled through so fast, the tip of his tail vanishing just as the door swung closed, that Ebony could only stand and stare, stunned. Neither she nor Zach spoke until the door stopped swinging and hung still.

'What was that?' asked Zach.

'I'm not sure; it looked like my uncle,' said Ebony, setting the whistle on the table so it would be easy to grab if the creature came back. 'But the tail … I think I'd have noticed if my uncle had a tail!'

'Where does the door lead to?'

'I have no idea.'

'Shall I go after him?' asked Zach, raising the gun.

Ebony looked at the weapon in Zach's hand and quivered. 'No! He doesn't seem very friendly,' she said. *In fact it seemed like he was the one that was scared*, thought Ebony. Zach smiled.

'I thought he seemed scared too,' he said.

Ebony frowned.

'Zach?'

'Yes?'

'Can you read my mind?'

'Yes,' he said, staring into her eyes.

The whispering voice tried to say something but Ebony forced it to be silent.

'Thank you,' she said. 'That's the first straight answer I've had since I got here.'

17

Seated in the kitchen, Ebony and Zach watched the door under the sink carefully.

'Do you think he'll come back?' asked Ebony.

'I don't think so. He seemed pretty terrified.'

'Did you read his mind?'

'Not really. Sometimes I can with the intelligent ones, but it's difficult with animals. I guess their brains work differently. I can get a glimpse but that's it. Just then, I read a flash of fear and desperate hunger. Is he always like that?'

'I don't know. If it *is* my uncle, I only met him this morning. He was eating breakfast rather greedily. And he did try to steal Winston.'

'Winston?'

'My pet rat.'

They both stared at the drips of blood on the floor, but neither said a word.

'A rat? That's a strange best friend for a girl,' said Zach.

Ebony chuckled. 'Back home, I have lots of animals: goats, dogs, cats and chickens. We used to have a horse but he got old and died.' She stared off into the distance for a moment.

Zach cleared his throat and Ebony rose to her feet, startled. 'Want a drink?' she asked.

'What do you have?'

Ebony opened the fridge. It was full of cartons of milk. She held the door open for Zach to see.

'Milk it is then,' said Zach.

'Zach?'

'Yes?'

'How did you know I needed help?'

'I was passing and heard a scream. Then I saw Icarus at the window. I didn't know it was you.'

'But how did you get into my room?'

'The front door was open.'

Ebony frowned. She had closed and locked the door herself. But then again, the locked window had suddenly opened, as well as the bedroom door next to hers, so she would give Zach the benefit of the doubt. Ebony paused, holding two large glasses of milk.

'I'm glad you believe me,' said Zach.

Ebony started; then relaxed. There could be advantages to having a friend who read your mind.

'So, how does this mind-reading thing work then?' asked Ebony, setting the glasses of milk on the table and sitting down.

Zach shrugged his shoulders and folded his arms on the table, staring at the patterns in the wood. The silence was long. Ebony felt the whispery voice trying to speak to her from the back of her mind. It seemed to be getting stronger but she pushed it away.

'I'm sorry,' Zach said. 'I'm not used to talking about it. It's not something that people are usually interested in.'

'Well I am.'

'Really? You don't think it's weird?'

'If you'd asked me that before I came to the city, I think I might have,' said Ebony. 'But in the short time I've been here, I've seen lots of weird things. Reading minds is the least of it!'

Zach chuckled and glanced towards the sink.

'When you put it like that …' His shoulders relaxed. He unfolded his arms and took a big gulp of milk. 'I don't really know how it works,' he said. 'I guess it's what you'd call a fluke.'

'A fluke?'

'It's something I discovered by accident.'

Ebony nodded. After all the accidental discoveries she'd made since arriving the night before, she didn't need him to explain any further.

'Is it difficult to do?' asked Ebony.

'No and yes. It happens naturally, but it can be tiring.'

'So do you have to make a conscious effort?'

'I can usually tell what someone's thinking if I try. But sometimes their thoughts find me. Like yours in the park.'

Ebony was happy that he hadn't purposely been probing into her mind. She felt silly now for running off.

'Can you shut them out if you want?' she asked.

'Sometimes, but other times the voices are so persistent I

have to stop what I'm doing and listen. The worst is when I'm cleaning. I get bombarded by stray thoughts.'

'A boy cleaning? Now *that's* weird,' said Ebony.

'My mum was sick for a long time,' said Zach. 'I had to help out.'

Ebony thought about her grandpa and hoped that Zach's mum had got better. For the first time since her grandpa had died, she felt less alone; but this made her feel guilty. She decided not to pry, partly because it was unfair but mainly so he wouldn't detect her selfish thoughts.

'So you can hear lots of voices at the same time?'

'Hundreds, I think. Often, I don't know who they belong to. They get confused. Muddled up. I have to filter them. But the closer I am to a person, the clearer the message,' said Zach.

Ebony leaned in, intrigued. 'What kind of things do you hear?'

'All sorts – boring stuff like what people had for dinner or what shoes they want to buy. But then I hear the good stuff too. Fears, hopes, dreams, lies – I get the lot!'

'Sounds like a lot of fun.'

'It can be, but it can also get you into trouble. People dislike their thoughts being pried into. Adults don't like me much. They decide I'm a bad kid, but really it's just cos they don't know why they feel so odd around me.' Zach's face fell. 'Then there's the other type of voice …' He trailed off and looked into the distance with a pained look.

'If you don't want to talk about it ...' said Ebony.

Zach shook his head. 'It's actually quite nice to be able to talk. It's horrible having secrets locked inside all the time.'

Nodding vigorously, Ebony shut out all thoughts of the stolen book, the lost roses and the locket in her pocket. She wished she could share them with Zach but something was stopping her.

'So what do these other voices say?' she asked, quickly clearing her mind. She didn't want Zach to know that she was keeping secrets from him. She needed a friend.

'I get messages for people that I have to pass on. I can't ignore these. I have no idea what they're on about, but when I deliver the message, the recipient usually seems to understand.'

'Why don't the people who give you the messages just pass them on themselves?'

'Because they're dead,' said Zach, as flippantly as if he was stating what he'd had for breakfast.

Ebony sat back in her chair, staring at the wall for a moment. 'So you believe the dead can talk?' she asked.

'I know they can,' Zach said, 'but you probably think I'm crazy now.'

'No,' said Ebony. 'Not at all. When my grandpa died, I thought I heard him speak. The doctor said he was gone, but I was certain ...'

'What did he say?'

Don't tell him, said the whisper, but something else

compelled her to speak. It felt as though her brain was battling itself.

'That we'd meet again,' she said.

'Really?' said Zach. 'That's interesting. Did he give you any clues as to how this would happen?'

'What sort of clues?' asked Ebony, guarded.

'Ignore me. I'm just getting carried away. Go on.'

Don't let him know any more, said the whisper. *Find out more about him.* Ebony looked at Zach's face. She decided he'd had enough questioning.

'More milk?'

Zach shook his head. 'I'm sorry to hear about your grandpa,' he said. 'When did he die?'

It was the one thing that she hoped he'd been able to read, so she wouldn't have to say it out loud.

'Yesterday. Yesterday morning.'

The words sounded unreal to Ebony as she spoke them. So much had happened since then that it felt like much longer. Zach squirmed in his seat. Ebony spun the glass around in her hands.

'Sorry,' said Zach after a while.

'It's OK,' Ebony replied, though, of course, it wasn't. 'I think my grandpa would have liked you. He wouldn't have thought you were odd.'

Zach gave a lopsided grin. 'What was he like?'

'He was the best grandpa ever: funny and kind and smart. He could do everything. He didn't finish school but he was very intelligent. Especially on the sea; he was a famous sailor – seafarers came from all around the world to meet him. And he was fantastic with animals. It was Grandpa who saved Winston.' Ebony sighed.

'If you don't want to talk …' said Zach.

'No, you're right. It feels good,' said Ebony. 'My grandpa found Winston when he was a tiny baby. He was all pink, without a scrap of hair on him; an orphan, just like me. My grandpa looked after him and, when he got stronger, gave him to me for my birthday. And now Winston's my best friend – he understands me better than anyone in the world.'

'Can I meet Winston?' asked Zach.

'Sure! He's upstairs. I'll go get him.'

'Do you want me to come with you?'

Be careful, whispered the voice in her head, *go check your things.*

'No, I'll be fine,' said Ebony and she disappeared off.

Thankfully, her rucksack was still there. But then a thought struck her: her grandpa's medal. Although she hadn't thought about it since arriving, she suddenly wanted to check that it was still safe. Her legs trembled as she approached the wardrobe door. Taking a deep breath, she flung it open. It was empty, except for her case and clothes. Feeling inside the lining of the case, she found the presentation box, the wooden disc still tucked neatly inside. The smooth, shiny mahogany felt warm and comforting the moment it was in her hands. Relieved, she popped it back and returned to the kitchen with

Winston in her sleeve. She shook him out and handed him to her new friend.

'Winston, meet Zach.'

As Zach took hold of the rat, Winston squealed as loudly as he could. His hair stood up on end like he'd had an electric shock. He darted off and cowered in the corner.

'That's odd,' said Ebony, glancing at Zach's reddening face. 'Winston! That's not very nice. Zach just saved my life!'

But Winston stayed put. Ebony turned to Zach. 'I'm sorry. He's been unsettled since we got here. He bit me yesterday – look.'

Ebony held out her finger for Zach to see.

'It seems adults aren't the only ones who dislike me,' said Zach.

'I'm sure he'll grow to like you. He just needs time to settle into his new surroundings. He's probably still in shock after being attacked by Uncle Cornelius this morning.' Then she added in a whisper, 'It's the first time he's been back in the kitchen since it happened.'

Winston scurried under the cooker.

'I hope I haven't scared him away completely,' said Zach.

Ebony smiled and shook her head. 'Poor Winston. He's been through a lot. But as my grandpa used to say, he was born a survivor. I'll let him calm down and then give him lots of attention.'

A brief silence followed. Zach checked his watch. 'I've got to go,' he said.

Feeling unexpectedly dismayed, Ebony shuffled in her chair.

'Can I see you again?' she asked.

'Sure. How about tomorrow?'

Ebony smiled.

'I'll meet you outside,' he said, 'at 5 a.m.'

'5 a.m.? The only time I ever got up at 5 a.m. was to help during calving season!'

'I have something exciting to show you, something that I can't let anyone else see.'

Ebony considered the proposition, her curiosity aroused. 'OK, 5 a.m. it is,' she said.

Zach got up to leave. 'Oh, and I wouldn't mention me to your aunt or uncle if I were you. As I say, grown-ups don't take kindly to me.'

Ebony nodded, even though she was certain they wouldn't care; adults were rarely interested in children's friends. But convincing them to let her out at that time would be difficult, so she had no problem with the idea of keeping it a secret.

'Thanks,' said Zach with a smile.

Ebony showed Zach out and made sure the front door was closed and locked. As soon as this was done she took out the piece of jewellery that she had found. It was a delicate crescent-moon-shaped locket hung on a silver chain. Shivers ran down Ebony's spine. How had an apparition managed to leave the locket behind? And why? Ebony opened it, her skin tingling. Inside there were two engravings: a vine on one side and a rose on the other. She fastened the locket around her neck for safekeeping and checked in the hallway mirror to make sure it was completely hidden. Satisfied, she returned to the kitchen to attend to Winston. She arrived just in time to see Winston's tail disappear through the strange door that the creature had gone through.

'Oh, Winston,' she cried.

She would have to follow to make sure he was safe. After all, Winston had no idea what was down there.

18

As Ebony passed through the door under the sink on all fours, the sound of dripping water assaulted her ears and a damp gust of wind hit her face. It was so dark she couldn't tell how low the ceiling of the passage was, but she could feel that it was lined with flagstones. These were icy to the touch, turning her fingers and knees numb as she crawled. The secret passageway felt like it was sloping down. Ebony pictured the beast she'd met in the kitchen – had it been Uncle Cornelius? Hopefully she'd get to Winston before it did so she wouldn't have to find out.

'Winston,' she called in a half whisper, not wanting to disturb whoever, or whatever, was down there.

At the end of what seemed like a very long corridor, the floor changed under her knees. It creaked and groaned like wood. Feeling around, she discovered that she was on a huge wooden platform. As she leaned on it tentatively, the wood whined but held her weight. Relieved, she continued on until she hit a wall. *Impossible! There's got to be a way to keep going,* she thought. *And where is Winston?* As she started to turn to go back the way she had come, something brushed her face and she reached out, hands trembling. There were two long ropes hanging down. She tugged on the ropes, pulling them in different directions like she would to hoist the sails on a yacht. They squeaked into action. She was definitely on a platform – some kind of dumbwaiter – and now it was sinking.

Ebony lowered herself though several dark metres of creaky wood. The temperature cooled as she got lower, but after a few moments lights flickered somewhere down below and the air grew very warm. All of a sudden the light became so bright that it took a few seconds for her eyes to adjust. When she could focus again, Ebony found herself at the back of a huge room with a wall facing her full of television screens. There was a massive chair in the centre facing the screens and a dark passageway leading off to the side. Hundreds of cages hung from the ceiling. Many of the cages were empty, their doors left open; these were covered with cobwebs and rust. But some were closed, gleaming and swinging with the weight of the bird or mouse or frog that they contained. The animals were deadly quiet. *I must have frightened them*, thought Ebony as she stepped off the platform and tiptoed towards the chair. She could feel the animals watching her in silence as she surveyed her surroundings.

It looked like the place was used for surveillance. Each of the screens showed a different scene. Some displayed pond-weed or leaves or clouds and sky. Others were in darkness. Then, in the corner, up high, she spotted a flash of goggle and a violet-coloured eye. The camera zoomed out and there was her Aunt Ruby, stuffed in the sidecar and whizzing at top speed along a busy road lined with houses. Uncle Cornelius was next to her, gripping the motorbike handlebars tightly, leaning into the wind. This confirmed her fears – the creature in the kitchen hadn't been Uncle Cornelius after all.

With her gut churning, Ebony watched as whoever was filming followed her aunt and uncle for a little while, until they could no longer keep up. The camera showed Aunt Ruby and Uncle Cornelius in the distance, growing increasingly small, with puffs of smoke chugging behind them. As they zipped around a bend out of sight, a sleek black motorbike purred its way along the road as though in pursuit. When the road had emptied, a face that Ebony didn't recognise popped out of the hedgerow and made a phonecall. Ebony gritted her teeth. It looked like her aunt was right: they weren't the only ones with surveillance. The man had clearly expected her aunt and uncle to take that route, so someone was watching every move they made. It didn't feel right, it was an invasion of privacy, but then, she thought, how much did she really know about her aunt? What if the spying was justified?

All of a sudden, the creatures in the cages burst into noise. Birds squawked and flapped their wings, frogs croaked and hopped around and mice squeaked, scratching the bottoms of their cages. Ebony ducked behind the chair as the pad of heavy feet could be distinguished over the clamour. She heard a squelching noise and a soft puff of air escape from the chair

– someone or something had sat down! Holding her breath, she crouched lower, trying to make herself as small as possible to avoid detection.

Whoever was on the chair started to fidget, making the chair swing from side to side with their shifting weight. Ebony winced as the bottom of an unruly curl caught in a gap in the floor. She yanked her hair free, concealing a squeal as her scalp pulled. Then she realised the floor was moving and that the chair was set on a large pivot wheel on which she too was crouching. *It must make the screens easier to view on that huge wall*, thought Ebony. The chair spun forty-five degrees, allowing her to peep out at some of the screens. She recognised many of the rooms shown: every communal part of her house was being watched. There was also the park, the street and several other locations that Ebony didn't recognise, including a giant glasshouse. Then on one of the screens flashed a gnarly hand, a lock of matted hair and a familiar bloodshot eye. Ebony recognised Icarus Bean immediately.

The screen crackled off and an image of Mercury Lane replaced it. Her aunt and uncle's motorbike could be seen approaching.

Thank goodness! thought Ebony. *They're back!*

Just as she was about to try to creep back the way she'd come, Ebony spotted Winston in the corner of the room. Not daring to move in case she created a shadow, she watched as her friend made his way along the skirting board before climbing the wall and scuttling across a pipe suspended from the ceiling. Winston stopped when he was directly above Ebony's head and he twitched his whiskers at her in recognition. All the creatures went deadly quiet.

Ebony waited for the noise to start up again, but it didn't – instead, a low growl sounded from the other side of the chair.

Winston blinked down at Ebony and then looked towards the screens. Ebony followed his gaze. All of the screens blinked off and then one by one they flickered back on at random. Each screen showed an enlarged image but Ebony couldn't make it out. She realised they were forming one gigantic picture like a mosaic. As more screens blinked on, the image became clear. She gasped. The whole wall was covered with a bird's-eye view of Ebony peering out from behind the armchair.

Ebony looked up at her pet rat and then back at the television screen, not believing her eyes. She was showing on the screen at exactly the same angle that Winston was viewing her. Winston was a spy? Impossible! He must have been set up – surely he wouldn't treat her like this. Ebony waved her hands in an attempt to shoo Winston away, but he stayed motionless, staring at her.

Whatever was on the chair sniffed the air, growling. Then the growl turned into a throaty chuckle. Ebony tucked her head back behind the chair. She had an awful feeling that something bad was about to happen and wished the creature would get it over with.

As though answering her thoughts, the creature spun the

chair around ninety degrees, then rotated again. It started to spin in a complete circle, slowly at first, but soon faster and faster, spinning around and around until Ebony felt sick. Then, as suddenly as the spinning had started, it stopped, and Ebony sprawled forward. Feeling hundreds of pairs of eyes on her, she didn't dare look up, but after a few moments, she had to peek. The surveillance screens had changed again: each showed a different angle of Ebony flopped on the floor. The realisation suddenly hit her that all the animals above her were acting as living cameras!

Ebony heard a slight cough and looked up. The creature from the kitchen glared down at her over the back of the chair – and it was definitely not her uncle. Its eyes were grey, not amber, and its silver hair had stripes of black running through it. Its face didn't look friendly at all.

'I'm sorry,' stammered Ebony. 'I didn't mean to intrude.'

The creature snarled and bared its teeth. Its incisors were long and sharp, tapering to a fine point. It leaped off the chair and landed on the floor in front of Ebony with a heavy thud. Creeping towards her on all fours, one slow step at a time, it flicked its long tail behind it, like a cross between a lion and a four-legged Uncle Cornelius. This was a creature unlike any she had ever seen before. Ebony backed off, wishing she hadn't left the whistle on the kitchen table. Then she noticed something moving along the pipes.

'No, Winston!' she cried.

But it was too late.

Winston hurled himself off the pipe in the direction of the beast. The rat spread out his claws as far as he could and opened his mouth wide. As he landed on the beast's nose, Winston chomped down hard, removing a clump of skin and hair. The creature howled and swatted at Winston with his paw. Winston dodged. He leaped for the relative safety of the chair, but the Uncle Cornelius lookalike saw his chance and swung at Winston, flipping him high up in the air and opening his jaws wide as he did so. Winston began to fall and landed in the middle of the gaping jaws. With one snap of the creature's teeth, Winston was caged.

'No!' shouted Ebony.

Winston's tail poked out from between the beast's teeth. As Ebony rushed forward to grab it, the creature sucked hard and the tail disappeared like a piece of spaghetti. She watched as the creature gulped. A lump travelled down his throat as he swallowed Winston whole.

'You animal,' shouted Ebony, tears welling up in her eyes. Then a loud crack made them both look up.

'Ebony Smart, what on earth are you doing down here?' asked Aunt Ruby.

She looked fierce in her neck-to-ankle dress. Her violet eyes flashed like an electrical storm. In her hand she held a great big leather whip which she slapped against the ground. The creature that looked like Uncle Cornelius cowered and moved backwards, snarling. Ebony gawped, red-faced – there was no getting out of this one.

'Back!' cried Aunt Ruby, brandishing the whip again. The creature backed off even further, staring at Ebony the whole time and licking his lips.

'He's eaten Winston,' shouted Ebony.

'Quiet!' shouted Aunt Ruby. 'Didn't I tell you the basement was out of bounds?'

'But I didn't know this was the basement! Who uses a secret passage under their sink to get into their basement?'

The beast made a sound like a snigger. Aunt Ruby spun the whip once more and this time it caught the creature's bottom. The beast roared and Winston flew out of his mouth, covered in sticky saliva and half-digested flesh.

Ebony ran to gather Winston up. But before she reached him, the beast ran straight towards her and reared up, sending her reeling back. Aunt Ruby lashed out again and this time the creature ran off along the passageway, squealing. The sound gradually faded until he couldn't be heard at all. Then the whip cracked again just in front of Ebony, narrowly missing her nose. She jumped, staring at her aunt in disbelief.

'I'm sorry, Aunt Ruby,' she mumbled.

'Sorry? You were nearly a goner.'

As Aunt Ruby's voice grew louder, Aunt Ruby herself seemed to be growing. Her hands shook with rage, making the whip quiver. She stomped towards Ebony.

In a flash, Uncle Cornelius appeared from the dumbwaiter shaft. He rushed to Ebony's side and put his arm around her, pulling her back slightly. Ebony was so surprised she nearly toppled over. Staring at her uncle's face, she was struck by how much it resembled the wild creature's. Winston stopped in his tracks, cowering. Aunt Ruby moved closer, her face still and mask-like; it looked as though she was in a trance.

'When I say it's out of bounds, I *mean* it's *out of bounds*,' she roared.

Aunt Ruby's hair blew wildly behind her even though there was no wind. She took another step closer and then Uncle Cornelius did the strangest thing: he opened his mouth wide and began to sing. The song was enchanting, like water bubbling into the sea, mixed with birdsong and the whisper of dragonfly wings. Ghostly images of butterflies and hummingbirds poured from his mouth and surrounded Aunt Ruby. She swatted at them playfully, letting them land on her shoulders and hair as she giggled like a young girl.

Suddenly, Uncle Cornelius stopped singing and Aunt Ruby fell to the floor. Rushing to her side, Uncle Cornelius lifted her arm. When he let go, it plopped to the ground. Aunt Ruby had fainted. Uncle Cornelius motioned for Ebony to come and help him lift her.

'But she tried to hit me,' said Ebony.

Angry tears threatened to fall. Uncle Cornelius cocked his moon-round head to one side and then picked up Winston and handed him to Ebony. Holding her breath, Ebony reached out and stroked Uncle Cornelius like she'd seen Aunt Ruby do. He smiled and pointed to the body on the floor then beckoned for Ebony's help.

Despite being angry, Ebony couldn't refuse. Taking her aunt by the arms while her uncle took the legs, they managed to lift Aunt Ruby on to the dumbwaiter. Uncle Cornelius kneeled next to Ruby, feeling her forehead and checking her pulse. When he was satisfied that Ruby was OK, he pulled at the ropes with all his might to haul them up.

19

Back in the living room they laid Aunt Ruby on the floor in front of the fire. While Uncle Cornelius dabbed Aunt Ruby's face with a cold flannel, Ebony picked the bits of bone and flesh off Winston's fur.

After several dabs of cold water, Aunt Ruby finally came around. She drank a cup of warm sweet tea that Uncle Cornelius brought her and slowly returned to normal. But that didn't stop Ebony sitting on the furthest beanbag possible from her, just in case. Uncle Cornelius seated himself by Ebony's side like a sentry. Ebony regretted the mean thoughts she'd had about him earlier that day, but she couldn't help wondering what his connection was to the creature in the basement.

Aunt Ruby was quiet. She looked thoughtful, glancing intermittently at Uncle Cornelius and Ebony in the far corner of the room. After a while, she lit her pipe and sucked on it. Then she leaned forward with a sad look. 'I'm sorry that you had to see me like that, Ebony.'

'Sorry? You tried to hit me with the whip! Just because you didn't want me finding out about your hidden cameras.'

Even though Ebony was afraid of angering her aunt again, she couldn't help her outburst. Fury raged in her veins – how dare her aunt turn Winston into a spy? Aunt Ruby groaned and covered her eyes, rubbing them between thumb and forefinger.

'I was worried about your safety! But I admit maybe I went about it the wrong way. I'm truly sorry. Forgive me?'

'For what? The violence or for using my rat against me? What did you do to him anyway?' Inside, Ebony was raging. There was no way she would forgive her aunt where Winston was concerned.

'We have cameras implanted in the creatures,' said Aunt Ruby. 'It's a necessary safety precaution.'

'It's sick,' spat Ebony. 'And you had no right to touch Winston. Just like you had no right to try to hit me.'

Aunt Ruby's eyes filled with tears. 'I can't help it. Everyone in the Order of Nine Lives is affected by their birth moon – and the power becomes stronger as you get older. Unfortunately, I was born under a negative new moon. It makes me have … funny turns, sometimes.'

'There are funny turns and then there's abuse,' said Ebony.

'You'll find out for yourself when you're old enough,' replied her aunt. 'You were born under a waxing crescent moon, which is even more unpredictable! Believe me, it's no fun. The stronger the moon, the stronger the effects.'

'Moon or no moon, I would never hurt those I care about,' responded Ebony, making a mental note of her birth moon, just in case.

Aunt Ruby shrugged. 'You'll see.'

Her eyes betrayed a tired look that Ebony had sometimes seen in her grandpa. It was the first similarity she'd noticed and it softened her mood.

'You're not *that* old – you look about thirty at the most,' said Ebony, considering her aunt's smooth, porcelain skin and bright red hair.

Aunt Ruby chuckled.

'I'm much older than that, dear. I've some clever lotions and potions that keep me looking young. There's no point being an inventor if you can't enjoy some perks! It's all about imagination.'

'Like that thing downstairs?' asked Ebony. 'Did I just imagine him?'

'Mulligan? Oh no, he is very real, my dear. He's a family heirloom. He was captured in one of your father's previous lives, during one of his expeditions. Your father was a very famous Victorian explorer, though he always hid what he was really searching for. He never did locate any more of our kind, no matter how many leads he followed, but Mulligan was his prize find: a prehistoric wildcat. He's very useful.'

'You're telling me that that thing is thousands of years old?' Ebony said sarcastically.

Her aunt let it pass. 'Easily. He makes me seem young.' She laughed.

Not really in the mood for laughing, Ebony glared at her aunt. She suddenly felt exhausted by all the bizarre events and stories. *I want out of here; I want to go home*, she thought.

'Will it happen again? One of your funny turns?' asked Ebony.

'I won't lie to you. It might, if I'm angry or upset,' said Aunt Ruby.

'So is that what Icarus Bean wanted to warn me about?'

'Icarus? When?' Her aunt's voice had suddenly become very high pitched.

'When I arrived,' said Ebony. 'He was waiting for me outside and told me I was in danger.'

'Why didn't you tell me?'

'I was going to … But you went all strange when I mentioned his name.'

'You said you heard his name during a phonecall. Meeting him in person is a completely different matter altogether!'

Hanging her head, Ebony mumbled, 'You could still have told me about him.'

Aunt Ruby thought hard. 'Yes, I could, but I thought you had enough to get your head around as it was. He's in exile by order of the High Court, so by rights we're not meant to talk about him. I can't believe he had the nerve to come here.'

'Doesn't exile mean you're sent away?' asked Ebony.

'Yes, banished to the Shadowlands. The exiled person becomes imprisoned, only able to move within the shadows. When the gateway to the Reflectory closed, it was realised that to prevent future wars and further attempts to break in the Order would need an official organisation to oversee our people. So the High Court was created. Because of our close relationship with the universe many of us had been able to access magic, but now its use was restricted to members of the High Court – though some of us do retain a special gift or two. As well as making the final decree on our Ultimation, the court was given the power to banish people who could potentially harm the Order. Icarus is not the only one; I'm sure that's what happened to many of our missing people. If I'm right, they're everywhere, these exiles, watching. But they can't harm us. They observe, like ghosts.'

'So how come Icarus could talk to me?'

Aunt Ruby smiled. 'When the High Court banished him, something unusual happened – he wasn't trapped in the Shadowlands like the others. He could move in and out of the shadows at will – it's as though the Reflectory somehow intervened.'

Ebony shuddered and touched her throat; she could still feel the grip of Icarus Bean's leathery hands choking her. If the Reflectory was this wonderful place of peace and light, as her aunt kept insisting, she couldn't understand why it would help someone like Icarus.

'But why do you think the High Court has banished everyone?'

'Like I said, power can be a terrible thing. They could simply have been forgotten about, or the High Court could know about them and want to keep them away.'

Aunt Ruby looked around nervously and shuffled in her chair. 'Icarus was blamed for a terrible crime for which the

Nine Lives High Court declared him an exile, but he has always maintained his innocence. He was very powerful within the Order until they stripped him of his title, and is both feared and respected in what's left of our community. There's a rumour that he has a few supporters who are protecting him, but he hasn't been seen publicly for years.'

'Hasn't been seen until now,' said Ebony, but something in the way her aunt had said the name Icarus struck her as odd. Almost like she cared about him. Suddenly Ebony started to wonder if Aunt Ruby was on the side of Icarus Bean – one of his supporters?

As far as she was concerned, she'd seen all the evidence of his guilt she needed through the binoculars. He had murdered her grandpa. *The Book of Learning* had helped her to find out the truth and she was determined to see Icarus brought to justice. If all this reincarnation stuff was true, then it was clearly the only way to achieve her destiny. And after all, wasn't her grandpa part of the Order? She'd do anything to see him again. But caution crept over Ebony like a protective shield and her mind raced – who could she trust to help her if her Aunt Ruby was a supporter of the murderer? An idea struck her – a way to find out how trustworthy her aunt really was.

'Aunt Ruby, have you heard anything yet about how grandpa died?'

'Not a thing, dear,' replied Aunt Ruby, almost too quickly and calmly. 'As I said earlier, I expect it will take some time.'

Clearly uncomfortable with the way the conversation was going, she patted her knee as a deflection and Uncle Cornelius ran straight over.

'He's such a good boy,' said Aunt Ruby, rubbing under his chin. 'You're nothing like your mean dad, are you? You wouldn't go attacking young girls in the basement.' She looked up at Ebony. 'His mother was of much milder temperament, easily trained. Thankfully, Uncle Cornelius took after her.'

'Is she in the basement too?' asked Ebony.

Uncle Cornelius whimpered and Aunt Ruby stroked under his chin.

'I'm afraid not. She died years ago.'

Uncle Cornelius flopped from two legs onto four. His shirt sleeves tightened, showing strong muscles. As Ebony stared at him, she realised for the first time just how inhuman he looked with his sharp teeth, huge hairy hands and scrunched-up face. Winston sat bolt upright, also watching her uncle.

'So Uncle Cornelius is a prehistoric wildcat too?'

'Well, he was born here, in captivity. But yes, he's the same species. Your grandpa helped me tame him.'

Her grandpa? He had never mentioned Aunt Ruby, never mind a wildcat! Other than the stickers on the boxes in the attic and the matching tiles in the locked room, there was nothing in 23 Mercury Lane that showed any link to home. But then again, maybe she hadn't looked hard enough.

Aunt Ruby continued. 'I trained him to walk on two legs and to pass through the world without drawing attention to himself. With a bit of dentistry and grooming, it was easy to make him look almost human. Your grandpa taught him how to drive and sing, though he never did grasp how to talk. Still, he communicates in his own way, through signals and actions. He really is a remarkable creature.' She ruffled the hair on Uncle Cornelius's neck. 'He's a whizz when it comes to surveillance.'

'And that thing in the basement?'

'The two of them are my security team. There's been a lot of odd goings on in the last while – and some grizzly things too – so they've become my eyes and ears. Mulligan is almost completely deaf now – he can't hear anything except for his dog whistle.' She waved the whistle in the air. 'But they both have acute eyesight and they're great at sensing anything unusual. Mulligan was way too wild to be trained to communicate, but Uncle Cornelius can communicate with him and passes on his messages.'

'Why do you call him my uncle?'

Aunt Ruby laughed, but there was a sad note in her voice. 'I named him in memory of my late husband. I need to get about and I need protection; I know too much about the inner sanctum of the Nine Lives High Court. I used to work there full time until Icarus was exiled – I was their weaponry specialist before they moved me to transport and travel. That knowledge would be useful in the wrong hands.'

Ebony listened carefully for more clues.

'It was an important position. I know too much and yet,

in many ways, I don't know enough. It makes things highly dangerous. There are people out there who would harm me the moment they got a chance. That's why I keep a low profile – I need to do my research in peace. But I wouldn't get very far if people knew I had a prehistoric wildcat by my side. Even if he is tame. Imagine!'

As strange as it sounded, this made sense to Ebony. But keeping a dangerous cold-blooded killer in the basement did not.

'But why keep Mulligan when he's so dangerous?'

'I can't very well turn him out – he'd have the city eaten up in a few months.'

'Can't you get him put down?'

'You sound like Judge Ambrose!' Ebony flinched at the accusation. 'That creature's survived an Ice Age, war and floods. How do *you* suggest I kill him?'

'A poison dart gun?' suggested Ebony.

Uncle Cornelius let out a high-pitched wail. Aunt Ruby grabbed hold of his hand to stop him from running away. She stared at Ebony in disbelief.

'I don't want to kill him. He's living history – and very good protection.'

'When he's not trying to kill you,' said Ebony.

'He's usually OK in the basement,' continued Aunt Ruby. 'I asked Cornelius to tell him only to check on you if you blew the whistle. The only reason he attacked you was because you went into his space – he doesn't like anyone he doesn't know being down there. Otherwise, he rarely surfaces without being called – unless there's a dangerous intruder in the house. Did you call him?' She looked quizzically at her niece.

'No.' Ebony carefully made no mention of Icarus being inside the house – now that it seemed like her aunt might support him, the trust she had felt growing was shattered. She also didn't want any questioning to lead to Zach – she'd made her friend a promise – so she didn't mention blowing the whistle either.

'So how did you find the secret passage?'

'I heard a noise downstairs and when I came down to investigate I caught Mulligan in the kitchen eating. When he saw me he dived back into the tunnel. Then Winston went after him and I had to go and get him – I was worried he'd be hurt.'

Ebony hoped the surveillance cameras weren't able to record – that her encounter with Icarus Bean had gone undetected and Mulligan wouldn't think of communicating that Zach had been there. It was a lot to hope for but there was nothing else she could do.

'Oh, Ebony,' said Aunt Ruby, her voice quivering. 'If this arrangement is going to work, we need to be straight with each other. Is there anything else you've not told us that we should know about?'

Straight? thought Ebony. *Like you're being about Icarus Bean?* But she knew that fighting about this now could damage any hope of finding out more about Icarus and bringing him to justice.

'No,' she lied. 'Except … I think someone was spying on you while you were out.' She had to get her aunt to believe she trusted her – how else would she get the information she needed? 'I saw you on the surveillance cameras, whizzing along a road. A man stuck his head up when you passed and made a phonecall. It was like he was waiting for you.'

'Ah, so that's why we failed.' Aunt Ruby sighed. 'He'll have been reporting to the judge. Ambrose obviously trusts us as much as we trust him.'

'What were you doing out there anyway? Was it something to do with my roses?' asked Ebony.

'We had hoped to get a peek inside the judge's car to see if they were still there without him knowing anything about it, but he was waiting for us when we arrived and I had to make up another reason for our presence. The spy had probably seen us passing by earlier and tipped him off. We'll try again soon.'

'Let me come with you – I can help.'

'No, it would be far too dangerous if we were caught. I won't risk taking you along.'

Unable to take any more, Ebony snatched up Winston and ran out of the room. She took the stairs two at a time, her face hot and her legs trembling.

20

When Ebony reached her room, she slammed the door shut and shoved Winston into his cage, covering it with a T-shirt so he couldn't spy on her any more. She kicked the bedpost, angry with the city and everyone in it, including Winston. Lifting up the T-shirt she peered in.

'I can't trust you – you're a traitor,' she said, 'even if you were forced into it. I can't risk it.'

Winston crept towards Ebony but she put the T-shirt back in place before he could get too close. She would never have felt this way if her grandpa was alive or if she was back at home. Oddley Cove seemed so very far away. Loneliness filled her heart, leaving a gaping hole she'd never felt before. Anger at her grandpa thundered inside her – why did he have to die and leave her in the care of such horrible people? At least she had Zach; he was the only person who seemed to understand her right now.

'I just want things to be normal!' Ebony cried out, slamming her fists into the duvet before burying her face and a loud scream in its folds.

Feeling a little better, she took the scrapbook she'd

brought from home out of the drawer in the bedside table and started to flick through it. Mitzi the one-eyed dog, George and Cassandra, the old horse that died – they were all there. But their friendly faces only made her loneliness worse. Overwhelmed by feelings of sadness, Ebony closed the scrapbook and stowed it back in the drawer. Her mind turned to Icarus Bean and the sadness turned to a fierce rage that made her blood boil. She might as well forget about Oddley Cove – that life was long gone. She had to focus on her life now, and that meant bringing Icarus to justice. But how?

Snatching up *The Book of Learning*, she managed to squeeze out a small drop of blood to open it, then flicked through its browned pages, scanning all the information she had uncovered so far. When she reached a fresh page, Ebony stopped. It showed a four-by-four grid almost completely filled with small tiles – fifteen in total – reminding her of the surveillance cameras. Each tile had squiggles or letters on it. One tile was missing, leaving a single empty space in the centre. She tapped the page impatiently, wondering what it meant. Then a movement caught her eye.

One of the tiles slid to the right, into the empty space. Then another moved up into the space, joining their letters perfectly to form a word: THE.

'It's one of those sliding puzzles!' cried Ebony out loud, forgetting her anger for a moment. 'It's another test! I'll start with the writing.'

Placing her finger on one of the tiles, she slid it across. Then she moved another and another. Within moments, after a few wrong moves, the writing was perfectly formed.

THE AMULET

'It looks like there's a picture of something above, but I can't make it out.' She sighed, realising the letters were meant to go at the top of the grid and the image below. She'd have to scramble what she'd done so far and start again. 'OK. Let's see what this amulet-thing looks like!'

As she shifted tile after tile, slowly moving the writing up, the image began to form. Eventually, a drawing of the amulet appeared.

The amulet was a tiny crescent-moon-shaped locket made of delicately engraved silver. Inside, a vine wended its way around the left-hand side, leading across to the delicate rose on the other. The drawing was very skilled, capturing glimmers of light on the chain and pendant so perfectly that it looked real, like it could be lifted out of the page.

Hardly believing her eyes, Ebony undid the clasp on the necklace the apparition had left her. She checked behind her to make absolutely sure that Winston couldn't see out of his cage and then flicked the locket open. Inside, the engravings matched those on the diagram perfectly.

Ebony realised that she held the amulet in her hand – but what did it mean? And why had it been given to her?

There was a knock on the door.

'Ebony, can I come in?' called Aunt Ruby.

Quickly fastening the locket around her neck again and tucking it under her jumper, Ebony hid *The Book of Learning* under her pillow. Then she smoothed down her clothes before sitting on the bed, trying to look as natural as possible. After a moment, her aunt popped her head around the door.

'I just came to see if you were OK,' said Aunt Ruby.

She held out a mug of warm milk and a sandwich. There was an uncomfortable silence. Ebony knew she should probably say sorry for shouting, but the words wouldn't come out of her mouth. She was still too angry with her aunt. But, unsure what else to do, she accepted the milk, cradling the mug in her hands.

After a while, the silence became unbearable. Ebony couldn't stop thinking about Mulligan – she kept seeing his snarling jaw coming towards her. Some prize find! She decided to try a different line of questioning, to see if it led to any new information.

'Aunt Ruby – will you tell me about my father's explorations in his Victorian reincarnation?'

Aunt Ruby's eyes sparkled.

'Lieutenant Rufus Smart was the best explorer that the Order has ever seen,' she said, sitting down. 'Or he was, until disaster struck.'

Ebony felt her heart skip. 'He got lost? Stampeded by wildebeest? Eaten by cannibals?' she asked.

'Nothing that dramatic, I'm afraid. He simply disappeared.'

'Just like my own father,' said Ebony falling quiet.

'He was involved in important work, in both lives,' said Aunt Ruby in a consoling voice.

'Like what? Finding more of the Order?'

'Yes. But something even more important. Back in the Victorian times, he was guarding the amulet.'

Ebony perked up at this new thread in the story. 'But you said only the guardian could use the amulet.'

'Use, yes. But when our guardian was killed in Victorian times, Rufus took it upon himself to keep the amulet safe.'

'So you have it? Can I see it?'

Her aunt's face fell. 'I'm afraid not. Rufus worried that, before he killed the guardian, the murderer might have first extracted the secret of how to use the amulet to get into the Reflectory. He decided to try to modify it, but then it too was lost.'

'Lost?'

'I'm afraid so. When he disappeared, it could not be found, and all memory of its possible whereabouts was erased from your father's memory. We have searched for it ever since, but we haven't discovered it yet. That's what your own parents were doing when they were lost at sea.'

Ebony hid her excitement. She didn't feel overly sad about her parents – she had grown up without them and their disappearance was an everyday fact in her life – but she did feel proud that she had found what her parents were seeking. The amulet was in her possession, and only she knew about it. However, until she was certain whom she could trust, she decided she wouldn't mention it to anyone. She would carry on as though she was ignorant and everything was completely normal.

'Can't you make another one?'

Aunt Ruby widened her eyes in horror, until they looked like giant bouncy balls. 'You can't just get an amulet from anywhere!'

'You recreated the roses.'

'The roses are powerful, but they were plentiful – there was only one amulet! It was forged by the ancients, using magic we no longer know. We don't even know what it looks like. Now that it is lost, unless it can be found, we must work without it.'

Ebony stared at her aunt, mouth agape. Was the necklace she wore really so powerful?

'And your records don't say when or where it was lost? Maybe Rufus hid it somewhere?'

Aunt Ruby shrugged her shoulders and sighed. 'Who knows? We only have stories and hearsay to go on. The amulet was a locket: that much we know, thanks to Rufus's diaries. But the page that held the drawing of it has been torn out.'

Ebony fought to hide her smile. But what good was having the amulet to enter the Reflectory without the roses to show her the entrance – and what use were either of them if she didn't know how to use them? She needed more information from her aunt.

'Aunt Ruby, I want to help you with your research,' she

said, placing her hand on top of her aunt's and giving it a squeeze. 'I want to help you find the amulet, and more people from the Order, to restore things to how they should be.'

'I'm worried, Ebony,' said Aunt Ruby, openly troubled. 'It goes against your grandpa's wishes, and there are many dangers involved.'

'I'm part of this heritage too,' argued Ebony. 'Grandpa may not have told me about it, but if he was involved, I want to be too. In his honour. Hope and perseverance – that's the motto, right?'

Aunt Ruby stared intensely into Ebony's eyes and sighed. 'OK, I'll think about it,' she said.

Ebony nodded and smiled, feeling a strange mix of fear and elation in her stomach. Suddenly exhausted, she went into the bathroom and changed into her pyjamas. Then she climbed into bed and let Aunt Ruby tuck her in. Her aunt kissed Ebony's head and disappeared through the door.

Despite her tiredness, with only a few hours left before she had to meet Zach, Ebony found it impossible to sleep. As the sounds of the night whistled through the house, she mulled the situation over in her head. She'd figured out who the murderer was, but how would she reveal Icarus Bean's guilt like the book demanded? Who was it that needed to know the truth? There was only one person she could think of: Judge Ambrose. Aunt Ruby had done everything she could to make him seem untrustworthy, but was it a trick? Mulligan, whips, apparitions: Ebony certainly didn't feel safe with her aunt. The judge was strict but he was clearly against Icarus, whereas her aunt ... Ebony just couldn't be sure. By the time she'd drifted off to sleep, Ebony had resolved to somehow get the judge on her side.

21

It was still dark at 5 a.m. when Ebony Smart peeped out of her window to see if Zach was outside. Her breath misted the window as she pressed her nose to the glass. As promised, Zach was there, standing in a pool of light cast by one of the streetlights.

Ebony stuffed *The Book of Learning* into her rucksack and left Winston snoozing in his locked cage, checking first that the T-shirt was still in place in case he woke up and spotted her leaving.

Sleep had reduced Ebony's feelings of resentment towards Winston and she felt guilty leaving him alone, but she couldn't risk him revealing her whereabouts on the surveillance cameras again. Ebony crept downstairs, checking for spiders and bugs along the way. She didn't know how the cameras worked, but she had realised that they used small creatures to provide the images. The coast was clear but it wasn't easy to unlock the door quietly in the sleeping house and the hinges groaned as Ebony pulled it open. She paused, making sure that she hadn't disturbed anyone. When no one stirred, she slipped outside, hoping she'd be back before her aunt or uncle woke up – leaving the house this early wouldn't be easy to explain.

'Hi,' Ebony whispered, when she had closed the door behind her. She felt a little shy but as soon as Zach grinned Ebony felt at ease. He beckoned to her to follow and they set off down the road in silence. A gentle wind blew and a drizzle, so light that she could hardly feel it on her bare hands, was falling. Ebony spotted a few stars and the bluish new moon high above the glare of the streetlights as she followed Zach down the street. They turned the corner – Zach was a little ahead and she had to jog to catch up – and headed towards the park, the only part of the city that Ebony recognised.

They passed the entrance that Ebony had used and circled round the boundary railing towards the huge gateway that she'd exited from – the thought of all the commotion she had caused with the horse and carriage made her cheeks burn. Thankfully, it was too dark for Zach to see. When they reached the iron gates, Ebony and Zach climbed over them, the stone pillars at either side looking even bigger in the dark. Excitement pumped through Ebony's veins as she paused for a moment, letting her eyes grow accustomed to the lack of streetlights. It was just like home.

As her eyes became used to the dark, Ebony could just make out Zach weaving his way towards the pond. She followed him. In the distance a splash of moonlight reflected off the water's surface. Zach stopped at a strangely carved marble seat. It was green and bronze. The back reared up to a point, with a bronze bauble on top which looked like a head. The stone had grooves cut into it: these curved down to a small basin which looked like it had once held water, like an elaborate bird bath. Above the basin was an intricate carving of a rose.

'It looks like a lady holding a rose,' said Ebony.

'That's exactly what it is,' said Zach, clearly impressed. 'Most people walk by without noticing it, which, as you'll see, is a bonus for me. Right, let's make sure there's no one around.'

Ebony wondered why they were bothering; surely no one else would be in the park at this hour. But she did as Zach asked. The park was dark and full of shadowy shapes, but none moved.

'I think the coast is clear,' said Ebony.

Zach reached out and took hold of the bronze rose. He twisted it to the right and then to the left. The rose clicked. Then it clunked. A noise like an elevator hummed from inside the marble chair and, to Ebony's amazement, the seat started sinking. Within seconds, they were facing a gaping hole. Inside the hole were mossy steps leading down into the earth.

'Welcome,' said Zach, bowing ceremoniously. Ebony giggled.

'What is this place?'

'Come and see.'

Zach bounded down the staircase. With each footfall, small lights appeared on either side of each step, making the moss glow.

Suddenly, her internal voice returned. It was a stronger whisper than before: *Don't go inside*, it said. But Ebony ignored it and followed close behind her friend. The softness of the stairs reminded her of walking through the woods in Oddley Cove. She sucked in the scent of damp earth and grass. As they went deeper, the air grew warmer and the whisper faded until it was gone completely. Behind, the entrance hummed as it closed.

At the bottom of the staircase, Zach clapped and the room lit up with flaming candelabras.

'How did you light those candles?' asked Ebony.

'Your aunt's not the only inventor around here – they're not real,' said Zach. 'Look.'

He swept his hand through the flame, unharmed. Ebony tried it. She couldn't feel anything as her hand passed through.

'That's amazing!' she said.

'Not as amazing as that,' said Zach, looking upwards.

Ebony followed his gaze. Above their heads was a vast glass ceiling. Beyond it, Ebony could see a reflection of the moon rippling like diamonds. Pondweed billowed and tiny fish swam in small schools, swirling their way across the liquid sky.

'We're under the pond?' asked Ebony. 'It's so beautiful.'

'It's nice to hear someone else appreciate it,' said Zach.

Looking around, Ebony felt immediately comfortable in the room. In front of her an ornate four-poster bed draped with burgundy curtains was pushed up against the wall. A hearth was built halfway along the far wall, with an old-fashioned black leather sofa facing it. To her right there was a small kitchen. Next to where they had come in there was a tiny wooden door, which she guessed concealed a bathroom. Ebony sniffed at the air. The place was filled with countryside smells: soil and fresh-cut grass, pine trees and water lilies. She inhaled deeply.

'This is where you live?' asked Ebony. 'It's incredible!' Dropping her rucksack to the floor, she stretched out her arms and spun slowly on the spot, her face raised to the ceiling. 'It's magical.'

'I'm glad you like it. It's the first time I've shown the place to anyone,' said Zach.

'Like it? I love it!'

Zach's cheeks coloured. Ebony pretended not to notice and returned to spinning. Then she stopped abruptly.

'Do you live here *completely* alone? How did you find this place?'

'It's where I grew up.'

Ebony looked about her, trying to figure out how a whole family could live in such a small space with only one bed.

'It's much bigger than it looks,' explained Zach. 'If you go through that door there's a whole heap of rooms. But now I'm alone, I just live in this one.'

Ebony fought the urge to peep behind the door. Zach had obviously closed it off for a reason.

'There are good memories here,' continued Zach. It made sense to stay when …'

He paused awkwardly, so Ebony hurriedly filled the uncomfortable silence. 'You're so lucky – but don't you have *anyone* to look after you?'

Zach's face darkened as he plopped down on the sofa. As Ebony joined him, she noticed that the wall was also made out of glass. Outside, a mass of worms, ants and other bugs could be seen building nests, collecting food, fighting.

'You're quite safe,' said Zach, before she could ask whether the bugs could be her aunt's spies.

Ebony stayed silent and patiently waited to see whether Zach wanted to discuss his family; he'd listened to her talking about her grandpa, after all.

'My parents are gone,' he said after a short while. 'My mother was sick for a very long time and …'

'Are your parents dead?'

When Zach didn't reply, Ebony felt her heart sink.

'But what about aunts or uncles – couldn't they look after you?'

'I don't have any other family,' he replied, after a moment's pause. 'Icarus Bean took care of that.'

Zach looked away, his brow locked in a deep frown. Ebony recognised that kind of look: it meant *I'm upset and I don't want to talk about it* more than it meant *I'm not bothered*. She suddenly felt guilty for feeling so alone. After all, she had Winston and her aunt and Uncle Cornelius, as strange as they were. Although they were many miles away, she knew that Old Joe and the villagers would be thinking about her. And she felt like her grandpa was still watching over her. Zach was completely alone – and somehow it was Icarus Bean's fault.

As hard as she tried, Ebony couldn't think of anything useful to say. So she decided to try to cheer Zach up another way.

'I also have something to show you,' she said, taking out *The Book of Learning* and handing it to him.

The distraction worked. Zach's eyes brightened as he tried to open the book. He dug his nails into the seam but, as Ebony expected, nothing happened. Intrigued, Zach looked up with a crinkled forehead.

'Go on, put me out of my misery,' he said, sitting back in his chair and holding the book out in front of him.

Taking it, Ebony crouched on the floor. 'There's a special way of opening it,' she said. 'Watch!'

She picked at the wound on her finger, even though it was getting quite sore by now, and wiped it on the casing to make the book spring open.

Zach leaned in. 'Did you open it using blood?'

Ebony didn't reply.

'Oh, that's gross,' said Zach, obviously impressed. He shuffled forward and rubbed his hands together.

'I found it in my uncle's study. He doesn't know I have it. No one does, except you.'

Now that they had both shared secrets, their friendship

was cemented. Zach looked pleased.

'I think it was written by one of my ancestors – also called Ebony Smart. Weird, hey? And in the library I discovered that another Ebony Smart lived in my aunt's house in the 1700s,' said Ebony. 'And guess what? She was murdered.'

'Murdered?' Zach raised his eyebrows and he leaned in close. 'Three Ebony Smarts?' he continued, a slight smirk playing on his lips. 'How is that possible?'

'Don't laugh! It seems my family has a severe lack of imagination!'

Zach chuckled. Relieved, Ebony continued. 'It's an unusual book, with moving pictures and everything. I don't quite understand it yet – but I will. Look!' She held the book open on the brown hangman page – the body forever frozen in mid-swing in the noose.

Zach smiled at her determined face and leaned in. But instead of showing interest, he recoiled and covered his eyes with his arm, a painful cry escaping from his downturned lips.

'Zach, what's wrong?' cried Ebony, jumping up.

The book fell to the floor at Zach's feet. 'Close it!' he cried, terrified.

'It's just a game of hangman, Zach. Can't you see that?'

'Ebony, *please*!' The request was drawn out, like he was in agony.

Snatching the book up, Ebony slammed it shut and shoved it in her pocket.

'Ever get the feeling you're not very popular?' said Zach, with a note of sadness in his voice.

'What did you see?'

Zach replied with a shake of his head. 'I can't really say … it was more impressions than actual images … fire, blood, screams … it was horrible.' A shudder ran through Zach's body, making him quiver.

Ebony cleared her throat, her mind going back to the eternal pain her aunt talked about when she first explained about the High Court signing the final decree – was this what Zach had seen?

'I'm sorry. I don't know why that happened.'

'It's not your fault. But whatever you have there, it's obviously very powerful.'

Ebony heaved a huge sigh of relief that he didn't seem to be holding her responsible. 'I really wish I knew what was going on. My aunt doesn't make much sense – she told me all this nonsense about being part of a reincarnated people.'

A smile played on Zach's lips. 'And do you believe her?'

'There's certainly been lots of weird stuff happening. Stuff that can't be explained any other way. Wouldn't you?'

Zach shrugged. 'You're talking to someone who hears voices and reads minds.'

Ebony laughed. 'I just wish I could figure Aunt Ruby out. She seems nervous of Judge Ambrose, the leader of this Order she believes in. But I don't know – he's odd but he can't be that bad. After all, he sent Icarus Bean into exile.' At the news, Zach perked up. Pleased, Ebony continued. 'My aunt's a total drama queen when it comes to the Order, but she seems to think Icarus Bean is OK while I'm certain he's trouble. It's so annoying – and it doesn't make any sense.'

Zach rolled his eyes in sympathy. Then his eyes danced mischievously. 'You know, I think there *is* a way we could find out what's going on.' Reaching over, he ruffled her hair like her grandpa used to, making Ebony feel both elated and miserable at the same time.

'How? Aunt Ruby won't tell you anything and I don't know who else to ask.'

'You're forgetting my special gift.'

Ebony brightened. 'You mean you could read my aunt's mind?'

Zach shrugged. 'Sure, why not?'

Ebony considered the idea for a moment, her mind racing. It was a brilliant idea: she could get all the information she needed and use it against Icarus Bean! But was it the right thing to do? She watched as a school of fish floated above her head, their scales glinting in the first rays of dawn. Then, slowly, she shook her head, imagining a look of disappointment on her grandpa's face. 'It doesn't seem right … She took me in and is trying to look after me.'

'As far as you know – but can you be certain? After all, she's keeping secrets, isn't she? We'll do it in secret. I bet there's plenty of stuff that she hasn't told you.' Zach's face twisted with concern. 'You're the only friend I have. I want to help.'

Ebony threw her arms around Zach and gave him a hug. It was her turn to go red and for Zach to ignore the blushes. She pulled away awkwardly.

'I appreciate it, I really do – but …'

'No buts – I insist!' Zach's voice betrayed a note of irritation.

They stared at each other in silence. Ebony squirmed. What better option did she have?

'OK, let's do it.'

All of a sudden, a strange noise rumbled from somewhere deep in the soil and the glass wall shook. Zach jumped to his feet. 'They've got the lawnmowers out,' he said. 'That means that the park will open soon. They always start on the lawns before letting the visitors in. You'd better go or else we won't be able to open the entrance and you'll be trapped here until nightfall.'

Ebony looked up at the glass ceiling. The sky was now blue, turning the pond a delicate eggshell colour which shimmered in the early morning sunlight. She thought of her aunt's sombre, old-fashioned house; there were worse places to be trapped all day.

'Don't forget, you have to get back before your aunt and uncle get up,' said Zach. He was reading her mind again.

Her temples throbbing, Ebony put her hand to her head and rubbed it to release the sudden pressure there.

'Sorry,' said Zach. 'I don't mean to hurt you. That often happens when I'm reading someone's mind.'

'It's OK,' said Ebony. 'It's not your fault.'

Gathering up her bag and coat, Ebony followed Zach up the mossy staircase. By the time they had reached the top, the exit leading to the park had appeared. Zach hesitated and turned, looking deep into Ebony's eyes. 'Do you remember that I said I got messages from dead people?'

Ebony nodded, her skin prickling.

'I have a message for you.'

Frozen to the spot, Ebony stared at her friend nervously.

'Your grandpa said to tell you that you didn't break your promise. He saw you give his last breath to the sea.'

Ebony's lip trembled and her shoulders shook. Could it be real? She wanted it to be true so badly.

There was the sound of jangling keys and Ebony could see a tall, lean man in a cap and uniform walking down the path towards the main gate.

'It's the park warden. Quick!' said Zach, pointing to a bush. 'Hide in there until you see the gate open, and then you can sneak out. You know how to get home from here, right?'

Darting for the bushes, Ebony gave Zach a thumbs-up sign just as the entrance began closing.

'Thank you for showing me the book,' he mouthed as she backed into the foliage.

Ebony watched her friend disappear back down the stairs; before the warden reached the park entrance, the ground had swallowed Zach up. She waited while the warden opened the gates. Suddenly, the pale morning light betrayed a slicked, grey-blond V underneath the back of his cap. Ebony's heart leaped as she recognised Judge Ambrose. Should she approach him now? This was her chance! As he turned from the gate, Ebony saw his cold eyes squint, scanning the park, and she felt a familiar, searing pain in her wrist.

Had he already spotted her? And why was he dressed like that?

Although Ebony knew that all she had to do was step out of the hedge, something stopped her; she couldn't risk involving Zach. So she waited in the bush until Judge Ambrose was gone, well out of sight, before heading home.

22

Back at the house, Ebony opened the locks carefully and sneaked inside. It was only just past dawn, but the sound of singing from the kitchen and the scent of frying bacon meant that Aunt Ruby was already up. Careful to avoid any creaky floorboards, Ebony crept up the stairs to the top of the house. As she got to the foot of the staircase leading to her room, she noticed that the door of the room next to her own was once again open. Gentle singing billowed out from behind the door – what was Uncle Cornelius doing in there? Ebony tiptoed up to the room and peeked inside. But it wasn't Uncle Cornelius – in fact, the room was empty. So empty that the cobwebs had completely disappeared and the tiles on the fire surround gleamed in the sunlight that streamed in through the window.

Ebony stepped into the room, amazed. Had Aunt Ruby been spring cleaning? The sunlight warmed her skin but a shiver travelled up her arm as she realised it was only just daylight outside and the sun would be hidden behind the buildings across the road. A ripping sound rang out behind her. Turning slowly, she spotted a crack on the wall zig-zagging its way down the middle. When it reached the bottom, the paint on the wall parted, like curtains.

'Show me,' whispered Ebony. 'What should I see?'

On the wall an image appeared, sepia and grainy, like that of an old-fashioned projector. It showed a girl identical to Ebony, but dressed in white nightclothes, seated near the window. Ebony recognised the girl as the same one who had dropped the locket – the one from the newspaper report. She noticed the girl's bare neck and instinctively touched the locket around her own neck.

At that moment, the scene in front of her burst into colour and the girl stared back at Ebony with big round eyes. Shocked, Ebony let go of the locket and the scene returned to sepia, but the girl continued to stare in Ebony's direction. She moved her lips, as though trying to communicate something, but Ebony couldn't hear the words. She crossed to the girl and waved her hand in front of the girl's face but there was no reaction. Couldn't the girl see her now?

Somehow, the locket and the image had connected, but no matter how much she poked or prodded it, Ebony couldn't make it happen again.

As the girl moved towards the window, Ebony edged closer. This time, when Ebony touched the necklace, the image disappeared completely and she saw everything in 3D technicolour. A searing heat shot down her back and she felt a shove from behind. Panic set in as the ground rushed towards her. She was falling through the sky! Faster and faster she plummeted. Then there was nothing. No pain, no light, no darkness.

Suddenly she was back in the room.

Only now the cobwebs had returned, the wall looked normal and the door was closed.

Ebony tried tugging on the handle but there was no way out: it was locked tight. A scratching sound came from behind her. Ebony spun around. On the window, spiky letters were forming. Ebony covered her ears and snapped her eyes shut, trying to block out her fear. When the noise stopped, she opened them again. On the window, the message was there again:

TO LIVE, FIND THE MURDERER AND REVEAL THE TRUTH.

'Who are you?' she said. 'I don't know what you want me to do.' Breathing heavily, Ebony tried one last tug of the handle. As the door flung open, Judge Ambrose was waiting on the landing.

'So you managed to sneak back in?' he said. 'Come with me.'

'Judge Ambrose, I was hoping to talk to you–' started Ebony.

'Now!' He turned and started down the stairs.

'You don't understand, I need–'

'Enough! I don't want to hear another word.'

Following the judge into the kitchen with her head bowed, Ebony hurriedly tried to think of an excuse as to why she had been outside when she should have been tucked up in bed, fast asleep. Her mind only drew blanks, so she decided silence was the best option.

In the kitchen, Aunt Ruby was busy cooking, looking hot and bothered in her neck-to-floor dress. Uncle Cornelius sat waiting for his stack of bacon and Winston hid behind a bowl of rat food, purposely avoiding her gaze. Someone must have collected him from his cage, and it felt like another small betrayal on Winston's part. He was her rat, no one else's. Ebony sat down, awaiting the questioning and confrontation, but it didn't come. No one even acknowledged her.

As the judge slid silently into a chair, Ebony noticed he was once again wearing a suit, but there was mud on his shoes. Aunt Ruby dished out the breakfast and then sat down, staring disinterestedly at her plate. Ebony didn't feel hungry at all but she picked up her fork gingerly. Aunt Ruby followed suit. Then everyone picked at their food in silence. Ebony wished that her aunt or the judge would say something – get mad at her even. It would be less torturous. Thankfully, Aunt Ruby must have been thinking similar thoughts.

'Perhaps your grandpa had the right idea keeping you away from here,' she said, lips pursed. 'This house brings nothing but trouble–'

'Were you out all night?' interrupted the judge.

Just as Ebony had thought, he'd come to check up on

her. Although relieved, hearing her grandpa mentioned still hurt.

'No. I just went for a walk,' she said.

The lie was on Ebony's lips instantly. She had to hope that they hadn't realised how early she had gone out. Aunt Ruby looked strangely pleased, so Ebony guessed she was OK.

The judge's eyes slid towards Ruby and then back to Ebony, as if checking that they weren't somehow communicating. 'Just like your aunt said … but in a locked park?'

'Everyone keeps telling me the city is dangerous. I thought it would be safer than walking the streets and it was easy to climb over the fence.'

The judge's eyebrows quivered slightly. 'I thought that perhaps you were getting mixed up with the wrong crowd. That perhaps you were being led astray.'

Ebony shook her head. 'I don't know anyone here.'

'A young girl can be vulnerable in an unfamiliar environment,' continued the judge. 'Are you sure you're not hanging around with anyone you shouldn't be?'

'I'm sure,' replied Ebony, desperately trying to think of how she could speak with the judge alone to discuss the coroner's report – once that was sorted, he would help her find her roses.

The judge continued. 'Your story matches what your aunt tells me and what my man in the park told me.'

'Your man?'

The judge coloured slightly.

'Don't be so surprised. I'm a powerful man. I have spies everywhere. One was planted in the park when you came to live here and he happened to see you. He reported it directly to me and–'

'I thought it was you,' said Ebony. 'I saw you, dressed as a warden.'

The judge snorted, but his face reddened further. 'Me? Dressed as a park warden? Don't be ridiculous.'

He diverted his attention to stirring his cup of tea, but Ebony wasn't fooled. It was definitely him she had seen – so why was he lying?

'Getting back to important matters,' said the judge, avoiding Ebony's eye and staring straight at Ruby. 'Be warned – if I get the slightest hint of something fishy going on ...' The judge paused just long enough to make everyone in the room uncomfortable, then rose from the table. 'I've heard all I need. Ruby, make sure you continue to comply with the Order's instructions to keep a close eye on this one, so she stays out of trouble.' His gaze settled on Ebony.

Aunt Ruby lowered her eyes and nodded.

'I'll see you out,' said Ebony, jumping to her feet.

'There's no need,' snapped the judge, striding out of the room towards the front door.

Ebony moved to follow, but her aunt caught her by the wrist, a concerned look on her face. 'There's no need to be overly enthusiastic,' she said.

As soon as the door slammed, Aunt Ruby rushed to the

hall and put her eye to the peephole. After a few minutes, she returned in her camouflage jumpsuit. Ebony decided to make the next move to deflect any uncomfortable questioning. She had to regain her aunt's trust for Zach's plan to work – how else would he be able to get close enough? And once she knew what was really going on, she could use her aunt to get to the judge.

Once they were all sitting at the table again she said, 'Aunt Ruby, I haven't been completely straight with you. There's something I need to tell you.'

All eyes turned to Ebony. Winston gulped.

'I have *The Book of Learning*.'

Covering his eyes with his paws, Winston rolled on his back. Ebony awaited the explosion but, instead, her aunt simply asked, 'How did you get your hands on it?'

Looking at the floor, Ebony's reply was barely audible. 'I broke into Uncle Cornelius's study and borrowed it.'

Certain she would be punished, Ebony sat quiet and waited. After a moment's silence she looked up. There was a huge grin on her aunt's face and she looked strangely proud. Uncle Cornelius began rocking on his chair with laughter, holding his tummy as though stopping it from splitting.

Ebony was confused. It was the last reaction she'd expected. 'You're not angry?' she asked.

'We can't condone breaking and entering for any old reason, but it shows us something positive: that you're interested in our work and that you now trust us enough to be honest,' said Aunt Ruby. 'Besides, we'd already seen it on the surveillance screens.'

'You've been watching me?' asked Ebony.

'Not us,' replied her aunt. 'Them.'

Uncle Cornelius pointed at a fly buzzing on the window and a spider in the crook of the skirting board. Winston hid his face in his bowl of food.

'You're not stupid. You must have had an idea we'd use them to keep an eye on you. That's why you hid Winston under a T-shirt before sneaking out.'

Ebony nodded.

'But that brings me to a more pressing question: why did you go out so early?'

'Didn't your spies tell you?' said Ebony haughtily, hiding her worry.

Winston stuck his face deeper into his food bowl.

'They only show the facts – they can't read your mind! We got a glimpse of you turning the corner, but that was it. Were you alone?'

'Yes. I wanted to clear my head so I went for a walk,' said Ebony, relieved the spies hadn't spotted Zach.

'Before dawn?' asked Aunt Ruby.

'Before dawn. I couldn't sleep. It wouldn't have been a problem back home.'

'Oddley Cove is much safer than the city.'

Sure, thought Ebony, *tell that to my poor grandpa*. But she kept quiet and concentrated her energy on winning Aunt

Ruby round so Zach could get near.

Aunt Ruby seemed lost in thought for a moment then sat up straight and adjusted the neck of her jumpsuit. 'So, come on then, girl – what has the book revealed?'

'I'll show you,' said Ebony, shocked that her aunt was willing to let the matter drop. As she pulled at the scab on her finger and moved towards the book cover, her aunt cried out in alarm, 'What on earth are you doing?'

'It's the only way I can open it.'

'Nonsense!' said Aunt Ruby. 'It just needs to recognise you. Of course, blood will work. But that's a little gruesome – try the right-handed fingerprint combination.'

'Try the *what*?' asked Ebony.

Aunt Ruby took hold of her niece's hand, pressing her fingers on the cover one at a time, showing Ebony the combination: index finger, middle finger, little finger, thumb. As soon as her thumb made contact, the *Book of Learning* opened. Ebony was relieved: no more blood.

'Now we've got that out of the way,' said Aunt Ruby, 'tell us what it's revealed.'

'But how did you know how to open the book? I thought it only reacted to me – that I was the only one who could read it.'

Aunt Ruby chuckled. 'You've got a lot to learn! Anyone from the Order can open it and read it. That book belongs to our people. It responds to whoever has it in their possession at that time.'

'I don't understand.'

'Pass it here ... See?' As Aunt Ruby turned the book over in her hands, the writing on the back changed.

Gasping, Ebony rubbed her eyes. Sure enough, the back cover read: *Property of Ruby Von Blanc*. Snatching it back, and checking the name had changed back to her own again, Ebony bit her lip thoughtfully. 'Go on.'

'This is one of the oldest books that the Order of Nine Lives possesses. It dates from the eleventh century, when Ireland was ruled by warlords and kings.'

'But who would have written it?'

'The daughter of the leading clansman – a priestess, we believe.'

The image of the girl in the brown tunic popped into Ebony's mind – that must have been who she'd seen! She kept quiet, wondering what it would be like to be a medieval priestess, as Aunt Ruby continued.

'With peace increasingly difficult to maintain, *The Book of Learning* was created as an instruction manual for our people to follow. But instead of giving generic guidelines, it was meant to be consulted on an individual basis. The book shows different messages to different readers.'

Ebony thought back to Zach's terrified reaction – he said he had seen terrible things. But why had it shown him horrors? Was it because he wasn't part of the Order? The thought caught her by surprise: she really did believe all this Nine Lives stuff. Just like her aunt had said, it now felt like a natural part of her existence, like she'd always known she was different.

'And how did you get to have it?'

'I borrowed it, just like you! Only I took it from the High Court's library, and when I read it, the book instructed me not to return it. I think someone there might have been trying to use it for a dark purpose. Although I'm not sure what that could be. I can only presume the reason it wanted me to keep it is linked to your destiny. The book was very persuasive.'

Smoothing her hands over the book's binding, Ebony could almost feel the power fizzing within. 'That's why you want to know what I saw.'

'The advice I received was limited. It told me about you coming, that I had to protect you from something terrible and … well, it didn't tell me anything I really need to know.'

'Such as?'

'How exactly I'm meant to protect you. So that's why we showed you the book and waited to see what would happen – to see if you're ready to be involved. I knew if you were interested in your destiny you would automatically be drawn to it.'

Surprised that her aunt was ready to trust her, Ebony took a moment to let the idea sink in. She watched as Uncle Cornelius and Winston shuffled closer, both sniffing at the book. They were friends now? Ebony felt a twinge of jealousy. She hoped Winston would forgive her and still be her friend too.

'Have you shown this book to anyone?' asked Aunt Ruby.

'No – like I said, I don't know anyone here.' There was no way she was going to tell them about Zach. He was going to do her such a big favour – she wouldn't betray him.

'What about the judge? You seemed like you wanted to speak to him about something.'

Feeling her face redden, Ebony blurted out the first thing that came into her head. 'You're the one who told me that I had to make it look like I was obeying him. I was only trying to play the part!'

Aunt Ruby eyed her niece carefully. 'If that's the case, then thank you. I just hope that we don't need to be so secretive from now on. It's important that you trust me. No more sneaking around. Are you ready to learn more, to get more involved?'

Although Ebony didn't know what her aunt was up to, she knew it would take her a step closer to achieving her own goals. 'I'm ready,' she said, her fists clenched.

23

'So what exactly did *The Book of Learning* tell you?' asked Aunt Ruby.

Ebony eyed her aunt cautiously.

'I haven't been able to make sense of it yet,' she lied, knowing that if the book showed different things to everyone, her aunt couldn't prove otherwise. 'But maybe if you shared what you know … especially what this terrible thing you have to protect me from is.'

'OK, but you have to understand that what I tell you is what the book revealed to me, and not my own ideas. You might not like what I have to say.'

'Please, Aunt Ruby!'

'The book confirmed one of our oldest family legends, that your destiny is extra special.'

Wanting to know how or why she was considered special, Ebony leaned in, eager for more. 'In what way?'

Pausing, Aunt Ruby's face turned stormy. 'As I explained before, people can't join the Order of Nine Lives unless they're specially chosen – and that only happens when one of the families has reached Ultimation. Yet there is a legend that there is a way to swap Nine Lives souls at will, kickstarting a new reincarnation cycle but bypassing the usual procedures – using bodies and souls that weren't chosen.'

'So the new body automatically gets a nine lives soul without having to wait to be reborn?'

'Exactly – when the soul is implanted, the person wakes in their new first life. People who shouldn't have been reincarnated suddenly can be. It's unnatural.'

'And what happens to the other soul – the one whose ability to reincarnate was removed?'

'Who knows? But I'm guessing the effects won't be pleasant.'

Ebony shuddered, thinking of the eternal torment her aunt had spoken of earlier.

'The story goes,' continued Aunt Ruby, 'that the swap has to take place inside the Reflectory. Until now, this was considered a myth, as it has never happened. But *The Book of Learning* told me that, driven mad with the desire for power, one of our people has now discovered the secret of how to swap souls and all they need to make it happen is access to the Reflectory. However, because they need the guardian, locket and rose to get into the Reflectory, this awful event has not yet come to pass.'

'But does it matter if souls are swapped at will? It can't make that much difference, surely.'

'It matters a great deal. Remember I told you that we make up the fabric of the universe? Well, if we allow people who hunger for reincarnation to become part of the Order, they'll create negative energy which is then fused into the universe. Their destiny won't necessarily be for the greater good – they'll have their own selfish interests at heart. And imagine the impact on a soul being ripped from its rightful being … The balance of good and evil in the world could alter irrevocably. The world could become a terrible, desolate place – if it survives at all. Nature has a way of dealing with things that interfere with its natural order – and the results are usually catastrophic. In this case, they most certainly will be.'

'So where do I come in?'

'Your destiny is linked to whether this soul swapping happens or not. You are the original and true guardian. According to what I saw, you will either save us from this aberration or be the first soul swapped. If it's the latter, then there'll be a domino effect and the whole Nine Lives existence – as well as the world – will be at risk.'

'But the book only showed this to you, right? So only you know?'

Aunt Ruby's face paled. 'That, I cannot guarantee. The book used to be in the High Court's possession. Who knows who else it told? There was certainly a lot of interest in you when your mum announced she was pregnant this time around. When your parents disappeared, the judge wanted you to remain in the city but my father fought for you – and won. There were more of us back then and our people voted in my father's favour as they respected him greatly.'

The room fell silent. Winston waddled over to Aunt Ruby

and curled up on her lap. Uncle Cornelius quivered and scratched his beard. Anxiety hung in the air, heavy and dark. Even Ebony felt a tremble ripple through her body. Feeling unsafe made her think of Icarus Bean and she touched her hand to her throat – she could still smell the stale whiskey and mould from him.

With the ghostly visitors and the weird goings-on, her aunt's claims no longer seemed so far-fetched. Feeling the amulet in its rightful place – it had been linked to her soul for centuries – gave little comfort. If the book was to be believed, she was in massive danger. Someone clearly wanted power for themselves, and they would have to go through her to get it.

Another thought came to her. Hadn't her aunt said that Icarus had been part of the High Court when the judge was elected? He must have had access to the book – he must know about the legend surrounding her destiny. Icarus Bean had killed her grandpa to get to her and clearly kidnapping her was his next move.

Since she was afraid that Aunt Ruby sympathised with Icarus, that meant she had to get the judge's protection fast – but how? Fighting to calm her racing mind, Ebony settled on an important question: the key to securing the judge's favour.

'What about the roses?'

Uncle Cornelius gave a twitch and Aunt Ruby looked pained.

'The roses must still be in Judge Ambrose's car. I'm sure if he'd found them then he would have wanted to rub our noses in it and question you about them. They must have fallen onto the floor and rolled under one of the seats. We're lucky he hasn't noticed them yet, but it's only a matter of time. We have to get them back as soon as possible.'

'Where does the judge live?' asked Ebony, not believing her luck. If she gave the judge the roses he would surely be happy to give her protection.

'He has a chamber in the Nine Lives Headquarters, hidden in the Botanic Gardens,' said Aunt Ruby. 'That's where we were headed when you saw us on the surveillance cameras, but the tip-off from the spy you saw meant the judge was waiting at the gate to meet us. We couldn't go snooping in front of him and had to pretend we came to report on your progress instead.'

'How can the headquarters be hidden in public gardens?'

'The best place to hide something is in plain sight because people don't expect it. All official business takes place at night when the gardens are locked up.'

'OK. So we sneak in and get them back,' said Ebony.

'Yes – but it's not as easy as it sounds. The Botanic Gardens are heavily guarded.'

'So what do we do?'

'We've been planning a pre-emptive strike in the dead of night. If you're up for it you can come too and we can steal the roses back together.'

'And if we get caught?'

'We'll sneakily replace them with this.'

Aunt Ruby held up an *Ebonius Tobinius* rose. Ebony gasped. 'You have one anyway! Why even bother getting mine?'

'Because we need them. Yours are real – this one's a decoy,' said Aunt Ruby.

Taking the flower, Ebony ran her fingers over its petals. 'It feels just like the real thing,' she said.

'Yes. If the judge catches us snooping around, he'll have us searched and will confiscate the roses. Rather than let that happen, we'll have these in case we need something to hand over.'

'Are you sure it's a decoy?' asked Ebony.

'I can prove it,' declared Aunt Ruby, matter-of-factly. 'It'll self-destruct in approximately three seconds.'

She counted down – three – two – one – and the rose burst into a puff of smoke. 'The ones I have for the High Court have a delay of forty-eight hours. I'd have preferred if they didn't self-destruct at all – or at least to have bought us more time – but I haven't quite perfected the formula.'

Ebony fought to hide a smile. Her aunt had just given her an advantage. Even if they didn't get caught, she could alert the judge and tell him about what was going on. When the roses self-destructed, he would have no choice but to believe her.

'I'm glad you're on board, Ebony,' continued her aunt. 'We've been hoping for so long to return the Order to its former glory – find the lost souls and restore our rightful position. And what is more powerful than hope?'

Ebony grimaced, gripping *The Book of Learning* tightly. 'If hope is so powerful, then why did grandpa die? I'd hoped we'd be together forever.'

Aunt Ruby smiled sadly. 'We all lose people close to us in some way or another, dear, but take heart – we're lucky. Achieve your destiny and you could be reunited.'

Ebony could tell that her aunt was thinking of her late husband and her heart softened; when her aunt reached out to take her hand, Ebony let her – but only, she told herself, to help convince her they were allies. They sat quietly, side by side, their hands linked and the air thick with remembrance.

After a moment, Ebony jumped to her feet. 'OK, so when do we go on this mission?' she asked.

'Tomorrow at midnight: Judge Ambrose will be caught up with official business so his car is guaranteed to be there,' said her aunt. 'But be warned. It could be extremely dangerous. The person who seeks to access the Reflectory will stop at nothing to get their hands on the roses.'

'If what you're saying is right, I'm in danger anyway,' said Ebony, nostrils flaring. 'I might as well try to do something about it.'

'That's what I like to hear,' said Aunt Ruby, grinning.

Feeling weirdly energised, yet too tired to talk, Ebony gave her a thumbs-up sign. Excusing herself and retrieving Winston from her aunt, she decided it was time to go back to reading *The Book of Learning*. Her grandpa had always told her to be prepared and that's exactly what she intended to do.

When she reached her bedroom, Winston hovered near

her, as though eager for the next adventure. Ebony opened the book, her face shadowy.

'Maybe there's some truth in what my aunt says,' she said aloud, flicking the pages over. When she got to the first new page, Winston squealed loudly and seemed to point to the book. It showed a bouncing arrow pointing to the edge of the page. Following orders, Ebony turned the page over to find her next message: YOU HAVE EARNED THREE QUESTIONS.

'Brilliant!' she cried. 'Do I speak them out loud like I did the hangman letters?'

YES. YOU HAVE TWO MORE QUESTIONS.

'Oh no! I didn't mean to waste one. That wasn't a question. I was thinking out loud!' pleaded Ebony.

But the message didn't change.

'I'll have to be extra careful,' she sighed, drawing her knees up. 'Now, let's see what I know … I've discovered a girl with the same name, the same address and a Georgian murder.'

But what does that have to do with me? she thought, too afraid to speak the words out loud in case she wasted another question. Flipping to the inside cover, Ebony stared at her name. A sudden thought struck her, one that filled her with dread.

If there was an Ebony Smart matching one of the dates, would it be possible that there was an Ebony Smart attached to each of the dates?

After all, she'd already seen five different girls who looked like her, each in clothes from a different era. Walking slowly over to the dressing table, Ebony removed the towel. Inside the mirror, a speck of light, barely visible, zipped around like a firefly. Shakily, Ebony sat back down and slid her finger down the list to the final date.

Seeing as she was born in 2003, wouldn't it be reasonable to assume that this final date referred to her?

Something in Ebony's stomach flipped. Her grandpa had always told her to trust her instincts. Many a time he had gone against the weather forecasts and had saved a life or prevented a terrible accident. He said it was a gift – one that she possessed too, if she chose to be mindful of it. Now, her instincts told her that she was on her way to uncovering some truths that had been lost for a very long time.

'According to this list, Winston,' she said, pointing to the inside cover, 'I'm the last Ebony Smart. The book's answer matches what Aunt Ruby said – we only have nine lives each.' She felt her friend tremble. 'So, if I'm right, 2015 – this year – is when I'm going to die.'

Hands quivering, Ebony turned back to the questions page and cleared her throat. Winston raced up her arm and onto her shoulder, stretching out his paws across her mouth as though trying to stop her from talking.

'I have my next question,' she said firmly. 'Do the dates represent my past lives?'

YES, came the reply. YOU HAVE ONE MORE QUESTION.

Struggling to keep her voice from wavering, Ebony spoke again. 'Will I see my grandpa again in my next life?'

The answer formed slowly.

THIS IS YOUR LAST LIFE.

QUESTIONS COMPLETED.

Falling back with shock, Ebony gasped for air. It was exactly as she'd guessed, but the confirmation made it all the more real. Suddenly feeling sick, she rushed into the bathroom and hung her head over the toilet until the nausea passed. She splashed cold water on her face then returned to her room, desperate to be close to Winston.

On the bed, Winston was shaking, his teeth rattling. Her window was slightly ajar and a note was waiting on her dressing table.

'How did that get here?' Ebony said aloud, scooping up Winston and slamming the window shut. Hurriedly, she read the note:

You've got to get out of there! Icarus Bean is your aunt's brother and I can prove it. Can you meet me tomorrow at the Natural History Museum at 11 a.m.? Your friend, always. Zach.

Terror crashed through Ebony's body like a giant wave. Holding Winston close, her body shaking, she tried to still her mind.

'He must be wrong, Winston – he *has* to be.'

24

Later that day, as Ebony cowered under her quilt, shakily leafing through her scrapbook, there was a tap on the door. Taking a deep breath, Ebony tried to still her fear as Aunt Ruby poked her head in.

'I hope I'm not disturbing you …'

'No, n-not at all. Come in.'

Ebony tried to sound cheery but her voice wavered. She couldn't get Zach's note out of her head. Aunt Ruby entered carrying a small bundle. She sat next to Ebony and admired the photos for a moment; Ebony stayed deadly still, fighting the urge to run.

'You must miss home,' said Aunt Ruby.

Unable to speak, Ebony nodded.

'I bet it's the sea you miss most. And the animals, of course.'

Again, Ebony nodded.

A faraway look in her aunt's eyes suggested that Aunt Ruby was also missing things from her past. When her aunt's eyes started to flicker back to the present, Ebony averted her gaze and pretended she hadn't noticed.

Aunt Ruby picked something up from the top of her bundle and handed it to Ebony. 'This came for you this morning ... maybe it'll help?'

She handed Ebony a postcard. It showed a calm blue sea and bright blue sky, with small boats dotted on the ocean and a white lighthouse in the distance. There were hills and green fields to one side.

'It's from home,' cried Ebony, momentarily forgetting her fears, 'from Old Joe!'

She quickly scanned the writing:

Dear Ebony,

The animals are fine – I've taken the dogs and cats to my place so they've got more company – and the leeks are coming along well. The weather has been mild for this time of the year so the garden is thriving. We're all missing you – especially the goats.

Your friend,
Joe.

Lifting the postcard to her nose, Ebony inhaled deeply – as though the scent of the sea could travel through the picture. She flipped it over again and stared at the image. Then she reread the words silently. Instead of feeling comforted, she missed home even more.

'Speaking of home,' said Ebony, 'I don't suppose you've heard anything from the hospital yet?'

'Not a thing,' said Aunt Ruby, unfazed.

Anger stirred in Ebony's gut and she inched away from her aunt. Seemingly unaware, Aunt Ruby patted the bundle in her arms.

'I hope you don't mind, but I made you these.'

Aunt Ruby held up a pair of jeans and a blue-green jumper. The colours on the jumper seemed to change, flowing like the ripples of a tide.

'I didn't replicate the holes,' continued her aunt. 'Easy movement at all times is a must when you're out in the field. I hope you like them. They're a little less old-fashioned, I trust?' She handed the outfit to her niece. 'Try them on.'

With mixed emotions – her aunt was being so kind but she was still lying about the coroner's report – Ebony did as she was asked. They fitted perfectly. The jumper had a fluid texture; it seemed to shape itself around Ebony's body. The jeans felt extremely light, not at all like denim, and they had pockets on both legs big enough to fit *The Book of Learning* in. She would have preferred a few rips in the jeans but they felt comfortable and looked much better than the original jumpsuit her aunt had tried to make her wear.

'I like them very much,' said Ebony.

Her aunt beamed. To really convince her that she liked the outfit, Ebony went to the wardrobe and pulled out the utility belt. She tied its bulky load around her waist and turned to Aunt Ruby to show her she was now fully equipped. Unexpectedly, Aunt Ruby fell about laughing.

'What are you doing with that old thing?' she asked.

'You said I'd need it,' said Ebony, a little hurt and very confused.

'Only to help you find *The Book of Learning*,' said Aunt Ruby. 'Why else do you think I let you see it in your uncle's study?'

'Why didn't you just give it to me?'

'Everyone knows that if you want someone to be interested in something, you have to tell them they can't have it. If I'd handed it directly to you and said what it was, would you have believed me?'

Ebony considered the question and then shook her head slowly. She removed the utility belt and Aunt Ruby took it from her.

'There's nothing this utility belt can do for you now. The answers you seek lie within the book,' she said.

And Zach's plan, thought Ebony, tucking her postcard into *The Book of Learning* and closing it tight. Then she placed the book in one of her pockets and climbed back onto the bed.

Aunt Ruby gave her a wink, before heading towards the door.

'Keep wearing the outfit if you like, to get a feel for it. You'll need it when we sneak into headquarters tomorrow at midnight.'

As soon as her aunt was out of sight, Ebony reread Zach's note several times, unable to take it in. Zach must be mistaken … But if her aunt still denied knowledge of the coroner's report – what else was she hiding? Although every part of Ebony's being yearned for it to not be true, she quickly wrote a note for Zach: *I'll be there.* Then she sat back, deflated.

'How am I going to get this to Zach?'

Scratching her head and heaving a big sigh, her eye caught Winston's. He scurried into his cage and pulled the T-shirt over the top with his teeth. Ebony lifted off the T-shirt and glared at him.

'I shouldn't even be talking to you after you grassed me up,' she said.

Winston put his head down.

'You're meant to be my friend, Winston. And instead, you were spying on me all this time.'

Winston flattened his body against the bottom of his cage and covered his eyes with his paws. Then something occurred to Ebony, something that was so obvious she couldn't believe she hadn't noticed until now.

'You understand me perfectly, don't you?'

Winston peeped out from behind his paws.

'You understand every word I say! Lift your left paw for yes and your right paw for no.' Sure enough, Winston's left paw went into the air. 'I should have known it; you're not a real rat after all, are you? You're probably one of Aunt Ruby's creations, sent to Oddley Cove to spy on me all along.'

The left paw stayed raised, then swapped for the right paw. The answer couldn't be yes, then no; Ebony realised that she'd made the questions too complicated.

'So you're an invention?'

Right paw. No.

'Then you *are* a real rat?'

Left paw. Yes.

Ebony sat back and sighed. Then she looked at Winston again.

'But how are you so smart?'

Winston blinked back at Ebony.

'I mean, did someone make you smart?'

Left paw.

Ebony paused. She would find out more about that later. Right now, she just wanted her friend back.

'Are you really my friend?'

When he raised his left paw, Ebony took Winston out of the cage.

'Good. Then it's only right that we make up.'

Winston did a somersault and Ebony laughed.

'I've never seen you do that before. You're amazing!'

Ebony laughed harder as Winston took a bow. Then she quietened.

'The cameras, inside you. Do you have control over them?'

Winston lifted his left paw, then his right, then his left again.

'Can you switch them off?'

Right paw.

'Well, can you make the transmission blurred or something? So it's difficult to see what's happening on the screen?'

Winston paused for a second, as though deep in thought. Then he raised his left paw and waved it emphatically.

'Winston, do you want to make it up to me?' Winston stopped and waited. Ebony showed him the note. 'I have to get this to Zach.'

Hanging his head, Winston shook it instead of raising his right paw. Ebony rubbed her eyes and repeated the sentence. Winston shook his head again.

'If you're going to be my friend again, I need to know I can trust you.'

The rat started hopping and leaping around, waving his paws and doing multiple somersaults.

'I don't know what you're trying to say, Winston.'

He paused for a moment, panting. Then he tried again even more emphatically, becoming a blur of fur, tail and legs. Ebony tried to make sense of it but impatience got the better of her.

'Winston, I haven't got time for games. I need to get this to Zach right away otherwise I'll never know what's going on and I'll … I'll die.'

Winston stopped immediately.

'Do you want that?'

The rat shook his head and raised his right paw.

'OK, then will you help me?'

Reluctantly Winston nodded and raised his left paw in the air. Ebony relayed the directions to Zach's underground hideout. She felt Winston's body shake and her heart did a flip as she realised why: there was only one place that Winston could go to try to find a way out – the basement. The room next door was once again locked so the roof wasn't an option, and she couldn't let Winston out of the front door – her aunt and uncle would hear her undoing all the locks. There wasn't even a letter box – at least, not one that opened. Thanks to her aunt's paranoia over security, all mail was delivered to the box on the wall outside. In such an old building, the basement was the most likely place to have a hole big enough for Winston to squeeze through – but that meant getting past Mulligan.

Ebony rolled the message up in a tight scroll. Winston quivered, but he jumped up and took it from her, wedging it between his teeth.

'Thank you, Winston. I really appreciate this.'

Winston's eyes dulled as he climbed from her lap onto her shoulder.

'I'm glad that we're friends again. I missed you,' said Ebony.

Winston nuzzled her neck the best he could with the scroll jammed in his mouth.

'Be careful,' she whispered.

An image of when Mulligan tried to catch Winston flashed in Ebony's mind, along with a close-up of Mulligan's snarling face. She wanted to call Winston back but it was too late; he was under the door already, on his way towards Mulligan's lair. *Good luck*, she thought, drawing her legs up and hugging her arms around them.

Night came, but there was no sign of Winston. Energy pumped though Ebony's veins. She was wide awake and she knew there was no way she could sleep until Winston returned. To make the time pass, Ebony took as long as possible getting ready for bed. She spent ages brushing her teeth and stayed in the shower until her fingertips turned crinkly. Eventually, she gave in and climbed into bed, leaving the bedroom door open just a crack. Propped up on her pillow, her body tensed, Ebony watched the door, jumping at every sound.

When she heard everyone else turn in, she waited long enough for them to fall asleep and then threw back the covers. Her feet cold on the polished floorboards, she carefully lifted her grandpa's suitcase out of the wardrobe. Quietly, she packed her few important belongings and put on her aunt's outfit – just in case – then she waited for Winston to come home.

An hour later, Winston returned.

He was wet and muddy and part of his tail was missing. Ebony gasped and leaped out of bed.

'Who did this to you? Mulligan?' she asked, reaching down for him and placing him gently on the pillow.

But Winston was either too tired or too shaken to respond. He curled his sore tail around his body, licking the bleeding stump.

'Did you deliver the note?' asked Ebony.

She felt selfish asking when he was clearly hurt but knew she wouldn't sleep otherwise. Winston managed a nod before exhaustion overtook him. Ebony kissed his head gently. Winston's tiny heart pounded and his body trembled as he slept.

'Thank you,' whispered Ebony and tucked herself in under the covers beside him. 'I'm glad I can trust you again.' Her aunt could try to hide whatever she liked; soon Ebony would know everything.

25

'Do you see them yet?' asked Ebony, peeking out from behind a case of stuffed puffins.

The museum would normally have fascinated her, with row upon row of glass cases filled with stuffed animals and skeletons. It was the kind of place she could have spent hours in, admiring tiny details like claws and eyebrows. But she wasn't there to look at the museum specimens. Zach had discovered that Aunt Ruby and Icarus Bean had arranged a secret meeting.

Summoning Ebony to the museum, Zach was certain that they would see Icarus Bean entering the building. Aunt Ruby had been distracted and fidgety all morning, as though trying to find an excuse for having to go out, so it had been easy for Ebony to leave. But now it was almost half past twelve and there was still no sign of either Icarus or her aunt.

'Are you sure my aunt was meant to meet him?'

'I'm sure,' said Zach irritably.

'Is it possible that you might have got mixed up with someone else's thoughts? You said you hear hundreds.'

'It was definitely your aunt. Her thoughts came through

very clearly, so she must have been somewhere nearby. This is the perfect opportunity for me to get even closer and read her mind to find out what's really going on.'

Zach ran his fingers through his hair and paced up and down near the butterfly cases. He lifted some of the protective covers and studied some of the specimens.

'I didn't know you were interested in butterflies,' said Ebony.

'I'm not,' snapped Zach, 'but it'll look suspicious if we're just hanging around.' Zach pointed towards a case of foxes. 'Go and look at something else, but keep your eye on the door. I've got a clear view from here but I want to make sure that we don't miss them.'

Not liking Zach's tone of voice, Ebony strode off towards the foxes, certain the two of them didn't look suspicious. The place was packed full of people: small girls in raincoats, little boys in tracksuits and pushchairs full of squalling babies. Many of the children were squabbling with their siblings or clambering up their parents to get a better view of the strange stuffed creatures that crowded the museum. The attendants were far too busy to notice Ebony and Zach; they had enough to worry about trying to stop mums from letting their children sit on the glass cases.

Settling herself on a broad wooden bench near a wall filled with sea creatures, Ebony looked up. A huge basking shark was suspended from the ceiling, hung on thick rusty chains. The shark reminded her of the one she saw every year off the coast back home that she'd named Cedric – only Cedric was a giant compared to this specimen.

Ebony was seven years old and in her grandpa's boat when she spotted Cedric for the first time. The sea was calm and blue – so blue, it could have been the Caribbean and not the Atlantic off the coast of a small fishing village in Ireland. She had spotted the fin first: a sharp black triangle with a small chunk missing near the top. It pierced the water like a blade, gleaming menacingly in the sun. Her grandpa had switched off the engine as soon as she pointed out the shark so that the noise and vibrations wouldn't scare it off. The tide had gently carried their boat up close to it.

That was when their eyes had met.

A warm glow enveloped her as she remembered staring into the blank eye of the shark, knowing it was looking back at her. It was a feeling that she could never forget and had never experienced since. After a moment, the shark had turned its attention to feeding, its huge gaping mouth combing the surface of the water for plankton.

She'd seen right into its jaws.

There were teeth missing at the front, reminding Ebony of an old man in the village called Cedric – that was how the shark got his name. Her grandpa found it so funny that word soon spread around the village. Everyone began to refer to the shark as Cedric whenever they spotted him and Ebony could never quite look the old man it was named after in the eye again.

Since that first encounter, Ebony had seen the shark many times. Although it was only ever his fin that she spied poking out of the water, she always remembered that moment when their eyes had connected.

Zach's hand on her shoulder shocked Ebony back to the present.

'I've got an idea,' he said. 'Let's check upstairs in case we missed them.'

They wound their way up a wide stone staircase and into a room filled with even bigger glass cases. These contained more exotic animals: polar bears, leopards, wildebeest and cassowaries. There were huge horned animal heads that Ebony didn't recognise mounted on the walls, next to giant birds with monstrous wingspans. Staring up at the medley of ferocious claws, razor-sharp beaks and piercing glass eyes, Ebony wondered whether the great explorer Lieutenant Rufus Smart had seen any of these on his expeditions. Then a horrible thought popped into her head: what if they were being used for surveillance? But she quickly relaxed – after all, these creatures were dead and her aunt needed spies that could stay on the move. Ebony looked around for any bug or insect that could be watching them. It looked all clear.

'This place gives me the creeps,' said Zach.

'I like it,' said Ebony. It was nice to be around animals again, even if they were dead.

'It seems weird that someone who loves animals so much would enjoy looking at a mausoleum.'

'I'm from the country,' she said. 'We deal with dead animals all the time. Where do you think the meat in supermarkets comes from?'

There was no reply. Something had caught Zach's eye. Ebony looked up to see a seagull walking along a skylight several storeys up.

'That's it!' he said.

'The gull? Do you think it's watching us?'

'No. But it's on the roof. I bet that's how they'll try to get in without us seeing them.'

'Aunt Ruby's not going to scale a building with Icarus Bean in broad daylight,' said Ebony. 'That would attract a heap of attention. And besides, they don't even know we're coming, so why would they have to hide?'

When Zach ignored her, she laid a hand on his arm. 'You know, it's OK to admit you're wrong.'

But Zach was undeterred. 'Think about what your aunt said: her brother is in exile. I'm sure she'd be in big trouble if she was found consorting with him, relation or no relation. That's why she's kept their meetings quiet. It's not us they're hiding from. It's the High Court.'

Ebony's eyes narrowed in thought as she looked up to the seagull.

'Fine. But how on earth would they get to the roof?' she asked.

'You have a staircase leading to yours, don't you? The museum has the same. They'll come in that way, just like

Icarus sneaked into your place that time.' Zach paused. 'Only that couldn't have been through the roof because you'd have seen him up there.'

Ebony frowned. How did Zach know she'd been up on the roof that day? She was certain she hadn't mentioned or even thought about it. But before she could ask, Zach pulled her over to the edge of the room to a closed-off staircase. On the chain across it was a sign: NO ENTRY.

'I bet you any money they're up here,' he said. Checking to make sure no one was watching, he climbed over the chain. Uncertain, Ebony followed.

At the top of the stairs a narrow corridor opened into a maze of rooms. Ebony and Zach sneaked through several of them, each filled with cases of bones, photographs and documents from expeditions.

Then, as she was passing one case, Ebony saw something that stopped her dead. Beside a pointed skull with spiral horns there was a photograph of her aunt Ruby and a serious-looking bearded gentleman. The inscription underneath read: Mr and Mrs C. Von Blanc, 1871. She called Zach back.

'Look!' she said. 'Except for the funny clothes, Aunt Ruby looks exactly the same as now.'

They peered in more closely at the photograph.

'Isn't that you?' asked Zach.

In the background, barely in view, was a small girl in a heavy black dress with a white lace collar. Ebony started; a cold shiver travelled from the bottom of her spine up to the hairs on the back of her neck. Goosebumps stood out on her arms. The shot was a little out of focus but he was right – once again, her face stared back. Ebony's stomach flipped – she'd now seen six different versions of herself. It wasn't a nice feeling knowing that her face had been used so many times.

'I hate all this reincarnation stuff,' said Ebony. But Zach was already through the next entranceway out of earshot. All of a sudden, he flew back in and grabbed Ebony, dragging her underneath a table of exhibits.

'What?' Ebony was about to pull away from him when the bottom of a floor-length black dress and a pair of shabby trousers and scuffed shoes came into view. Approaching the table, they stopped right in front of it. Zach and Ebony both held their breath, but it seemed they hadn't been detected.

Aunt Ruby's voice rang out clearly. 'What shall we do with her, Icarus?'

'I'm not sure, but we have to do something. We can't have her messing things up.'

Icarus Bean's voice was like a fork scraping on a porcelain plate. A surge of hate flooded through Ebony and her heart felt black.

'We certainly can't. This is a very serious business indeed,' said Aunt Ruby.

Ebony turned to Zach, her cheeks flushed with fear. Zach's face was solemn and stern, crinkled with worry. She could tell he was reading someone's mind. Going by the expression on

Zach's face, she wasn't sure whether she wanted to know what that mind was thinking.

'Does she trust us yet?' asked Icarus Bean.

'I think so. She shared *The Book of Learning*.'

'But not what it revealed.'

So Aunt Ruby knew that Icarus Bean was familiar with The Book of Learning? Any slight hope of ever trusting her faded.

'That's not a good sign,' continued Icarus.

'What if Ebony doesn't figure out how to break the cycle quick enough, brother? Look what happened to Father … He was so close to bringing this all to an end.'

Ebony's eyes narrowed. She curled her hands into fists and pressed them into the floor as hard as she could. *Didn't Ruby know that Icarus had murdered her grandpa?*

'I still haven't figured out who in the Order has learned the secret of soul swapping,' said Icarus Bean, 'but I think I know who's helping. I think it is time for me to act.'

'You don't mean …'

'Yes. Maybe the day has come to wage war on my own flesh and blood.' His voice sounded determined.

The look of fear on Zach's face told Ebony that he had reached the same realisation that she had: if Icarus was Aunt Ruby's brother, then that made him her uncle.

'Do you mean …?' Aunt Ruby's voice wobbled.

'Elimination,' said Icarus Bean.

Aunt Ruby took a deep breath. 'Elimination,' she repeated,

in a way that was very final and somehow also signalled that their conversation was over.

They walked off in silence.

Ebony turned to Zach. *He killed my grandpa and they're going to kill me,* she thought. *Aunt Ruby is just pretending to be on my side – she's one of the bad guys.* Zach had turned a strange shade of grey. He took hold of her hand and they listened as the dull thump of footsteps died away.

A small spider suddenly climbed in under the case above Zach's head. Surprising herself, Ebony reached out and did something awful. She squished it.

Sitting in Zach's underground hideout a little later, Ebony sipped hot sugary tea. Zach had risked opening the door during the day because it was raining heavily, there was no one around and they desperately needed to be somewhere they could feel safe to talk. The sky above was dark with clouds, casting shadows on the surface of the pond above them. Ebony's nerves were so raw she had to grip the cup with both hands to stop the tea spilling out.

'Are you sure we don't need to cover this wall?' said Ebony, grimacing at the bugs and worms that had previously fascinated her.

'I'm sure,' said Zach. 'They've not surfaced. There's no way your aunt could have got to them.'

'But what if there's a marauder?'

'Then I'd pick it up. Your aunt needs intelligent creatures to act as her spies so, although I wouldn't be able to read their thoughts, I'd be able to detect some heightened activity.' Zach's hair fell into his face, framing his green eyes. 'I'm more worried about what you're going to do.'

'It's simple: if my aunt is afraid of the judge, then it's his protection I need.'

A smile spread across Zach's face. 'You're an intelligent girl, Ebony Smart,' he said admiringly.

Ebony blushed.

'So how will you get to the judge?'

'I have to go back and play along with my aunt's plan. I can't bring Icarus Bean to justice alone. I'll help her get the roses from the judge's car and then turn them in. She thinks she's smart but–'

'She's no match for you,' said Zach, and Ebony felt her heart glow.

26

At midnight on the dot, Ebony Smart stepped out of 23 Mercury Lane in her special new outfit, accompanied by Aunt Ruby. There was no one around to see the pair leaving at that strange hour. Even if there had been, it would be hard to tell who they were: Mercury Lane was full of fog, which gathered around the streetlights in thick clumps.

Ebony heard a purring noise travelling towards them on the road. Dipped headlights crawled out of the fog as a wide silver hatchback with blacked-out windows approached. When it reached Ebony and Aunt Ruby, the passenger door opened. Uncle Cornelius sat behind the wheel looking very solemn. Despite the fact that it was night-time, he wore a pair of sunglasses.

'Uncle Cornelius can see very well in the dark,' explained Aunt Ruby as she clambered into the back seat of the car, snapping the front seat back into place and motioning for Ebony to get in. 'These streetlights play havoc with his eyes. It's irresponsible, really. It could cause a terrible crash. Now, buckle up!'

Ebony didn't feel like it was the right time to point out

that most people didn't have a prehistoric wildcat as a driver – after all, Uncle Cornelius might not be able to protect her while driving if her aunt had another funny turn.

As soon as Ebony clambered in, slamming the door shut, a strange musty smell hit her nostrils. Sinking into her seat, Ebony's legs squashed up against the glove compartment. She glanced towards Aunt Ruby: her long legs were sticking into the back of Uncle Cornelius' seat and she looked nervous. As the car sped off, Ebony was forced to face the front so she wouldn't feel carsick.

The car interior was alive with lights, dials and levers, but Uncle Cornelius didn't use any of the special equipment; he used the gear stick and steering wheel just like her grandpa used to do. Ebony guessed that the extras were for her aunt's benefit.

As the car cruised through the streets, Ebony thought she heard a low growl coming from the back of the car, then a snuffling sound, like someone being silenced with a hand over their mouth. She pulled down the visor above her which, as she thought it would, had a mirror on it but couldn't see anything out of the ordinary. The bright lights in the front made the back of the car incredibly dark.

'Are you OK, dear?' asked Aunt Ruby.

'I thought I heard something,' said Ebony.

'It's probably just the engine,' replied Aunt Ruby. 'I've been doing some tinkering ...'

Ebony snapped the visor back into place and stared out

into the night. She'd have to stop being so jumpy if she was going to succeed on her mission.

The car cruised smoothly along the city streets. Lights from nightclubs and poker rooms whizzed past them, along with crowds of faces, lines of taxis and rows of burger vans. After a short while, the car turned a sharp left and the busy city streets were replaced by a row of houses with small gardens on one side and a canal on the other. The fog lifted and the sky filled with twinkling stars. There was another sharp turn, and then not long afterwards Ebony noticed a stone tower that marked the start of a high wall to her right. Where the wall ended there was what looked like an old house and a pair of tall wrought-iron gates. Uncle Cornelius pulled the car over to a stop outside the gates. Ebony could see that they led into a cemetery.

'We'll walk from here,' said Aunt Ruby.

The three of them climbed out of the car and Uncle Cornelius picked the lock on the gate, forcing it open. Cautiously easing the gate ajar, they started along the dark, unlit pathway with Cornelius in the lead. A low growl echoed through the chill night air, making Ebony stop dead in her tracks. She tried not to look at the tall tombstones that loomed over her head like giant monsters.

'Keep going!' whispered Aunt Ruby, giving her niece a push. 'Don't lose sight of Uncle Cornelius, whatever you do.'

Ebony hurried on, her legs trembling with every step. The trees whispered and wailed in the north-west wind. An owl hooted. Rustling and shuffling noises came from every direction and what sounded like twigs and boughs snapping underfoot rang out. It felt as though hidden eyes watched their every move. The cemetery pathway was so dark that Ebony couldn't see where she was going. She could only just make out the silhouettes of gnarled trees and endless rows of gravestones surrounding her in every direction, and she had to hold onto her aunt's utility belt to keep up.

Blindly, they stumbled along behind Cornelius. Every now and again, wings flapped overhead, carrying invisible creatures across the sky. This cemetery was nothing like the one at home that overlooked the Atlantic, with its low stone walls and pretty flower bouquets and rosaries decorating every grave; this place was sinister and unwelcoming. Ebony's veins pulsed and, despite the chill, she was drenched in sweat.

After what seemed like a very long time, they stopped at a low stone wall, topped with a spiked fence. Once again, Uncle Cornelius fiddled with the lock on the gate and, as they pushed their way through to the other side, Ebony spotted lights flickering through the trees. As the trio made their way towards the lights, a huge glasshouse structure emerged, glistening under the moon. Inside, giant cacti and leafy palms with leaves the size of umbrellas reached up to the sky; above them was a panoramic room dotted with bodies and floating candlelight.

'That's the meeting chamber,' whispered Aunt Ruby. 'Once the candles stop moving, you know the meeting is in progress.'

Within minutes, the tiny flickering lights stopped moving and the figures stood still. Aunt Ruby began to jog across the grass, with Ebony and Uncle Cornelius following close behind. Even in the dark, the park looked spectacular: huge, carefully manicured shrubs gave way to vast mounds of unusual flowers that spilled out onto meadow grass. The trees were alive with bats and insects. Ebony half expected the judge to leap out of the shadows as they padded along, but there was no sign of him. After a few moments, they stopped in a well-hidden, tree-lined car park.

Aunt Ruby signalled to Uncle Cornelius that they would be OK continuing alone from here, and he started off back towards the car. Ebony watched his retreating back with dismay then looked up at the new moon and shivered.

Aunt Ruby followed her gaze. 'It's almost a waxing crescent moon – the power isn't as strong. You're safe.'

Excitement whipped through Ebony: that was her birth moon! She couldn't help wondering what effects it would have. But first – the roses! She turned and surveyed the cars in silence. They all looked the same in the dark. How on earth would they find the right one? Aunt Ruby pulled out a slim torch and clicked it on. A powerful beam shot out. Aunt Ruby flicked it along a few rows of vehicles. After a moment, Ebony recognised the judge's number plate: N1NE L1VE5.

'It's there! That's it!' she whispered.

Aunt Ruby headed straight for it and peered inside, with Ebony following close behind.

'It's too dark, I can't see a thing,' said Aunt Ruby.

Ebony took the torch and shone the beam into the car. Pulling out a small implement like a mathematical compass, Aunt Ruby scratched a circle onto the glass.

'Keep watch, Ebony.'

Taking out a small hammer, Aunt Ruby lifted her arm to strike, but a crunching sound, like someone stepping on a snail, stopped her in her tracks. Ebony checked around them but nothing stirred, not even a breeze. In some ways, it seemed too still.

'All clear,' she said.

Aunt Ruby tapped the car window with a sharp thwack. The glass fell onto the back seat.

'Can you get your hand in?'

With a bit of effort, Ebony managed to reach through the hole and unlock the car door. Her aunt was straight inside, shining her torch on the floor.

'They're not here,' she whispered.

'They must be!' cried Ebony, slithering inside and poking her hands under the driver's seat. When her fingers found the edge of a plastic bag, she gave a small cry of joy. She pulled the bag from under the seat and took out the roses. Keeping a tight hold on them, she climbed out.

'They're here,' she said.

At that moment, a bright spotlight flicked on, startling both Ebony and her aunt. They turned around slowly.

'Stay right where you are,' said a cool voice from behind

the spotlight. Ebony recognised the voice instantly: it was Judge Ambrose.

'Hide the roses,' whispered Aunt Ruby, before stepping forwards with her hand shielding her eyes, blocking Ebony from view. Ebony tucked two roses into her waistband and covered them with her jumper, then slid the other into her pocket.

The spotlight swung from side to side, surveying the rest of the car park, and then shut off. In an instant, Judge Ambrose was up close, his face extra taut and his lips stretched angrily across his teeth. Ebony's heart beat fast.

'Inside,' he said, turning on his heels and heading back towards the main door.

When Aunt Ruby failed to move, he spun around. 'Don't mess with me, Ruby, or you'll be sorry,' he snarled.

Ebony didn't like the look she'd seen on his face and wished there was someone else she could turn to for help, but she had no option other than to follow him, Ruby close behind.

The High Court headquarters was a labyrinth of heavy iron doors and exotic plants; coral vines, orchids and flame lilies climbed out of giant pots and tangled their way around door frames. As they passed through atrium after atrium, Ebony noticed that several of the beds had been freshly prepared for planting. Many were already planted with rows of small, spiked stems – the plants were too small to have developed blooms but their stems perfumed the air with an unmistakable scent: *Ebonius Tobinius* roses. Aunt Ruby eyed the beds also. Catching Ebony by the hand, she pulled her back.

'It looks like they're trying to farm the roses,' she said through gritted teeth, 'in some sort of mass production. But if they didn't find our roses, where did they get these cuttings?'

'It's rude to whisper,' called the judge, slowing his pace until they caught up.

They turned up a winding stone stairwell that was concealed by a heavy floor-length curtain and followed it until they reached a wooden door. Pushing through, Ebony held her breath, expecting a room full of High Court officials angry at her and her aunt – but the room was empty. Stars twinkled overhead and candles flickered gently around the room. The candles were set in holders shaped like life-sized people. Otherwise, the judge seemed to be alone.

Judge Ambrose noticed Ebony's puzzled expression, but his face remained tight and emotionless. The vice-like grip Ebony had felt before began to burn her wrists and she felt herself being pulled to a chair. One glance at her aunt showed she too was under the judge's power.

As soon as they were both seated, the pain lessened and the judge leaned over Aunt Ruby.

'So, why are you here in the dead of night?'

Aunt Ruby held out the three decoy black roses, a fake pained look on her face. Judge Ambrose raised an eyebrow, then reached for them.

'Interesting ...' he said. It sounded like an accusation.

'Wait! They're not real!' cried Ebony. 'Don't take them – they'll blow up!'

She leaned forward slightly, reaching for the real roses hidden in the back of her jeans.

Aunt Ruby lunged at Ebony to stop her, but she seemed to have difficulty grasping the jumper – the material swirled and slipped through her fingers. Frustrated, Aunt Ruby caught Ebony by the wrist and yanked her close; the two roses fell to the floor. The judge scooped them up right away, a thin hiss of laughter escaping from behind his teeth. 'Good girl, Ebony.'

Reaching behind a giant palm trunk, he pulled out a thick rope and flung it in Ebony's direction.

'Dear oh dear, Ruby. You know you're not sanctioned to be involved in these matters any more. I thought you'd learned your lesson. You and that brother of yours.'

He motioned for Ebony to gather up the rope. Pulling away from her aunt's grip, Ebony obeyed. Then she tied her aunt's wrists and ankles securely with the fat, scratchy rope, careful to avoid her eyes.

Triumphantly, Judge Ambrose held the flowers up to his long, thin nostrils and took a deep sniff.

Aunt Ruby's cheeks grew hot and pink as she wriggled furiously, trying to break free of the bindings. Judge Ambrose fixed his cool gaze on her. As her aunt's face twisted in discomfort, Ebony knew he must be controlling her somehow, filling her with that searing pain. Aunt Ruby turned red in the face. Then purple. Her body shook and her skin seemed to sizzle and fizz. It was horrible to see, but Ebony couldn't tear her eyes away.

I hope I've made the right decision, she thought. She didn't like the judge's actions one bit, but then she thought of Icarus Bean and the vision of her grandpa's murder and any doubts faded.

'It didn't have to be this way, Ruby,' said Judge Ambrose. 'You should have followed orders.'

Aunt Ruby caught the judge's gaze; her violet irises sparkled with fury. 'I have! I've been looking after her and educating her, as you requested.'

The judge laughed loudly. 'So why has she been snooping around the National Library and running around the city with Zachariah Stone?'

Her eyes wide, Aunt Ruby shook her head vehemently. A noise sounded in the stairwell and a tall blue-haired woman burst into the room – Ebony recognised her immediately as the librarian who had helped her.

'Ah, Miss Malone,' said Judge Ambrose. He turned back to Ebony and Ruby and smiled. 'I told you I had spies everywhere.'

The woman looked surprised to see Ruby and Ebony, then a slow, wide grin spread across her face. She leaned against the wall and, as she did so, there was a loud click. The candles began to move around the edges of the room.

'Miss Malone!' shouted the judge.

The woman flinched and she quickly turned and flicked the switch she'd accidentally knocked. The candles stopped moving. Ebony thought about how the room had looked from outside – filled with people ready for a meeting. She realised that the judge was trying to make it look like he had more supporters than he did – that's why he'd pretended he wasn't in the park dressed as a warden.

'A fine choice of comrade you have here, Ruby,' said the judge, walking to Ebony and placing an arm around her shoulder. 'She's on my side now.'

Ebony felt a tremor run through the judge's body. He strode towards Aunt Ruby and lifted his hand high. Sensing something bad coming, Ebony averted her eyes.

'This'll teach you to disobey me!' cried the judge. Ebony heard a loud slap, followed by a thud, as the chair with Aunt Ruby in it toppled on its side.

All of a sudden, there was a loud roar. The judge looked towards the atrium window, startled, and then opened his mouth in a silent scream as Mulligan smashed his way through the glass, shattering it into millions of tiny shards. Ebony tried to shield herself from the shower of splinters, sinking down behind her aunt's slumped form as the judge threw his arms in front of his face for protection.

With a powerful flick of his tail, Mulligan knocked the judge to the ground, sending him sprawling – he landed face first with his bottom sticking up in the air. Then Mulligan flicked him over, lifting him high off the ground by the throat, before throwing him across the room with all his might. The judge slammed into the glass, sending shards and splinters out into the dark night; they caught the light as they fell, like dying fireworks. The judge landed on the floor, dazed, glass dusting his face and body.

Footsteps echoed in the stairwell – it sounded like people were charging towards the room. Dashing to Aunt Ruby, Mulligan chewed off the ropes before pinning Ebony to the wall with his paw. His breath was warm against Ebony's face and his fur stank of moss and old dirty socks. That's what she'd smelled in the car – he must have been in the boot for the whole journey! Letting out a low growl, the beast pushed his face into hers.

'Good boy, Mulligan,' cried Aunt Ruby. She beckoned to him. 'Bring her!'

Mulligan tucked Ebony under one arm then bounded over to the judge and snatched up the real roses with his mouth. He let out a long, low growl at the prone figure before running across to Aunt Ruby and tucking her under his other arm. Just as he leaped out of the window, the door at the top of the stairs burst open and three men ran in. Safely landed on the lawn outside, Aunt Ruby climbed onto Mulligan's back and clung on as they raced towards the cemetery. Ebony, jolted out of her state of shock by the cold air, kicked to get free. She could hear the whine of something whizzing past their heads.

'They're firing at us,' cried her aunt, and Mulligan reacted instantly; he zigged and zagged as he ran, dodging the bullets.

Uncle Cornelius was waiting with the car engine running. When they reached the car, Mulligan shoved Ebony inside. 'No!' she cried, trying to pull herself out, but Aunt Ruby dived in and held her niece fast.

'Ebony, stop – believe me, you don't want to go back there!'

'How do you know what I want? You're trying to murder me!'

'What?' cried Aunt Ruby, before being temporarily silenced by an elbow to the jaw.

Ebony continued to flail, but Aunt Ruby was strong. She recovered quickly and Ebony hardly had time to catch her breath before the door slammed shut and the car sped off.

Looking in the rear-view mirror, Ebony spotted Mulligan chasing after them. Uncle Cornelius pressed one of the flashing orange dials and the car rocked from side to side, like a boat in a storm. In the mirror, Ebony watched as a trailer emerged from under the car. Once the trailer was stabilised, the car continued on smoothly. Mulligan quickened his pace and took a flying leap, landing on the trailer with a loud thud. Ebony jumped and shivered as she watched the beast bare his teeth, crouching low behind the car, his fur billowing in the wind as they raced through the night.

Back at Mercury Lane, Aunt Ruby and Uncle Cornelius carried a struggling Ebony into the house and put her in the kitchen, with Mulligan standing guard. At first, Ebony thought of trying to escape, but she quickly realised it would be futile and eventually slumped down at the kitchen table, quietly plotting her next move. When Ruby and Cornelius returned Mulligan was rewarded with what looked like the thigh of a large animal and sent back to the basement. Ebony was certain he had a strange glint in his eye as he headed through the cupboard door.

'Winston!' she cried, jumping up, suddenly desperate to be near her friend.

At that moment, Winston poked his head under the kitchen door and slipped in to join them. Ebony sat back down, relieved. She stroked his head and let him run up and down her arm.

'That was close.' Aunt Ruby sighed, rubbing her wrists where the ropes had been. 'I thought we'd lost you.'

Ebony winced – she hadn't realised the ropes had left burn marks; she'd been too busy obeying orders.

'You can't keep me here against my will,' said Ebony defiantly. 'The judge will come and get me. He'll protect me.'

'Protect you? Didn't you hear him talking about sides? We're meant to be a people, a community. The supporters shooting at us, the secret roses – doesn't this make you wonder what he's up to? The power has obviously gone to his head.'

Ebony glared at the kitchen table. Winston perched himself on her shoulder, nibbling nervously at her hair. Suddenly she burst out, 'He's probably growing them to help the guardian, just like you pretended you were doing. And why should I believe anything you say? You've been lying to me since I got here. I know that Icarus is your brother; you want the power of soul-swapping for yourself and you're trying to kill me.'

She waited for her aunt to try to deny it, but instead Ruby let out a huge sigh, then took out her pipe and lit it. After chugging on the crackling tobacco for a moment, she spoke. 'Yes, Icarus is my brother. But you have to believe me, he wouldn't harm you. He's trying to protect you.'

Snorting loudly, Ebony couldn't help raising her voice. '*Protect* me? That man is evil! He killed my grandpa and now he wants to kill me. Well, it's not going to happen!'

'Ebony – what are you talking about?' asked Aunt Ruby, her face white as chalk.

'I heard him with my own ears, in the museum – elimination – that's what you both said! And I saw him kill my grandpa. *The Book of Learning* showed me, through the binoculars in the study. It said I have to reveal the truth and that's exactly what I intend to do.'

Smashing her pipe down and grabbing Ebony by the arms, Aunt Ruby shook her niece in frustration. 'The book couldn't have showed him killing your grandpa – he was trying to save him, you foolish girl. Do you see where your lies have got you? You said you didn't understand *The Book of Learning* yet! If you'd come to me and told me what you saw, we could have sorted this out before tonight's fiasco. Now, what else did the book show you? And what have you been up to with Zach? It's important!'

'I won't tell you! And I won't stay!' cried Ebony, nostrils flaring.

'It's for your own good, Ebony,' said her aunt coolly, letting go. 'You can stay of your own free will or–'

'No!' shouted Ebony, jumping to her feet.

'Fine, then you leave me with no choice!' Aunt Ruby blew loudly on Mulligan's whistle.

Ebony froze. Her eyes followed the trail of blood where Mulligan had dragged his prized slab of meat down into his lair. Within moments, the beast was pushing his giant head through the door, an evil gleam in his eye.

'Take Ebony to her room, please, and guard her door,' said Aunt Ruby. Cornelius signalled to Mulligan so he could understand her orders.

Mulligan plodded over to Ebony, only stopping when

their eyelashes nearly touched. A mean growl escaped his lips as he butted her with his big, hairy nose.

'I think you'd better go quietly,' said Aunt Ruby, rubbing her temples wearily.

Snatching up Winston, knees trembling, Ebony pounded angrily up the stairs. Mulligan was so close behind her she could feel his breath on her heels.

Once inside her room, Ebony slammed the door shut. She let out a loud howl of frustration and kicked the door, her mind racing.

How was she going to get back to the judge? Yes, his behaviour was odd, but no more odd than anyone else's. How else was he meant to defeat Icarus Bean? She was certain those bullets hadn't been meant for her – they were fired at Aunt Ruby and Mulligan. Aunt Ruby was wrong – Judge Ambrose was the only one she could trust. She had seen and felt his power – only he could help her break her curse and stop her dying within the year.

Edging quietly towards the window, Ebony gave it a sharp jerk. Disappointed, she found that it once more appeared to be nailed shut. Pressing her face against the glass, she stared out into the night, searching for a safe way down. However, she quickly realised that, even if she smashed the window, she was too high up to jump and the drainpipe was probably too far away to grab and, if she could reach it, it mightn't hold her weight.

Certain she could hear distant singing, Ebony paused. The

gentle voices carried like birdsong – only sweeter – drawing her in. Enraptured, she almost forgot her predicament for a moment. But then a loud rattling sound broke the spell: it sounded as if someone was trying to force the lock on her door. Where was Mulligan – had he left his post? Bracing herself for an assault, Ebony's jaw dropped as the door opened and another past self, one she hadn't seen before, crept in, dressed in a cap, black short trousers and a white shirt. Mulligan's muscular back was visible in the doorway. He was still guarding the bedroom, completely unawares. Her aunt had said he was almost deaf, and clearly she was right. The rattling sound had been loud enough to wake the dead.

Casually, the girl crossed the room, picked up the battered suitcase and held out her hand. When Ebony took it, a warm sensation spread through her body. As she let the girl lead her across the room, terrified at every footfall that Mulligan would suddenly turn round and attack, Ebony's heart felt like it might leap out of her throat. Reaching the doorway, she held Winston tightly, extra careful to avoid Mulligan's flicking tail.

She held her breath – Mulligan might be deaf, but would he see or sense them?

As they stepped out towards the stairs, passing the wild-cat's vicious face, it was clear they were somehow invisible. Mulligan was admiring his claws and scratching at his chin, as though bored. Relieved, but still not wanting to take any chances, Ebony let out a slow, quiet breath and closed the door slowly and silently behind her. Gripping the ghostly hand tightly, she started down the stairs, her head turned back and her eyes fixed on the prehistoric wildcat. A few steps down, Ebony saw Mulligan's nose twitch. He let out a deep, uncertain growl and sniffed around him. The growl grew louder. *He might not be able to see us*, thought Ebony, *but he's detected our scent!*

As the invisible pair quickened their pace, Ebony felt Winston start to shake uncontrollably, but she couldn't offer any words of encouragement – she was just as scared! Dashing down the stairs two at a time, they reached the bottom unharmed. Her past self whispered what sounded like an enchantment and the locks fell away. Ebony checked the stairs, expecting to see Mulligan charge down them at any moment. But before she knew what was happening, she was pulled out into the night, with just her suitcase and rat for company.

'Run!' said the girl. 'You have to go home. You must open the gateway to the Reflectory there.'

When Ebony turned, the girl had completely disappeared. *What now?* thought Ebony, her skin prickling in the cool night breeze.

As though on cue, a rhythmic purring filled the air and a sleek black motorbike turned in to Mercury Lane, lights dipped. Its body was smooth and curved like a panther. Stopping outside Number 23, the rider pulled off his helmet and offered up another – it was Zach!

'Come on,' he called in a loud whisper. 'We haven't much time!'

Winston tugged on her hair and squealed in protest, but Ebony was already running towards the bike.

'They know about us,' said Ebony.

'Who?'

'Aunt Ruby and the judge.'

'The judge? You said he was the good guy, right? Then we're safe. Come on!'

Hurriedly, Zach grabbed her case and tied it onto the bike. Without a backwards glance, Ebony forced the helmet down over her hair, shoved Winston in her pocket with *The Book of Learning* and climbed aboard.

28

As they rode into the night, Ebony clung on tightly. When they'd been travelling for an hour or more, certain that no one was following, Zach pulled in to the side of the road for a rest. Removing their helmets, they slumped down onto a boulder and stared into the night.

'Where did you get the motorbike?' asked Ebony.

'I, er, *borrowed* it.'

'I didn't know you could ride … you're not old enough.'

Zach chuckled. 'I'm too young to be on the roads but I've been riding bikes for years. When I was younger, my dad and I used to go out on dirt bikes. We'd race through mud and jump ramps. That was before it all went wrong.'

'Won't the owner notify the police? Then they'll come looking for us and we'll end up in prison – or worse, I'll be brought back there.' Ebony nodded in the direction of Dublin and shuddered.

'I've borrowed this bike a few times before,' said Zach. 'It gets parked up around six and it's not used again till noon the next day. I've never had any trouble before. And guess what?'

'What?' said Ebony.

'This is the best bit … It belongs to Icarus Bean.'

As Zach's face spread into a huge grin, Ebony's jaw dropped.

'Icarus Bean? What are you thinking? What if it has some sort of tracking device attached to it?'

'Even if it does, if his bike is gone then he has no way of coming after us.'

'He could call Aunt Ruby,' said Ebony. 'She has transport.'

'That's true – but that would take organising, which gives us time to get where we are going. So we win again.'

'Where exactly are we going?'

'I'm taking you home – to Oddley Cove.'

'Will it be safe?'

'Safer than back there,' he said.

'But they'll come after me – even if they're not tracking us, it's the first place they'll look. I never want to see Dublin or my lying, cheating aunt ever again. I hate her! Oh, Zach – what should I do?'

She felt her resolve draining out of her so she avoided Zach's gaze.

'The only thing I can think of is to try to get into this Reflectory place before your aunt and Icarus Bean. But you must work alone – you can't really trust anyone other than the judge, not until you know exactly what's going on. Send word to him and I'm sure he'll come and protect you. If everyone is looking for this place and you find it, then the power is yours.'

'Zach – that's genius! There are loads of *Ebonius Tobinius* roses outside my bedroom window. But you shouldn't come – it could be dangerous!'

Zach snorted.

'More dangerous than a twelve-year-old girl travelling across the country alone? Anyway, how else are you going to get there? If it wasn't for me you'd still be standing in the middle of Mercury Lane looking lost.'

'How did you manage to turn up just in time anyway?'

'I sensed your panic. I was planning on breaking in and rescuing you.'

'I didn't need rescuing, I'm not a baby.'

'Let's not argue. You're here with me now and that's all that matters. I'll make sure you get home safely and then turn back.'

Ebony felt the blood rush to her face in indignation. She hated being patronised. How old was *he* anyway?

'I'm a whole year older than you,' said Zach with a wink.

Ebony coloured with guilt. Zach was trying to help and he was the only friend who hadn't let her down; even Winston had spied on her.

'Thank you, Zach,' she said, even though it was difficult to say.

Zach grinned. 'We should get going.'

When Ebony hesitated, he bowed deeply. 'The lady's carriage awaits.'

The night was heavy and cold, filled with steely grey

clouds. Ebony shuddered, checked Winston was safe then hugged into Zach's back to signal she was ready to leave.

Zach took off instantly and they cruised out into the night, heading for the west coast.

It felt good to be home, even without the usual warm welcome from her dogs and cats – and, of course, her grandpa. The low ceilings felt snug after the draughtiness of 23 Mercury Lane and the walls seemed to welcome Ebony in a gentle embrace. The pale blue tiles on the fireplace gleamed; the clouds and larks decorating them were a comforting sight. Her heart warmed as she drank in the familiar smells of turf, goats, old carpets and sea air. Winston was also happy to be back, poking around his favourite nooks and crannies.

The cottage was cold, having been empty for a few days; Zach shivered and their breath formed puffs of moisture in the air, but Ebony couldn't light the fire because she didn't want to signal her return. She couldn't chance someone alerting the authorities. One of her grandpa's thick knitted jumpers would have to do.

Heading to her grandpa's room, Ebony paused outside the door and inhaled several deep breaths before shoving it open. The room looked exactly the same as she remembered it – like he might come back at any minute – and it smelled of sea-fresh tobacco. Ebony inhaled the scent; it was both comforting and painful at the same time. She picked out her grandpa's favourite jumper and brought it to Zach. Then she made two steaming cups of black tea.

'No milk,' she said.

As Ebony leaned forward to set Zach's tea on the floor in front of him, the locket swung out from underneath her jumper.

'What's that?' asked Zach, grabbing the locket, his eyes gleaming.

'What?' asked Ebony, straightening up; the chain snapped and the locket fell to the floor.

'I'm sorry,' said Zach. 'I didn't mean to break it.'

As Zach stooped to pick up the necklace, Winston skidded across the room, snatched the locket in his mouth and ran off. The locket swung from Winston's jaws like a pendulum.

'Come here with that!' shouted Zach angrily and gave chase.

Winston shot along the skirting board with Zach in pursuit.

'Winston,' Ebony shouted. 'Bring it here! Zach, leave him alone!'

Neither of them listened. Winston scurried up the wall to the top of the kitchen cupboard and peered down. Zach looked ready to follow him.

'Zach, please, you're scaring him – I'm sure he'll bring it back in a bit,' said Ebony, hoping with all her heart that he would.

But Zach ignored her words. Climbing onto the washing

machine, he stretched up as far as he could. Just as he managed to touch the tip of the rat's fur, Winston did a flying leap from the top of the cupboard to the sofa, settling on Ebony's lap.

Then Winston did something very bizarre indeed – he swallowed the necklace, locket and all. Zach and Ebony looked stunned.

'Did he just do what I think he did?' asked Zach.

'He did,' said Ebony, an odd sense of foreboding filling her stomach.

They watched Winston for a moment to see what he would do next. The rat simply laid his head on his paws and closed his eyes, looking quite happy with the outcome of his little escapade.

'That's too weird,' said Zach. 'Will he be all right? Maybe I should take him to a vet?'

Winston's ear twitched but his eyes stayed firmly shut.

'I think he'll be OK. He's eaten some strange things in the past and has always been fine – but it's going to hurt when it comes out the other end, that's for sure,' said Ebony.

Zach's expression lightened and they both chuckled.

'Poor Winston,' said Ebony, stroking his fur. 'You have no idea what you've done.'

Winston peeped open one glossy eye then settled back to sleep.

'Well, at least I've warmed up now,' said Zach lightheartedly, but his brow was deeply furrowed and his eyes gleamed darkly. 'I am sorry, though,' he added, as an afterthought.

'It's just a dumb necklace,' said Ebony, her tone deliberately nonchalant.

There was something about the way Zach had reacted, something she couldn't quite put her finger on. She knew the amulet was meant to open the gateway to the Reflectory – but for reasons she didn't understand, her instincts told her to conceal this information from Zach.

Anyway, she didn't want him to feel any worse than he already did; she could tell by his quiet demeanour and flushed skin that he was already feeling guilty enough. She owed him; after all, he'd rescued her. She looked up at her friend. To her dismay, Zach stood up to leave.

'It's time for me to go. I'd better get this motorbike back before Icarus discovers it's gone. I'll be in touch.'

Not wanting to be alone, especially in a house that now felt so empty and nothing like home, Ebony realised how much she wanted Zach to stay. She felt safer with him around but she didn't know how to say it and she couldn't think of anything to stall him. She willed him to read her mind, but Zach seemed intent on leaving.

'Will you be OK riding back alone in the dark?' she asked.

'It's safer than with a passenger. If I set off now, and replace the petrol, there'll be no trace that the bike was used, so even if there are tracking devices on it no one will notice. It buys you some time; they won't expect you to have made it this far yet.'

Crossing her fingers, Ebony hoped that that was true.

'But how will I contact the judge?'

'Through me. He's in the Botanic Gardens, right?'

She nodded, thankful for his mind-reading skills. 'Thanks for your help, Zach,' she said, reluctantly showing him to the door.

Ebony's knees twitched and her legs wobbled. She hoped that Zach would change his mind and stay, but it wasn't to be. Minutes later, he was cruising off down the lane, his headlight dipped and one arm raised, waving goodbye. Ebony watched until the light from the bike faded, then went inside and closed the curtains before cuddling on the sofa with Winston.

'It looks like it's just me and you, buddy,' she said.

The words echoed around the room. Her grandpa's absence thick in the air, she couldn't face going to sleep in her old bedroom – not without him coming to say goodnight. Instead, Ebony fetched the quilt from her bed and decided to sleep on the sofa next to Winston, in case he needed her. He'd been through a lot, and she was quite sure the locket would give him a terrible tummy ache.

Flicking through the used pages of *The Book of Learning* for comfort, Ebony felt her eyelids droop. As she slumped down into the sofa cushions, the relief of being home comforted her sore heart and aching limbs. Drifting off, she thought about the sea, imagined being carried off in its waves. As sleep took her, *The Book of Learning* fell onto the floor, open on a new page. As Ebony slipped more deeply into sleep, the page glimmered then a video-image appeared, showing Zach's bike doing a U-turn on the road. Winston jumped up, his tail sticking out poker straight. Scampering up Ebony's shoulder, he patted her face with his paws. But Ebony was fast asleep. Trying one last time to wake Ebony and failing, Winston scurried over to his favourite little hole in the bottom left corner of the doorframe. Squeezing his way through, he scurried out into the night and positioned himself on the bend in the lane just before the cottage. Quietly, he waited to see whether Zach would return.

The clang of the letter box woke Ebony early the next morning. Fingers of light poked through the gap in the curtains, but it didn't help alleviate her fear – had they come for her so soon? Dropping to the floor, Ebony held her breath and waited. She heard footsteps, but they faded quickly – whoever it was wasn't sticking around. Whether this was a good thing or a bad thing, she couldn't be sure, so she stayed put for a while. When it had been silent for some time, Ebony crawled to the doorway and peeked out into the porch. There was no one there, but an envelope sat on the mat just inside the door. She picked it up – it had her name on it but there was no address or stamp. It hadn't come through the post. She tore the envelope open. Inside was a bright blue card. It read:

We have your rat. If you want him, come to the underground cave on Gallows Island.

Ebony flung the cottage door open wide and ran outside, but whoever had posted the letter had disappeared. She closed and locked the door before racing around the cottage, checking all of Winston's favourite places: he wasn't in the bread bin, on the shelf above the water boiler or even in the bottom of the linen basket. He was nowhere to be seen. Had the kidnappers somehow snatched Winston from under her nose while she was asleep? How could she be so useless? She was the worst friend ever!

But who would steal him – and why? Guessing Aunt Ruby was involved – they must have been spying on her more successfully than she'd thought – Ebony scowled. A horrible thought crept into her mind. Did they know Winston had swallowed the amulet? If so, she was certain they'd stop at nothing to get it.

Elimination – that was the word Icarus Bean had used in the museum.

Ebony wasn't going to let that happen. There was only one thing for it: she would have to get Winston back before he came to any harm.

Gallows Island was a small green mound surrounded by rocky cliffs on the other side of Gun Point. She had shot lobster pots there with her grandpa many times and had explored the entrance of the cave with him once or twice on sunny days, but she had never been underground. Neither had she sailed to the island alone, because of the treacherous currents and hidden rocks that surrounded it. There was a small pier for mooring boats, but it was tricky to reach and Ebony wasn't sure she could manage it alone. But for Winston, she'd brave it.

Realising she might need something to bargain with in exchange for her pet – if they wanted roses, they could have roses – Ebony dashed outside. But a terrible scene was waiting: the soil was mashed up into lumpy craters, and all the rose bushes were gone. Horror cut through her like a blade. Crouching, Ebony dug desperately into the ground with her fingers, but even the roots had been removed. And looking at the condition of the soil, they'd been taken days ago. This was not one of her animals: this was a carefully managed operation. Someone had stolen her roses! Without them, what would she trade for Winston? Then she remembered the one she'd managed to conceal at the Botanic Gardens. Slipping her hand into her pocket, she felt its soft velveteen petals against her fingertips and breathed a sigh of relief.

Taking the rose out for a sniff, Ebony suddenly remembered the scent from the cuttings at the Nine Lives headquarters – could it have been the judge who had taken them? He couldn't have seen them when he collected her after her grandpa died because he didn't go out the back – the dogs had stopped him – but he'd told her he had spies everywhere. Maybe one of them had found them and told the judge. If this was the case, rescuing Winston was going to be even harder than she'd expected – a single rose wouldn't be much of a bargaining tool.

Without another moment to lose, Ebony snatched up *The Book of Learning* and stuffed it into her pocket. She also retrieved her grandpa's medal from the case – once again, it felt warm and comforting in her hands – and dropped it into her other pocket for luck. Then she grabbed the boat ignition key and her pocket knife, just in case. She had a feeling this was going to get hairy.

29

Running down to the end of the garden and through the gate, Ebony was pleased to find that her grandpa's fishing boat was still moored to their private quay. The sea seemed calm but Ebony knew that it could be deceptive. She glanced up at the sky – it was pale blue, covered with a smattering of wispy clouds – to check the wind direction. Some of the clouds looked like the pattern on a mackerel's back; others spread out like flying horses' tails. Ebony's heart sank as the words her grandpa used to say sang in her mind:

> ♪ **Mackerel skies and horses' tails,**
> **Moor your boats and lower the sails.** ♫

Squinting out over the sea like her grandpa had done, Ebony took a proper look, trying to read the sea's mood. The channel between the mainland and Gun Point was calm enough, but Ebony had to get round to Gallows Island – the next island to the north – and she knew the water would turn choppy and dangerous. She probably only had an hour or two before the weather turned really bad, but Winston's well-being had to come first.

The boat bobbed in the water as Ebony untied the painter rope from the bollard on the quay, the blue hull and the small white cabin beckoning her in time with the tide. She climbed aboard and pulled on her life jacket. Then she fired up the engine; it chugged into action immediately. The vibrations from the engine reminded her of the last voyage with her grandpa, but there was no time for sadness now.

Without a moment to lose, she undid the bow and stern lines and shoved the boat away from the wall with a long hook. Tucking into the shelter of the spray cabin, Ebony gripped the steering wheel, her eyes fixed on the waves as the boat pushed against the tide.

The sea smashed against the hull as Ebony steered her way past the buoys and shrimp pots of her childhood. With the weather threatening to turn nasty, no one else was out sailing except for the huge fishing boats pair-trawling in the distance. Those massive vessels were at least a day away from shore and built for the sea's angry ways, but her boat was not. Her grandpa would usually keep their boat moored until mid-May. She shook the thought from her mind and increased the speed a little more.

Getting out into the channel took longer than Ebony had hoped. The wind was already strong and picking up fast. On the horizon rain covered the trawlers with a thick, perilous downpour, and it was heading her way.

As Ebony pushed on, every minute seemed like a lifetime. There was nothing more that she could do; the little boat was already at full throttle. Every now and again, she touched her grandpa's medal for luck. At the mercy of the sea, anything that gave her comfort was welcome.

Eventually she reached the end of Gun Point and turned the boat out into the open sea. The wind sneaked around the edges of the cabin, whipping her hair across her face and trying to force the boat off course. Gulls caterwauled above her head as they headed for shore. Spray splashed up over the sides, stinging her eyes and drenching her hair; yet the clothes her aunt had made somehow deflected the water, keeping the rest of her bone dry.

Ebony pushed on.

A second later the wind changed direction, helping the boat along. It whistled in her ears and Ebony's heart warmed. It was as though she could feel her grandpa's presence beside her. The boat started to pick up speed and Ebony steered towards Gallows Island. Soon she was nearing the small pier and slowed the boat down, guiding the little vessel towards it as she edged carefully past the dangerous rocks that lurked beneath the surface. All along the pier were big, solid bollards for her to tie her ropes to, but getting to one of them proved even trickier than she had expected. Ebony knew it was dangerous to moor at the pier in such unpredictable weather, but she had to leave her boat somewhere and the inside moorings would offer some shelter from the wind.

Without help to steady the boat it took Ebony several attempts to get close enough to the pier to tie the painter rope around a bollard. All the while, the hull groaned as it scraped and bashed against the pier's barnacled sides. She had to move quickly. High tide was a few hours away and the water would continue to rise. If Ebony didn't make it back, her boat might be forced up onto the pier or crushed against its side; if the rope got damaged, the boat could be pulled out to sea by the tide.

Eventually, she managed to secure the rope and climb out to attach the stern line, making sure to leave a bit of slack for the boat to move with the tide – 'the draw' her grandpa had called it. When she was satisfied that the boat was as secure as she could make it, Ebony climbed up the vertical ladder, tucking in her chin to shield her eyes from the roaring wind and waves that threatened to engulf the pier.

The pier turned wet and slippery as the waves crashed around her. She had to lean into the wind, walking slowly and carefully, to prevent being dragged into the angry water. Salt stung her face, but she knew that as soon as she hit the path she would be sheltered by the grassy banks on either side. But when she reached the path there was no time to catch her breath: she had to save Winston. She ran east along the road in the direction of the underground cave, aided by the wind behind her. It hurt her lungs to suck in the cold air as she ran, but she concentrated on getting to Winston, allowing the sound of rushing wind to drown out her fears.

When she reached the entrance to the cave, it was covered by a boulder. Ebony was surprised; it hadn't been there the previous times she had visited. She pushed at the huge rock but couldn't make it budge, then searched around the edges, looking for some sort of opening mechanism. As she moved from one side to the other, her foot stubbed against something on the ground. She crouched down and found a bronze rose. It was the same as the one in the park that opened the entrance to Zach's underground hideout. Ebony twisted the bronze rose one way and then the other. Sure enough, the boulder began to sink into the ground, revealing the cave entrance.

'Thank you, Zach,' she said aloud, hoping her words would reach him under the pond in Dublin.

The cave was damp, its sides lined with the thick roots of marram grass. She had only ever explored the entrance before, and as she ventured further back, the cave got darker and gloomier, eventually turning into a sheer wall of stone and shadows. So where was Winston? Feeling her way along the wall – there had to be some way to keep going – she found the opening to a thin, dark passage, just wide enough for her to squeeze into if she turned sideways. Ebony took a deep breath, then headed inside. It was pitch black and the walls were wet and slimy, the air rank with damp and decay. As her face grazed the passage wall in front of her, her head pushed back against the opposite wall as she side-stepped along and it felt like she was suffocating in the dampness. The further she got, the thinner the air became. Blood pumping, Ebony had no idea what was waiting for her.

After a few moments, the tunnel widened slightly and she could turn her head. There was light up ahead. As she pushed her way towards the light, the passage came to a sudden end and she found herself in a proper tunnel, which stretched away to her left and right. Each way was gently lit by candles, but which should she choose?

Ebony paused, listening for voices. For a moment all she could hear was her breathing and the thump of her blood in her ears. Focusing on each direction in turn, she strained her ears. Nothing. Certain it was all clear, she turned left, following her gut instinct and hoping desperately that it was the correct way to go. The tunnel started off spacious, but as she progressed, the roof remained high but the sides narrowed. The candles became few and far between, lit only where there was enough room, so sometimes she found herself in complete darkness. Ebony had to squeeze her way through sideways in these spots, fighting off her claustrophobia.

The tunnel seemed never-ending and Ebony started to wonder whether she had made a huge mistake. Then, just as she was tempted to stop for a rest, she heard a loud thud in the distance. It jolted her out of her growing despair as she realised that she had to stay strong: she had to get to Winston.

Pushing on quietly, she came to the end of the tunnel and cautiously peered out. The tunnel opened into a huge cavern carved out of sparkling granite and she saw that she was about twenty feet above the floor. Water dripped down the walls and old fishermen's oil lamps hung on the walls, making the cave glow and the shadows loom large.

The cave was filled with scaffolding, tracks and pulleys. It reminded Ebony of her aunt's kitchen and she took this as positive evidence of Ruby's involvement. She shuddered, thinking of the dark corners of 23 Mercury Lane and the monster in its basement.

Looking around the cave, there was no one to be seen. She had expected guards, but the place was empty and still, like it had been suddenly evacuated. She figured that Winston's kidnappers probably hadn't expected her to figure out how to get in and had meant to meet her at the blocked entrance – maybe she'd managed to get there quicker than they'd predicted.

Ebony listened carefully. She could just make out a faint noise, like the soft padding of feet, coming from a hole on the opposite side of the cave, which she guessed must be the end of the other fork in the tunnel. She heaved a sigh of relief; it seemed her instinct to go left had been right.

The footsteps sounded distant so, reaching for the nearest bit of scaffolding, Ebony started to climb down as quietly as she could. If she was right about the footsteps, any noise she made would echo loudly and she would be discovered right away. Checking behind her, Ebony spotted Winston and stifled a gasp.

Her rat was tied to a stone slab in the centre of the cave. His back was flat against the stone, his legs stretched away from his body and secured with straps. He had a metal band around his head, pulling it back so his throat was bared. A trolley next to him carried a gun and a scalpel; both glinted menacingly. Tears welled in Ebony's eyes.

How could they do that to Winston? He was her best friend.

With his body limp and motionless, and his tongue lolling out of his mouth, it looked like Winston was dead. *Oh no*, she thought, *am I too late?*

The padding of feet grew louder as someone neared the opening of the opposite tunnel. Ebony quickly finished climbing down and ducked behind a conveyor belt. From this hiding place she had a good view through the latticed metal-work and hoped she wouldn't be visible from the other side.

Poised, breath held, she fixed her gaze on the tunnel entrance – would Icarus emerge? And if not Icarus, who? Ebony felt an unusually black feeling swirl in her gut as violently as the sea. She tried to quell it, not liking the shadows in her heart.

Suddenly, Mulligan padded out of the opposite tunnel. She was right – Aunt Ruby *was* to blame! The wildcat crossed the cave, and when he reached Winston he lifted a sharp claw and slashed the straps.

'Stop!' cried Ebony, rushing out from her hiding place and, without thinking what she was doing, launching herself at the beast. Although no match for Mulligan's bulk, her attack knocked him off balance. As he slammed into the trolley behind, the gun slid off and skidded across the floor. Without hesitation, Ebony threw herself at the weapon and snatched it up. Gesturing at Mulligan with the gun, she growled, 'Step away from my friend.'

Ebony had held Old Joe's shotgun before, but not a weapon like this. It looked like a pistol but buzzed gently as though an electric current was running through it. She hoped that as long as she looked like she knew what she was doing, she would be OK.

Mulligan froze to the spot, his teeth bared in an ugly smile.

'Move *right* away,' said Ebony, gesturing more emphatically to try to make him understand.

Mulligan stayed put.

'I mean it.' As she took a step forward, Mulligan took a step back.

Ebony moved quickly. Keeping the gun trained on Mulligan, she approached the table and put her hand on Winston's chest, almost crying with relief when she felt the faint thump of his heart – he was alive but he didn't respond to her touch, so she realised he must be anaesthetised. Lifting Winston's limp body from the table, she slipped him into the spare side pocket of her special trousers as carefully as she could. The pocket seemed to shape itself around him as support. She hoped he wasn't too uncomfortable in there, but she had nowhere else for him to go; in his drugged state, Winston couldn't cling on to her shoulder.

Without taking her eyes off Mulligan, Ebony felt her way back to the scaffolding one step at a time. The moment cold steel touched her hand, she turned, shoved the gun into the waistband of her trousers and raced up it. Hand over hand she headed for the tunnel entrance above. Behind her, Mulligan let out a low growl.

In moments, Ebony was level with the tunnel. She glanced back towards the wildcat to check he wasn't following her, but Mulligan was facing the opposite tunnel growling, shoulders taut and tail twitching, as though angered by something. Not waiting to see what, Ebony thrust herself through the entranceway and started back along the tunnel.

With the knowledge that Mulligan would soon be after her, the tunnel seemed even longer than before, but Ebony pushed on fearlessly. Eventually, she reached the place where the tunnel widened and she took off as fast as her legs would allow, hoping that she wasn't bashing Winston around too much. But a few bumps were nothing compared to what Mulligan had probably been planning – Winston would surely understand.

As she ran on, Ebony heard the echoes of a ferocious roar. She guessed that Mulligan would be unable to follow her because the tunnel was initially too narrow, so he would be forced to use the other tunnel to catch her. Running as fast as she could, she drew near to the entrance to the other tunnel, but came to an abrupt stop as she saw she hadn't been quick enough. Mulligan had reached it first. He was up ahead, blocking her way back through the passage to the cave entrance. Sweat pouring from her forehead and down her neck, she looked around frantically. What was she going to do? There was nowhere to go. Was this how she was going to die? Ripped apart by a prehistoric wildcat?

Instinctively searching the walls for a way to escape Mulligan's clutches, Ebony could just make out a few cracks of light high up in the tunnel ceiling. If she could climb up, there might be a way out.

Somewhere in the tunnel behind her, footsteps rang out – she didn't know who they belonged to, but she couldn't imagine it was anyone friendly. The floor vibrated slightly and Mulligan threw himself into a crouching position, staring towards her like he was waiting to pounce. Ebony knew she only had seconds to work out how to escape. *Use the gun*, a voice whispered in her head.

As the footsteps drew closer, the vibration in the floor grew stronger. Suddenly Mulligan launched his huge body in her direction. Ebony ducked and, after he sailed over her head, she started to climb. She heard a thwack, like something slamming into the wall. Whether it was Mulligan or whoever the footsteps had belonged to, she didn't look round to find out. Finding the jagged rocks easy to climb, Ebony scaled the walls. When she reached the highest point possible, she checked Mulligan's position: he was now directly below her, facing the tunnel she had come through, looking fierce. It looked almost like he was guarding her.

Grabbing the gun, she pointed it at the largest crack in the ceiling and fired. It jerked violently, sending out a ray of blinding light and a tiny see-through bullet, which flew skywards, silently striking the rock. The ceiling exploded in an avalanche of rock, chippings and dust. Ebony clung to the tunnel wall, tilting her head to shield her face, her ears ringing painfully with the noise. When the pain in her ears subsided and the dust cleared, Ebony blinked her eyes at the bright light flooding in.

There was no time to waste – but she quickly realised the tunnel ceiling was too smooth to allow her to climb as far as the gap. She had to figure out a way to get to it.

Ebony looked about her in panic. She couldn't see anything that could help, but she spied Mulligan below, flattened on the floor and half covered with rocks and debris. A particularly large rock lay next to his head – it must have hit him when the ceiling shattered. Was he dead?

A sharp whistle sounded from above and Ebony tore her gaze away, trying to locate the source of the noise. The girl in the cowboy hat from the library was leaning over the hole the gun had made. She winked, then threw down the end of a long rope. It clattered in Ebony's direction and swung from side to side. She grabbed it and gave it a tug: it would take her weight.

'Thanks,' she called, but the girl had already gone.

Stuffing the gun back into her waistband, Ebony swung from the wall and started pulling herself up the rope. Her shoulders burned, the rope swung and lurched but her clothes seemed to affix themselves to the rope threads and give her extra support. When she reached the top, Ebony was panting hard – her lungs and throat burned with the effort – but she had to keep going. She hauled herself through the hole, then peered back over the edge.

At the bottom of the cave, Mulligan remained lifeless, his limbs twisted and splayed under the rubble. It looked like she was safe.

Then, as she turned to leave, Ebony heard another set of footsteps scrambling up the rocks. She had no idea who it was, but she wasn't keen to find out. Pulling up the rope so it couldn't be used by anyone else to escape, she ran towards the shore. The sky was now petrol grey and the wind was strong. If she didn't hurry, her boat would be smashed to smithereens and there'd be no way to escape. She had to get off Gallows Island before her enemies caught up with her.

30

Back at the mooring, the ropes had held but the boat was in difficulty. Waves smashed up and over the pier, sending silt and seaweed flying. Wind howled like lost sea-ghosts. Despite being sheltered from the wind, the boat hurled and tossed in the angry water. Ebony leaped on board and untied the bow rope, but the thinner stern line snapped before she could get to it. Waiting until there was a lull in the wind, Ebony wiped the salt water from her eyes and turned the key in the ignition to fire the engine. It took three tries to get it going, the dull thwack of the engine suddenly leaping into life with a growl.

The boat shuddered as the tide rocked it from side to side. Ebony fumbled with the wheel, her eyes fixed to the horizon where waves frothed and foamed like angry white horses. She had to get out of there. She pushed away from the pier but it was impossible to steer; the conditions were too fierce. A huge wave broke over the bow, thrusting the boat back against the pier. There was a loud grating sound as it scraped the pier's barnacled sides and Ebony hoped there was no damage to the hull. Water poured over the gunwale; if it got any deeper, she'd have to try to bale and steer at the same time. Ebony clenched the steering wheel tightly. If she could make it to the channel between her village and Gun Point, she'd be fine, but there was a long stretch of perilous sea to conquer first.

Pushing the engine as hard as she could, Ebony steered out into the open water. She tried skimming along the inside of the bigger waves, but they lifted her high, each time threatening to overturn the boat. The rain and the waves battered her face and the windows of the cabin so she couldn't see where she was going. Her grandpa would never have taken the boat out in these conditions. She hoped deep down that, wherever he was, he understood her actions.

Keep your eyes on the sea, warned the whisper, *you're at the mercy of the elements*. Ebony gasped. It was something her grandpa used to say to her all the time. *Grandpa?* she thought. Then she shouted it out loud. 'Grandpa!'

As she expected, there was no reply. Her words were caught by the wind and scattered in the violent sea spray.

The boat shuddered on the high swells and lifted high in the air. Her grandpa's life jacket flew over the side, lost in the churning depths – Ebony checked the one she was wearing to make sure it was secure. *Turn the boat around*, said the whisper. But Ebony couldn't turn, so she had no choice but to push on. She felt her pocket wriggling. Winston must have woken up. He'd been jiggled and bashed and would be both sore and confused, but there was no time to explain.

'It's all right, Winston,' she shouted, but thunder rumbled

overhead and her voice was lost. A crack of lightning split the sky and for an instant lit the scene in front of her. She was going the wrong way, heading towards land! She tried again to turn the boat but the waves were too strong.

The steering wheel lurched in her hands and rain lashed against her face. A whole wave engulfed the boat, shoving Ebony to the floor and away from the wheel. Desperately she stumbled to her feet and rushed forward to grab it, but it was spinning wildly and she didn't have the strength to stop it.

All of a sudden, she was facing a steep cliff. Although she tried her best to steer the boat away, it was out of her hands. The sea flung the boat against the rocks. The wood groaned and splintered. Huge planks cracked and exploded in all directions. Ebony was thrown backwards into the icy water, paralysed for an instant. The waves whirled around her and bits of broken boat smacked her limbs and face. She tried to grab hold of a piece of wood to stay adrift, but she couldn't get a grip on it. The sea whizzed her around like a giant food processor. She imagined Zach's face peering down at her, smiling. Something stabbed into her side and she felt her life jacket deflate.

Ebony sank into the water's depths. The misty sea was filled with sand, seaweed and ship wreckage. Her head started to feel light and she felt the bitter cold seep in through her clothes. The urge to breathe coursed through her body. *Poor Winston*, she thought. By trying to save him, she'd brought him to his death.

Suddenly a hand grabbed hers. Using all her remaining energy to look up to see who was helping her, Ebony saw a girl with long black curls in pirate garb kicking her way to the surface.

And a pair of familiar beady eyes approaching.

Cedric the giant shark was making his way through the tumult. His huge mouth gaped open, and he appeared to be consuming the wreckage of her boat as he heaved his bulk in her direction. Confused and weak from the lack of air, it was all too much and Ebony blacked out.

3¹

Water spewed from Ebony's lips and her body convulsed as she choked out mouthfuls of bitter sea water. Lying on her side, she coughed until her ribs felt bruised, her throat burning with sea salt. Lights twinkled all around and a metal ceiling yawned above her, punctuated by smooth white pipes which glinted in the glare of the lights. Ebony wondered whether she was dead and this was the Reflectory. A strange hollow echo sounded all around her and it felt like the ground was rocking gently from side to side. Ebony sat up and rubbed her eyes. As her vision cleared, she saw Uncle Cornelius crouching next to her.

'Where am I?' asked Ebony, shrinking back. She felt the gun still wedged in the back of her trousers and it gave her courage.

Uncle Cornelius wiggled his hand in a line like a wave, pointing underneath it with his other hand. Ebony thought for a moment.

'I'm under the sea?'

Uncle Cornelius nodded.

'But how?' asked Ebony. 'Is this a submarine?'

Nodding, Uncle Cornelius pressed his hands together to make the shape of a fin.

'I'm inside *Cedric*?'

Sticking up his thumb, Uncle Cornelius grinned.

'So even Cedric is fake,' said Ebony sadly.

Looking to the floor, Uncle Cornelius swayed from foot to foot. His wild hair stood on end. All of a sudden he sprang up, raced away and then came back a moment later, *The Book of Learning* in his hand. She opened it up: the pages were damp and salt-edged, but otherwise it seemed OK. Snapping the book shut, she shoved it into her pocket, relieved to find the medal and rose were still there. Then she gasped and quickly checked the other leg – Winston was gone!

'Where's Winston?'

Uncle Cornelius pointed towards the back of the room. It was too dark for Ebony to see anything. As he gave her another thumb's up sign, she noticed his claw was covered with dried red blood.

'You murderer!' shouted Ebony.

Uncle Cornelius twitched and rubbed his ears, cowering. Ebony hauled herself up amidst a fit of coughing.

'You're wrong,' said an old, gruff voice.

Out of the shadows stepped Old Joe – the last person she had expected to see. His face was soft and warm in the twinkling light. Ebony stumbled towards him as quickly as she could and flung her arms around him, sobbing hot tears.

'Joe, help me!'

'Calm down, girl.' He held her tightly, until the sobbing subsided. 'Whatever's the matter?'

Uncle Cornelius stepped towards Ebony but she hid behind Joe.

'Don't let him get me, Joe. He's working with her. They're trying to kill me.'

Old Joe gave a deep throaty chuckle, then stopped when he noticed the look of terror on Ebony's face. 'Why on earth would you think that?' he said.

'I heard her with my own ears. She didn't know I was hiding in the museum. I heard her talking with Icarus Bean. You don't know Icarus Bean but …'

'Yes, I do,' he said, with a calm look in his eye.

'… he attacked me; she left me alone on purpose so he could get to me. Oh, Joe, please don't make me go back there.' Ebony was speaking so fast, the words tumbling over themselves, that she had missed Old Joe's reply.

Old Joe tightened his arm around Ebony as Uncle Cornelius hopped from one leg to the other, glancing in her direction. He hid his face every time she looked his way.

'And that monster's eaten Winston,' she shouted, pointing in Uncle Cornelius's direction.

'Winston is quite fine. Cornelius saved his life.'

'But the blood on his nails …'

'He extracted a locket from his stomach. Winston would be a goner if it wasn't for your uncle. Connie, go and get Winston.'

As Uncle Cornelius shuffled off, deep into the belly of the

shark submarine, Ebony huddled into Old Joe. Then, as the reality of the situation dawned on her and she realised what he had said about Icarus Bean, she stepped away, squinting at him suspiciously.

'How did you know I was here?' she asked.

'When I called round to check on the animals, I could tell you'd been at the cottage. I noticed the boat had gone, so I phoned your aunt. She confirmed you'd run away and she was on her way to find you.'

'You know my aunt? Why didn't you say?' But Ebony didn't give him time to answer. 'And what about Uncle Cornelius? How did he get here?'

'They're all here – your aunt, Icarus, Cornelius. You were spotted by one of their surveillance team, heading out of town on the back of a bike. They came to find you.'

'To harm me, more like. But that doesn't explain how you knew I would be heading out to Gallows Island – unless you were in on the kidnapping.'

'We found the ransom note, so Cornelius fired Cedric up. This may be a mechanical shark, but it can still pick up sound and scent from miles away, just like a real one. It was our best hope of finding you. And it's a good job we did. Otherwise, you'd have drowned.'

Ebony pulled the gun from her waistband and pointed it towards Old Joe, hoping it would still work if needed. She felt bad, but if he was working with her aunt, she would have to be cautious.

'Where's Aunt Ruby?'

'She's back at the cottage, monitoring the enemy.'

'She is the enemy!' cried Ebony, feeling anger flush her face. 'She sent Mulligan to attack me.'

Old Joe glanced at the gun in Ebony's shaking hand. 'Calm down, Ebony, I'm on your side. I swear, your aunt sent Mulligan to help you – we brought him to the island in Cedric so that he could find you and protect you from whoever took Winston.'

Ebony held his gaze. Old Joe had been her grandpa's best friend and here he was helping Aunt Ruby and bringing a wildcat to supposedly help her. Zach was right – she couldn't trust anyone except for the judge.

'Get me back to land, Joe.'

The old man cocked his head to one side and listened to the groan of the shark's hull making its way through the water.

'We're already heading that way. It'll not take long now. We're only a few miles away.'

Uncle Cornelius returned but stopped in the door when he saw Ebony with the gun. Then he approached her slowly and handed over a washed-out looking Winston in an open shoebox padded with old socks – and the amulet. At least, it looked like the amulet – of course it might self-destruct like the roses, but Ebony had no option but to hope that it was the real thing, as her aunt had claimed she didn't know what the amulet looked like.

As Cornelius backed away slowly to stand with Old Joe,

Ebony crouched down and set the box on the floor. She reached in to give Winston's nose a stroke. She could feel his body trembling. Winston rolled onto his side, revealing a tummy full of angry red stitches. The rat was clearly exhausted, but he lifted his head towards Ebony and gave her a little wink. A tear formed in Ebony's eye, but she wiped it away then stood up and waved the gun at the two men.

'I'm sorry to have to do this,' she said, 'but put your backs against the wall.'

Both of them edged up against the wall she was indicating with the gun. For a moment there was silence and then, 'Your uncle needs to steer Cedric,' said Old Joe.

Ebony nodded reluctantly and Uncle Cornelius disappeared towards the head of the shark. She hated having to trust that he wasn't up to any mischief.

After a moment Joe cleared his throat. 'Ebony, you've got to believe me. There's no way Ruby is trying to kill you. She's looking after you.'

'How would you know?'

'She used to live at the cottage – along with Icarus. When your parents disappeared, they helped look after you for the first year. It was your grandpa that fired her interest in all this invention stuff.' He held up his hands and gestured to the shark submarine surrounding them. 'Ruby was your grandpa's favourite.'

Finding it suddenly difficult to breathe, Ebony's heart curled like razor wire. She didn't like the thought of someone else being adored by her grandpa. He was *hers*. Everything had been taken away from her since he had died. No one was going to take their closeness away from her as well.

Old Joe registered the look of pain on Ebony's face and, realising his mistake, took a tentative step forward. 'Apart from you, of course!'

Tears spilled from Ebony's eyes and her gun hand shook. Although she didn't want to hear what else Old Joe had to say, she felt she had to listen. She was getting closer to the truth about her past and the Order of Nine Lives, about how she fit into this new world she'd been thrown into.

'Go on,' she said.

'Your grandpa and aunt were very close, but then the judge ordered her to live in the city. There was too much dangerous activity there and the High Court needed her help. Your grandpa was heartbroken to lose her from his protection.'

'Why didn't he teach me about the Order?' said Ebony.

'He thought you were too young. He wanted to wait until you were older. His aim was to keep you safe until you passed your twelfth year, then reveal everything to you once you were out of immediate danger. He didn't want to repeat the mistakes he'd made with Ruby – she got into so much trouble. He blamed himself – the fact that he'd taught her too much too soon. If he hadn't, she might never have been forced to move to the city. He would never have lost her.'

'But I'm not my aunt! If he'd only given me a chance–'

'He felt there weren't enough certainties; he'd failed you

too many times already, losing your parents like that and having to keep the rest of the family from you.'

'I don't understand why we had to be kept apart.'

'The judge ordered it. For your grandpa to keep you, he had to give up Ruby.'

'Why should I believe you? You pretended you didn't know my aunt a few days ago.'

'I didn't pretend; I just didn't mention it. It's not my place to tell you these things. A family's business is its own. Your grandpa wanted to tell you everything when the time was right.'

'But he told you! And you're not even part of the Order … are you?'

As he shook his head, Old Joe's eyes turned red and watery. 'No, I'm afraid I only have this life. I was just lucky enough to have met your grandpa and become his friend. I saved his life once on a fishing trip and gained his confidence. Over time, I saw enough things with my own eyes to know his stories were true …' His voice trailed off. Ebony wanted to feel sorry for him, but hurt and anger bubbled up inside her.

'My grandpa is dead!' she shouted. 'You should have told me.' As a fit of coughing took over, Ebony's body convulsed.

'How could I? I haven't seen you. Anyway, the responsibility passed to your aunt,' said Old Joe, looking concerned. 'She's doing her best.'

'So why is she consorting with Icarus Bean?'

'They're brother and sister, Ebony. You must have heard the saying blood is thicker than water.'

'But he's a murderer!' she said.

'No! Ask your aunt–'

'I won't ask her anything! She's a liar. I have to prove that Icarus Bean killed my grandpa – only when the truth is revealed will I be safe,' cried Ebony. 'Maybe then I'll make it past twelve this time. Maybe I won't be obliterated – maybe I'll be able to save the Order after all.'

Ebony fell silent. She realised it was the first time she had ever referred to her soul with such belief. The internal voice whispered to her, *That's good.*

From somewhere deep inside the submarine, a siren blared.

'Land!' said Old Joe.

A sudden bump shook the shark's body. Ebony stumbled, dropping the gun. It skidded to Old Joe's feet. To Ebony's amazement, he kicked it back in her direction. 'You might need it,' he said.

Ebony cautiously picked up the gun. A moment later, a hatch in the side of the chamber opened. Daylight flooded in – the storm had passed and the sky now smouldered with weak sunlight – and Ebony realised she was looking through the open mouth of the shark. She shaded her eyes with her hand. She could make out the quay. They'd brought her home.

Putting the gun in her pocket, she put on the amulet and picked up the box with Winston inside. Stepping out of the mouth of the shark and into the glare, Ebony was careful not to look back. She had to stay focused on survival, on revealing the truth about Icarus Bean. If she could get into the Reflectory, she still had a chance of winning the judge's support and there may even be more clues waiting for her there. She had everything she needed – Winston, the rose, the amulet and her grandpa's medal for luck – now she just had to try to figure out how to open the gateway.

Ebony pretended to walk up to the cottage in case she was being watched, but when she reached a hump in the field where the goats were kept, she crouched down and sneaked away. Careful not to bump Winston too much, she only dared to stand when she had pushed her way through a hole in the bushes that lined the field.

Ebony kept on walking until she reached the path to the woods that overlooked Gun Point, determined not to check behind her. If Aunt Ruby was in the cottage, she was keeping well away. The woods were the safest place to hide. When she was safely hidden by the cover of the trees, Ebony looked back at the ocean and saw Cedric's black fin patrolling the shore.

32

After finding a well-hidden spot, the exhaustion and stress of the last few days hit Ebony. Her brain felt fuzzy and she decided she'd better take a quick rest before she tried to figure out how to get into the Reflectory. Cuddled up to Winston in the moss, deep in the woods, sleep overcame her, but when she woke up, she realised she'd slept for longer than intended and darkness had blanketed the sky. Looking up through the tangle of branches, she saw the waxing crescent moon – her birth moon. It seemed like a good omen. It was time to act. She wasn't sure how the amulet and roses would get her into the Reflectory, but if it really existed, she would have to figure it out.

Ebony made her way to a small copse of oak trees where she would be well hidden. Although it overlooked the sea, it was too dark to see the water properly, but Ebony sensed that Cedric was still circling. Despite wearing her aunt's special clothes, Ebony shivered. The trees provided shelter and the mossy ground offered a little warmth, but her tiredness made her vulnerable to the dropping temperatures. Her teeth chattering, she laid Winston on a bed of warm moss and took off the amulet.

Holding it in her hands, she took a deep breath and searched her mind for possibilities. But it felt pointless; she couldn't think of anything that would work. Deep down, she still doubted the place was even real.

'This is not the time to be hopeless, Ebony Smart,' she chided herself.

She wished Zach was there with her; he would know how to handle the situation. Ebony's heart thumped. She missed her friend.

As soon as the thought entered her head, *The Book of Learning* began to rumble in her pocket. As she pulled it out and inputted the special combination, it leaped out of her hands and – landing open – projected an image of Zach onto an old oak trunk. It was broad daylight and he was back in Ebony's cottage: she recognised the fireplace. But what was he doing there? She thought he'd gone home. His back was turned and he was pacing, clearly agitated. He stopped abruptly and looked behind him, as if he felt her watching. Ebony hardly recognised him. Zach's face was deathly white and his lips stretched tight and mean. His eyes gleamed with anger and his hair was wild, with strands sticking out from his ponytail in all directions as though he'd been battling against a strong wind.

Her heart contracted. *What is it? What's wrong, Zach?*

Suddenly a leg kicked out in Zach's direction. Ebony watched as her friend strode forward and gave whoever was trying to kick him a hard slap. A shock of red hair burst into her view as the body fell over.

'Aunt Ruby!' cried Ebony.

Confusion pulsed through her veins. Why would Zach be hurting Aunt Ruby? Maybe her aunt had been on Ebony's trail and Zach had intervened. Had Aunt Ruby turned on him? If so, Zach would have had to restrain her … Her brain tried to rationalise the scene, and yet in her heart she knew that his actions were overly brutal. No matter what Aunt Ruby had done, this was extreme, and Zach's face was twisted into a terrifying expression, full of malice.

Ebony covered her face with her hands and rubbed her eyes. When she looked up again, Zach's face was in close up. His eyes bored into her, full of hatred. Ebony's head began to throb and her blood ran cold. She hadn't seen this side of Zach before and she didn't like it one bit.

Thankfully, the image began to shrink, retreating back towards the book until it disappeared altogether, leaving the imprint of Zach's hate-filled face frozen on the page. Ebony quickly turned it with a shudder.

Overleaf was some sort of experiment entitled **GATE-WAY**. It read:

Apparatus:	The amulet; Ebonius Tobinius
Method:	Combine with a pure heart by moonlight
Result:	The gateway will reveal itself
Conclusion:	Access to the Reflectory

Ebony was disappointed. It was clearly meant to be directions for how to get in, but there wasn't enough information. She had the elements required but no idea how to combine the amulet and rose and how to do this with a pure heart.

'Sitting here doing nothing won't help, will it, Winston?' she said.

Holding Winston's box close to her chest, with the amulet secured around her neck and the rose and her grandpa's medal wedged in her pocket, Ebony passed through the trees into a clearing where the pale glow of the waxing crescent moon was most visible. Judging by the position of the moon, it was the early hours of the morning. Bathed in a silvery light, she placed the items on a low, mossy tree stump and put Winston gently on the ground next to it. She observed his slow, shallow breathing for a moment until it hurt too much to watch. What if he didn't get better? The thought made her feel physically sick. Focusing back on the task in hand, she stared at the objects on the stump, not knowing where to start. She reread the book, unable to find any further clues in the words. She tried desperately to recall something she'd seen or read on the rose diagrams on her aunt's wall, but to no avail.

The rose, amulet and moon had to connect in some way to trigger the gateway to the Reflectory – but how do you combine them with a pure heart? She tried slipping the amulet between the petals, covering it up, rubbing it against the petals, but nothing worked. She stamped her foot and growled with frustration.

Then she froze as Winston took a loud, rasping gasp of air.

Ebony slowly turned around, waiting for him to breathe out. But he didn't. Winston's belly was swollen with air but there was no sign of him being able to expel it.

'Winston!' cried Ebony. She dropped the rose and amulet and crouched beside his box. She tried pushing on his tummy and giving it a rub, but to no avail. Leaning in, she blew a little air into his mouth to try to shock him into breathing, but he continued to lie there lifeless. Tears formed in her eyes but she fought them back, flipped him over in the box and patted and rubbed his back like she was winding a baby. Suddenly he gave a small wheeze, then a huge cough and struggled to his feet.

Her voice wobbling as tears of relief rolled down her face, Ebony said, 'Don't ever do that to me again.'

As he looked up at her, Winston's eyes glowed. He was clearly as happy to be up and about as she was to see him. Ebony scooped him up and cuddled him close.

Winston nuzzled in to her neck. All of a sudden, he went stiff.

'What's wrong?' she said, thinking he was about to relapse.

Winston's eyes were fixed on the amulet and the rose, which were spattered with Ebony's tears.

'Don't worry, Winston. I know it's dangerous, but I have to try. I must find out if this place is real, once and for all. It'll help me win the judge's favour. I need his protection.'

Winston shook his head and lifted a foot to point. The

rose and amulet were glowing and it wasn't just the light of the moon – the glow was ethereal, like it came from another world. Then a sprinkling of dust glimmered in the air around them. It was the same as the silvery sky-mist she'd seen at the beginning of the story in *The Book of Learning* – Ebony guessed she must have triggered something with her tears.

'What's happening? Is it working?' She was too scared to touch the items in case it broke the spell.

The mist rose higher and higher and the moon glowed so brightly that Ebony had to squint to protect her eyes from its glare. *Hold everything in the mist*, said the internal whisper. Ebony snatched up Winston onto her shoulder, grabbed the amulet and rose and held them out, one in the palm of each hand, hoping for the best.

The mist swirled around her, glittering like dark crystal. Ebony felt the rose shudder and a loud rumble came from its centre. The middle of the rose, where the petals folded together the tightest, lit up. She touched her finger to it and as she did so the petals chimed like bells and their soft texture hardened into a cool, smooth metal. One by one, the petals began to unfurl.

Each bronze petal had a series of glowing grids and codes on it. As the petals unfolded, these mysterious symbols slid into the mist, toppling on top of each other to form a strange, web-like structure. It all happened so fast that, before she knew it, she was standing in the centre of a spidery scaffold made up of different coloured lights and beams. Winston clung onto her jumper with all his might. Not daring to move in case she interfered with the magic, Ebony waited to see what would happen next.

When the final petal opened, the lights surrounding Ebony began to blink out and disappear. It was as though they were being rubbed out by an eraser.

'We've done something wrong!' cried Ebony, clasping the rose tightly but not daring to move while the lights continued to vanish, in case she disappeared with them.

Darkness closed in on her but Ebony stood her ground. Then, when the last light blinked out, the earth shuddered and split as a huge ivy-covered stone pushed its way up. Now Ebony jumped back, putting the hand in which she held the amulet over Winston to protect him.

When the commotion stopped, she couldn't believe her eyes: in the centre of the stone was a giant mahogany door with thick, black bolts and a small peephole.

It was real! This was the gateway they'd all been looking for!

Ebony pocketed the bronze rose, put the amulet back around her neck and walked towards the door, then peered through the peephole. Behind the door swirled the silver-grey mist. Leaves rustled in a soft breeze and the air smelled of *Ebonius Tobinius* roses.

'Yes!' Ebony whispered, punching the air. 'We've done it!'

She tried to push the door open, but it appeared to be locked and there was no handle or sign of a lock. No matter how hard she pushed, the door wouldn't budge. Frustration tore through her. She was so close – she couldn't fail now!

Ebony kicked the door as hard as she could. As her foot made impact with the wood, sparks lit up the night and she found herself thrown through the air, a sharp pain splicing through her leg; it was as though the door had kicked her back. Ebony landed on the ground with a thump, her belongings scattered around her.

As she gathered them up she noticed that her grandpa's medal was glowing the colour of daffodils. She picked up the wooden disc and held it up, the side with the engraving facing her. The scene before her matched the engraving on the disc exactly. As she held it in the air, the peephole gave off a shimmer of light and she realised that the medal must be part of the key to the Reflectory.

Taking a deep breath, Ebony stood up and dusted herself off. She perched Winston on her shoulder again and walked to the door, placing the medal in the peephole. It fitted perfectly and a crescent-shaped hole appeared in its centre as soon as it was snugly in place. It was the exact size and shape of the amulet. There had been no mention of needing the medal in the *Book of Learning* and she wondered if this was the modification her clever father had made two centuries ago, rather than modifying the amulet like Aunt Ruby had thought? Hands trembling, she undid the clasp of the amulet and carefully inserted it into the hole, letting the chain dangle. The door swung open, silently. Ebony paused. *Don't forget the key*, whispered the internal voice. Ebony pulled the amulet out by its chain, bringing the medal with it, and stepped quickly through the door.

When she passed through to the other side, only the mist remained – there was no sign of the door. She reached out her hands to see if she could feel it, but there was no indication the door had ever existed. She had no idea how she was going to get out of the Reflectory but, against the odds, she had made it this far.

Taking her first step within the Reflectory, a sense of triumph filled Ebony's heart. She really was the guardian – and there was no going back.

33

Like her aunt had said, the Reflectory was a beautiful place, full of lush trees and blooming flowers. The magical fog christened each sprig and spray with a gentle luminosity. The air smelled like freshly cut grass and a warm breeze rustled harmoniously around her. The ground felt soft and springy, like woodland moss. Somewhere in the distance, she could hear the gentle ebb and flow of waves. It was like all of Ebony's favourite places had combined.

But on her shoulder, Ebony could feel that Winston was uneasy. He twitched his nose, looking around nervously, so Ebony checked her pocket to make sure the gun was still there.

'It's OK, Winston, we've got protection,' she said. But Winston didn't relax.

Ebony walked forward into the mist; although there was no path, it didn't seem to matter. All around her was endless beauty: foliage, buds, new shoots. Her heart fluttered at the abundance of life. As she accepted in her heart that the Order of Nine Lives was truly real – and that she belonged – Ebony felt as though the world was suddenly full of new possibilities.

'Maybe we'll find Grandpa,' she said.

But the memory of her grandpa's face was growing hazy. It seemed that with each step she took, it grew fuzzier still, as though the energy around her was sucking her memories away.

After a while, all the trees and flowers disappeared and only the mist remained. The sound of rustling foliage and distant waves could still be heard, but Ebony found herself in a vast landscape of nothingness. Yet it wasn't frightening; she felt strangely relaxed and at home. It was as though Ebony's spirit was part of the surroundings and her body irrelevant. She felt calm and complete. Was this what eternal life would feel like?

'It's wonderful, isn't it, Winston?' she said as he snuggled into her curly hair.

At that moment, something whooshed past her head. It looked like a hand slapping the air. Ebony ducked and it melted away as quickly as it had appeared. Then a foot kicked out in front of them before vanishing. An angry face appeared and opened its mouth wide as though trying to shout before floating off. Then an army of faces passed by, all twisted with anger and sadness and regret. Winston ducked and dived and covered his eyes, daring only to peep now and then. But Ebony walked on without emotion, watching the images as if she was watching a film.

'We must be close to where the souls are,' she said. 'These must be the memories the souls are trying to forget – just like Aunt Ruby said.'

In the distance, a tiny light glowed.

'Look!'

Winston ran from shoulder to shoulder excitedly. The light grew to the size of a balloon; it was coming towards them and seemed to be closing in quickly.

'We're in the right place, Winston.'

They continued towards the light, which soon engulfed them. Ebony blinked, adjusting to the brightness. When her vision cleared, she looked around in amazement: they were in a vast room filled with seemingly endless rows of transparent bodies. Her aunt was right: their number should be much greater. She had found the missing souls of the Order of Nine Lives – or at least some of them! Each sat in a director's chair facing a mirror surrounded by light bulbs. The mirrors stretched as far as the eye could see. Some of the bulbs were lit; others were switched off. Ebony felt herself drawn to them.

'Let's take a closer look,' she said, 'and keep an eye out for Grandpa.'

Winston tugged on Ebony's hair, as though he was trying to rein in a horse, but Ebony could not be stopped. She moved further into the room. As she got closer, Ebony could see that the figures had an unusual glowing quality about them – they were almost transparent. They certainly weren't human, yet they still had human qualities. She could hardly believe her eyes.

As Ebony leaned in to the closest mirror, Winston jumped

down in fright. The glass was fuzzy, as though it had been wiped with Vaseline. Ebony couldn't see herself in there; the mirror only reflected the face of the soul sitting in front of it.

In the reflection, a cloud of shimmering mist swirled furiously. Images poured out of the mist, cascading fuzzily inside the mirror – Ebony could make out iced birthday cakes, tumbling circus clowns, a wriggling puppy, wellies splashing in puddles and cascading spring blossoms. She tried to recall some of her own happy memories – like her grandpa's smile – but she could only conjure up a colourful blur. *I mustn't forget*, she thought, and the kind eyes and rough features of her grandpa's face formed in her mind.

Feeling encouraged, Ebony looked from the mirror to the soul's face – it was soft and carefree. But as she watched, the body began to shake and the image of a couple arguing shot out of the mirror and flew off into the distance like a comet. The face relaxed again. Winston squealed.

'The mirrors must deflect the bad things away,' said Ebony.

She reached out and touched the soul's face – her hand passed straight through it, but she could feel a warm sensation, like breath on her skin. Winston squealed and ran on; Ebony followed, her desire to find her grandpa intensifying. She noticed that the souls with lights on their mirrors looked at peace, while the souls without any lights had contorted expressions on their faces, like they were in lots of pain. Every now and again, they let out a blood-curdling shriek, so she avoided getting too close to them. As Ebony and Winston walked on, the pair ducked every now and again to avoid any bad memories flying past. Within minutes, Winston was jumping up and down on the spot. Ebony's heart skipped a beat. Winston had found him.

In his chair, her grandpa looked translucent. His kindly eyes and determined brow hadn't lost their character; but his expression was lifeless. His face was frozen, yet peaceful; at least he didn't look in pain. Ebony rushed at him and tried to hug him, but his body seemed to evaporate in her grasp. Peering into the mirror, she saw images of home: their fishing boat, the goats, Ebony's first glimpse of Winston – all these images floated by. Then her grandpa's body started to judder and shake and a bright flash escaped out of the mirror, flying across the room at top speed and exploding against a wall of a building she hadn't noticed before.

Turning her attention back to her grandpa, Ebony felt an overwhelming sensation – not of sadness or loss like she would have expected, but of happiness and calm. It seemed the perfect place for her grandpa to be. Reaching out, she touched her grandpa's face. His body shook again and another light sparked across the air, smashing against the same wall.

Follow! said the internal voice.

'Grandpa?'

Just like at the hospital, she felt a ripple run through his body. His eyes turned towards her for a split second, then settled on the wall that the light kept hitting. This time, Ebony took notice. What she saw was another smaller room, perfectly square with a huge sign above the entrance – the sign flashed with red neon lights like at a film premiere.

It read EMERGENCY ROOM.

Ebony looked at her grandpa for an instant and smiled, then she headed straight for the door with Winston in tow. The door was made of metal, covered in engravings of ivy, like those on the amulet. When they pushed their way inside, Ebony gasped.

Inside, there were two souls that looked very different to the others she had encountered. On one chair the soul was gnarled and badly damaged, dull yellow in colour, not transparent like the others had been. It was covered in scars and fissures, making the face unrecognisable. But above the soul's head was a mirror – it showed images of a younger-looking Aunt Ruby in her camouflage jumpsuit in the entrance hall of 23 Mercury Lane. The gilt mirror in the hallway showed a man's face with deep-set eyes, a black beard and serious expression. It took a moment, but suddenly she realised that it was the face she'd seen on the photo in the Natural History Museum. This was the soul of Aunt Ruby's husband – the real Uncle Cornelius! But what had happened to him?

Horrified, Ebony hardly dared look at the other soul but forced herself to take a quick glance. This soul belonged to a golden-haired lady that she didn't recognise – but it was ashen grey and looked like it was made of something different, a substance more like clay. A mask fastened over the soul's face was attached to a machine containing a pressure pump. The pump pushed up and down in slow, rhythmic movements, keeping the soul's life force charged. And then Ebony realised – this soul didn't have a mirror.

As she leaned in for a closer look, Icarus Bean burst through the door, panting, his eyes red and swollen and his matted hair sticking out. He looked like a wild animal.

Ebony snatched out her gun and lifted it towards him. A white dot of light quivered on his chest, threateningly.

'Don't move, murderer,' she said. 'Stay right where you are.'

34

In the eerie light of the Emergency Room, Icarus Bean slowly raised his arms in surrender.

'It's not what it looks like,' he said.

'Nothing's what it looks like since my grandpa died, *uncle*,' replied Ebony coldly.

Icarus flinched.

'How did you get in here?' she asked, keeping the gun on him.

'I've been following you ever since you left Cedric and returned to land. I waited and watched, and then I sneaked in behind you. You left the gateway open.'

Terror made her blood run cold.

'I was meant to close it? But how? The door disappeared when I passed through it.'

Icarus shrugged. 'Not on my side, it didn't. I even waited a few minutes before following. You're the one who's meant to know what to do. Let's hope I'm the only one who noticed.'

Ebony's confidence drained away. She had been so sure of herself – how could she have made such a stupid mistake? It was her fault that Icarus was there and there was no telling what he would do now that he had access to all of the Nine Lives souls.

'How could you do this?' she asked, pointing to the soul of Aunt Ruby's husband.

'It wasn't me!'

His lies made Ebony even angrier.

'What about her?' she asked, pointing to the lady. 'Who is she?'

Icarus didn't get a chance to answer as a shuffling noise came from outside the door. Icarus looked nervous as Ebony scooped up Winston. The rat's hair was standing on end and his claws dug into her skin.

'Show yourself! I know it's you, Aunt Ruby,' said Ebony, pointing her gun towards the noise but staying on her guard in case Icarus used the opportunity to attack her.

But to Ebony's surprise, it wasn't her aunt.

In stepped Zach, his face battered and bruised. Angry purple lumps stood out on his cheekbones. He held his ribs awkwardly. Ebony's heart missed a beat.

'I saw you with Aunt Ruby in *The Book of Learning*. Did she do this to you?'

In reply, Zach groaned and shook his head. He looked in the direction of Icarus Bean.

'You!' she cried, turning back to Icarus. 'I should have known!'

Icarus stayed silent and tight-lipped. Ebony stared at her prisoner, the gun held steady.

'Don't do anything rash, Ebony,' said Icarus. 'You're making a mistake.'

Ebony held the weapon fast. 'The book told me that, to live, I had to find my grandpa's murderer and reveal the truth. I've caught you in action, Icarus. I'll make sure the judge hears about this and sends you to prison where you belong. That's if I don't kill you first.'

Then suddenly the whisper in her head returned: *Don't do it.*

Ebony didn't know what to do – all along the voice had been the one thing she could rely on, helping her when she was in need. But did Icarus deserve to live? If she killed him now, he wouldn't be able to do any more harm and she would be safe. The truth would be revealed and she could go on to achieve whatever her destiny had in store for her. She could help the Order of Nine Lives to return to its proper function, without having to worry about being murdered. Her mind racing, Ebony stared into Icarus Bean's eyes. They pleaded with her. Winston's nails dug into Ebony's skin.

'I know what you're thinking,' said Icarus, slowly lowering his arms, 'but I'm not trying to kill you – that's what you're being made to believe. Use your instinct. The answer is staring you in the face.'

'Don't tell me what to do,' said Ebony furiously. 'I *did* use my instinct and look what I found: the murderer Icarus Bean trying to swap souls.'

'I'm not!'

'Why else would you be here?' interrupted Ebony. 'What exactly were you planning to do, *uncle*? Sell my soul to the highest bidder?'

'I'm not selling anything to anyone! I'm trying to protect it. Protect you!'

'From what?' asked Ebony.

'From him!' Icarus pointed at Zach. 'It's him you should be aiming that thing at.'

'Don't listen to him, Ebony. He's a fool.' Zach's lips pulled into a tight snarl.

'We're all fools,' said Icarus.

'Especially you,' said Zach. 'Takes one to know one.'

'This is not the time, son.'

'I'm not your–'

'Stop!' Ebony shouted. She looked from Zach to Icarus. 'You sound like squabbling children. I can't hear myself think!'

Zach shuffled closer to Ebony and Winston hissed and spat in his direction. Suddenly Ebony realised that Winston always behaved peculiarly whenever Zach was around. She started to wonder if she had been wrong about Zach all along.

As she swung the gun around to Zach, it felt like the world had tipped upside down.

'Don't move, Zach,' she said. 'I want to hear him out.' Zach stood still and glared. Ebony turned to Icarus. 'Go on, explain to me exactly why I should trust you.'

Icarus spoke slowly and firmly, with one eye on Zach the whole time.

'Our family has long suspected that someone in the Nine Lives High Court was trying to discover the power of soul swapping and find a way into the Reflectory themselves. Your grandpa figured out their intent and we all swore an oath – me, your parents, your aunt – to try to stop them, but we've had no definite proof until now. Years ago, when I got too close, I was framed for something I didn't do and the High Court tried to exile me. It didn't quite work, but even though I'm not imprisoned like the others, it's not easy to help from the Shadowlands. It takes a lot of energy. And despite the oath, we couldn't really act until we were certain, but now we know it is Judge Ambrose who is seeking this power.'

Ebony snorted. 'But he's already powerful. Why would he bother?'

'Firstly, he wants to sell our secrets to some very powerful people and use them to control the destiny of the entire earth. But that's not what the power is meant for. More importantly, when you swap souls, the reincarnation cycle starts all over again, so the body that soul inhabits gets nine fresh chances at life. The judge could use the power to make himself immortal.'

Icarus paused, as though trying to come to terms with his own words. Ebony narrowed her eyes.

'So why did you kill your father – my grandpa?' she asked.

'I didn't! You misunderstood what you saw in the vision.'

Zach interrupted with a snort. Ebony waggled the gun at him to remind him not to move. Then she turned back to Icarus as he continued.

'Your grandpa had contacted me to say he had a lead he was following and that he could use my help. But as I approached the meeting point I could see him struggling with someone. I ran to help but by the time I reached him his attacker had fled and he was unconscious. I carried him to the hospital for treatment, but it was too late.'

Doubt started to creep into Ebony's mind. She had been so sure she was right, but what if *The Book of Learning* had been showing her Icarus *helping* her grandpa? She was supposed to reveal the truth, but now she realised that she had no idea what that truth was!

'The coroner's report said his death was from natural causes, so how was he killed?'

'The coroner couldn't have known otherwise. The bullet used to kill him is of a kind that ordinary humans don't know about – created by the Order's magic, it can pass through flesh leaving no trace and then activate inside the body, exploding and damaging the organs. Because there was no external wound, it looked to the doctors like your grandfather simply had a heart attack and, because of his age, they had no reason to investigate further. And I'm pretty sure the judge will have made sure they didn't. With your grandpa and me both out of the way, the spotlight was off the judge and those helping him. With so few of us left, this made it easier for them to move forward with their plans to find the way into the Reflectory and steal a Nine Lives' soul – your soul – to put into someone else's body.'

Ebony rubbed her forehead. Now that she'd found the Reflectory, she felt closer to her destiny; she didn't want her soul going anywhere.

'They've been working hard to get in here,' continued Icarus, 'but what we didn't realise was that they'd already succeeded.'

'But how, if I'm the guardian?'

'Remember how one of our kind infiltrated the Reflectory in ancient times? And how your aunt explained that some souls remember their past lives, while others forget?'

Ebony gasped. 'That soul remembered?'

Nodding, Icarus's face darkened.

'Yes. But what it took all this time to realise was that it was the judge. His soul was so greedy for the extra power, it couldn't let go of the idea. He's been brewing this plan for centuries – he just needed to gather enough supporters or get as many of our people as possible out of the way to reduce opposition. Anyone who stood in his way or got close to stopping him was removed.'

'How?'

'Our guess is that the judge has been refusing to sign their final decrees. This refusal prevents people from passing through to Ultimation, which means replacements can't be found and, as a result, our numbers have dwindled over the centuries as people reach the end of their nine lives but can't move on. I've also seen lots of our people banished so they too can't achieve their goals or die, and in turn, their relatives can't reincarnate.'

Ebony pointed towards the door. 'So the souls out there, my grandpa?'

'They're being held in some kind of stasis. I wouldn't have believed it possible that there were so many of us if I hadn't seen them with my own eyes. But for some reason you are the key to the soul-swapping process, so Ambrose couldn't move any further along with his plan. He needs you to be on your last incarnation, with all your lives used and your soul ready to reach Ultimation. He wants control of the guardian. That's why in each of your earlier lives he made sure you didn't pass your twelfth year and reach your full potential – if you had you might have been able to stop him before now. But now that we can get in here, together we can figure out a way to release all those souls back to their own destinies.'

'After the mess I've made of everything?'

'*The Book of Learning* told Ruby that only you could save us. Either you'll prevent the soul-swapping from coming to fruition or you'll be the first. And that's why I'm here. Saving you is the only way to save us all.' Icarus nodded his head towards Zach. 'It's a pity *my son* doesn't understand that.'

Ebony's jaw dropped and her head reeled as realisation hit. She glared at Zach. 'You said your father was dead!'

'No, I said he was gone,' Zach snarled. 'I didn't actually say he was dead; you decided that for yourself. But it's not completely untrue – as far as I'm concerned, he doesn't exist. He's dead to me. That's why I use my mother's surname.'

Tears welled in his eyes as he flicked his eyes towards the

female soul, but Ebony was too busy figuring out the facts to notice.

'You said you had no family but this makes us … cousins?'

Zach shrugged. 'So what?' he said. 'It doesn't change anything. Didn't I tell you when we met that first time in the park that whatever is looking for you will always find you? All my life I had to listen to how the wonderful Ebony Smart would eventually save us all from some terrible curse. But not once did they consider that swapping souls isn't a curse – it's a gift. Think of the power, the possibilities!'

Ebony felt her face grow hot with anger. She turned the gun and pointed it at Zach's forehead.

'Icarus, go on,' she said.

'My son,' spat Icarus, 'has sided with the judge. He's been under his jurisdiction since I was exiled, but I suspect they probably conspired in past lives too. He's always found reasons to hate me, every lifetime, but this time it's different because there's more at stake. They've been working together to conjure up the Reflectory and get to your soul. Only my son doesn't realise he's being used. As soon as the judge has what he needs, Zach will be discarded.'

'That's not true!' shouted Zach. 'The judge picked me to help him, and he has promised me that I'll be at his side in his new world. So I won't stop until I get what he wants and what I want.'

'But you know you cannot have what it is you want,' said Icarus.

'What is it you want?' asked Ebony, confused.

'I want my mother back. And once we've harnessed the power, the judge has promised me she will be the first soul to be swapped. Then, all those useless souls out there will be sold to the highest bidders. The judge will be rich and powerful beyond our wildest dreams and I'll be his number one guy – with my mother there to share the glory. All I have to do is kill you and capture your soul in this.' Zach held up a small black device, the size of a matchbox. It had a tiny screen showing data and two buttons on the top, one red and one green. It didn't look at all frightening or harmful. 'And then we can start the procedure.'

Zach's face was ugly with hatred – it barely resembled the boy she knew.

'But why do you have to kill me if you're so powerful?' Ebony could hardly get the words out.

'It's nothing personal. We need the guardian's soul at its final incarnation, at the exact time when the reincarnation part of your soul would be separated for transfer to the new guardian. When I transfer that to mum's body, not only will she be reset with nine new lives and have another shot at achieving her destiny, she'll also be the guardian of this place, with control over all those souls out there.'

'But what if she doesn't recognise you? And what will happen to her old soul? Have you thought about that? I've heard it'll be left in eternal agony and torment …'

Again, Zach's eyes flickered towards the soul attached

to the breathing machine. 'The judge has promised that the procedure will be painless. Most of her personality will attach to the bit of your soul that we implant, so she won't know a thing about the bit that was discarded.'

Ebony's gaze followed his. 'Is that your mum?' she asked, recoiling. 'What happened to her?'

'The judge was angry with my father and signed her Obliteration decree. But, before she passed through, I argued for her life. I convinced the judge that she would be perfect for our mission and he retracted his signature. It's never been done before – and this is what happened.' He glared at his father.

'Well I like my body the way it is,' said Ebony. 'I don't want to live inside *that*.'

Choked, Zach took a moment to recover himself. When he spoke again, he sounded angrier than ever.

'Who cares what you want? Your soul is finally ours for the taking and we'll do what we want with it! This hasn't been easy with so many people in the way – but what they didn't realise was that by helping you they were also helping us. We needed you to find the amulet and the rose and enter the Reflectory, as this is the only place the soul swapping will work. Although we've found a way in, we've only succeeded in getting one person into the Reflectory at a time so far. We had to let you find it for yourself so we could follow you in – and as a bonus, I'll have the rose and amulet for my mum, the new guardian, so she can access the Reflectory at will once the procedure is complete.'

'So why didn't you just let me get on with it? Why even bother pretending to be my friend?'

'We had to alienate you from your family so you wouldn't turn to them for help or let them know what was going on. We had to make you believe I was on your side. My stupid father kept trying to help you but, as usual, he went about things the wrong way.' He turned to Icarus and grinned. 'You managed to make yourself look crazy and dangerous, Father, so instead of helping her, you pushed her further in our direction.'

Icarus hung his head in shame.

'But poor Winston – why did you have to kidnap him?' asked Ebony.

'To convince you further that your aunt was at fault. We knew your family would come to your rescue and that you'd get the wrong idea and blame them for the kidnapping. We'd sown enough seeds of doubt in your mind. If only we'd managed to get rid of that mangy rat for good by cutting the amulet out of him … then you'd have been completely reliant on me.'

'But the storm – I nearly died coming to his rescue. What good would that have been to you then?'

'That was out of our control and something we definitely didn't intend. We were very lucky your aunt sent people to look for you. Once again, they did us a big favour.'

Ebony looked at Icarus in amazement. He had been preventing Zach from hurting her, along with all the others. When he'd mentioned having to wage war on his own flesh and blood, it was his own son he was talking about, not her! *That* was why Zach had been so scared in the museum. She searched out Icarus's eyes apologetically as Zach continued.

'My father is finally right about something, however: this quest is centuries old. Our records date back to the ninth century, before *The Book of Learning* was created. Aunt Ruby isn't the only one with an inquisitive mind; how could I have resisted such an opportunity? Time after time we've managed to bump you off, trying to bring your final incarnation closer. We've improved our methods along the way until we've finally got you where we've always wanted you – and now, with my mother's life at stake, I won't fail.'

Ebony's heart burned with hatred, but she felt a certain pity for Zach.

'Why did she fail to reach Ultimation?' she asked through gritted teeth.

Zach zipped his lips up tight. Icarus Bean hung his head.

'It's *my* fault,' said Icarus, pointing at the female soul. 'Zach's mother came as backup when I was following a lead. We knew she was on her last life; I was meant to be looking out for her, but I didn't see one of the High Court men sneaking up behind us. He killed her and because she hadn't reached her destiny, her soul was destined to be wiped out, obliterated.'

'That's why there's no mirror,' added Zach. 'There are no more lives. If the judge hadn't created this machine, she'd be lost forever. Unless you die, and we get your soul swapped into her body, I will still lose her and all memory of her existence will be erased. She can't stay like this forever.'

Icarus held his face in his hands for a moment before looking up with bloodshot eyes. 'Zach couldn't forgive me for not saving his mother and, despite the fact that it was one of the judge's men who killed her, Ambrose was able to manipulate his feelings to turn him against me. The guilt I felt meant that I didn't intervene. What I didn't know was the extent of the judge's ambition, that he had planted these terrible ideas in Zach's head a long time ago and that darkness had already taken over my son's soul many incarnations earlier.'

'The judge promised me that her death was nothing to do with him – and to prove it, he is going to reincarnate her as the guardian. You lied to me – you said there was nothing we could do for her!' interrupted Zach. 'It's not fair. I don't want to spend eternity alone. I want her to pass through to Ultimation so that we can be together always.'

Ebony stared at Zach – all of this trouble, all of her family's pain, was because he wanted his mother back. Her heart felt torn. Zach was a danger to everyone, but his actions were all to do with saving his mum and she sympathised with that. She looked from father to son to the clay-like figure of Zach's mum. She felt her arm weaken and had to fight to keep the gun trained.

'It's not right, son,' said Icarus, stepping forward. 'We shouldn't be meddling in such things. There is no guarantee that the soul swapping will work, and if it does, it'll only bring disaster upon us if we interfere with the true order of things.'

'Your words mean nothing. We have to try! Her death was your fault! I wish you'd died, not her.'

'It was a mistake and I would give anything to have that day over again,' said Icarus, hiding his face in his hands.

'Mistake or not, now I'll be able to save her.' He turned his cold gaze on Ebony.

Perspiration and tears stung Ebony's eyes. She felt like such a fool. How could she have been so stupid? Her arm wavered, and as she dropped her guard, Zach lurched forward and grabbed the gun from her hand. He aimed it at his father and pulled the trigger. Ebony watched in horror as Icarus's body glowed. His mouth moved but the words were no longer audible – they were lost in another dimension, lost to the shadows. His face and body crackled, then disappeared. In an instant, he was gone.

Zach looked as shocked as Ebony felt, but he composed himself quickly and closed in on Ebony with his entrancing stare.

'Let's get this over with!'

35

As Zach pushed Ebony back through the door, out into the Reflectory, she tried to reason with him.

'Zach, don't do this.' Her voice was calm even though her insides were tied up in knots. But he didn't look at her. 'Zach, we're friends. Maybe my aunt can find a way to help your mother.'

'I doubt it. Anyway, it'll be a while before she's back in action.'

'What have you done to her?'

'What do you care? You hate her, remember?'

Guilt punched at Ebony's stomach. 'I only hated her because I thought she was trying to kill me. I was angry with her.'

'Well I'm angry too,' said Zach in a soft, trembling voice. Tears glistened in his eyes. 'I want my mother back.'

Ebony couldn't help feeling a bit sorry for him, but nothing could outweigh her anger or fear.

'I'm sorry,' said Ebony. 'I know what it feels like.'

'No you don't … You have no idea,' he shouted. 'You could have been with your family forever if you'd been smart enough.'

Zach's finger hovered over the trigger, but Ebony knew it was an empty threat – after what had happened with Icarus, Zach couldn't risk the same thing happening to her and have her simply disappear on him. And the surprise she'd seen on his face meant the weapon hadn't acted in the way he'd expected. It gave her the confidence to shout back.

'You tricked me! At least you met your parents … I never even knew mine! And I just lost my grandpa,' she seethed.

Zach sniggered. 'You still don't get it, do you?' he said, his eyes turning icy.

Dumbstruck as his meaning clicked into place, Ebony's jaw dropped. Her whole body shook and her legs weakened. 'You – you're the murderer!'

'Of course I am. Stupid old man thought he was a match for me, but it took just one shot from this special weapon to here,' Zach patted his chest, 'and he was down. I'm actually surprised it took him so long to die. I have to say, I was annoyed when I realised you'd taken the gun from the cave, but we never thought you would get there so quickly or I'd never have left it sitting around.'

'But I don't understand. Icarus said the gun that killed my grandpa shot him with an exploding bullet. If that's the same gun why did it make Icarus disappear? Is he dead?'

Caught off guard, Zach paused. 'It's never done that before,' he said. 'I should have known something created by your aunt would be faulty.'

Ebony ignored the comment. She remembered her aunt

telling her that she had been the Order's weaponry specialist. Zach was just trying to rile her.

'You should have heard your grandpa call your name into the night. I'd have finished him off there and then if my father hadn't arrived on the scene when he did.

Ebony's rage overwhelmed her. Disregarding the danger, she threw herself at Zach. As her hands wrapped around his throat, the gun went off and the Reflectory splintered and shattered around them. The glittery mist exploded, sending a hot blast of air which catapulted them off the ground. Winston clung on to Ebony's shoulder for dear life. Ebony's body suddenly felt weightless and she began to spin uncontrollably. She closed her eyes tightly, feeling way too dizzy and sick to open them as she hurtled to wherever they were going.

Then she felt a calloused but gentle hand grab hers, steadying her. A whiff of tobacco smoke filled her nostrils. *Grandpa*, she thought.

I've been here all along, the voice replied.

Ebony's heart fluttered with hope.

The hand left as quickly as it had arrived and Ebony landed in a heap on a hard floor. It was dark, but a streetlamp outside the window threw a warm glow across the room. She looked around, recognising the blue tiles, sash windows and door in the corner – she was back in the forbidden bedroom in 23 Mercury Lane. The window was wide open and a cold wind gushed in. Zach was already upright, the gun trained on her, his eyes red and his mouth curled into a snarl. Wondering how she had got there and why she wasn't dead, Ebony stood up, straight backed, matching his glare.

'Take us back to the Reflectory!' cried Zach.

'I don't know how!'

Zach growled like a wild beast.

'We'll have to go back to Oddley Cove and retrace your steps.'

'No!' cried Ebony.

Zach quietened for a moment, then he gave her a cold smile. 'You'll do as you're told. You can't defeat us, Ebony.'

When she didn't reply, he continued in a mean voice. 'Your grandpa must be very disappointed in you. There he was, all along, meddling from beyond the grave, and you were too dumb to figure out what he was telling you.'

'You heard his voice when you were reading my mind and knew it was my grandpa?'

'Yes – and I know all about your little friends visiting too: in the mirror, the girl in the room I pretended I couldn't see. You've had endless help, with your past selves finding some ingenious ways to contact you – only you were too stupid to realise I was your enemy all along.'

Ebony fought to keep her temper. She knew he was trying to get to her so he could somehow use it to his advantage. She decided to keep him talking while she came up with a plan of her own.

'If you hate me so much, why did you give me the message from my grandpa?'

Zach continued, the contempt clear in his voice. 'I made that up. I read your mind to find out how to snare you. You fell for my tricks every time. Pretending to be your friend, your grandpa's tobacco on the roof – I even tricked my father into believing I was going to attack you so he'd hide in your wardrobe and I could make it look like I was saving you. You were easy game. All I had to do was let you see and hear what you wanted.'

'But you did help me – you took me to your home, helped me get back to mine!'

'They say keep your friends close and your enemies even closer. I had to earn your trust so I could get you away from your protectors. It was the judge's idea: the perfect opportunity to separate you from those who could help you, to keep you isolated with only the judge and your *friend* Zach to turn to. It worked, didn't it? It also meant that once you'd recaptured Winston and rejected your family's help, I could stay close enough to hear your thoughts and know when you'd succeeded in opening the doorway. Then it was just a matter of sneaking into the Reflectory behind Icarus.'

'But it doesn't have to be this way. We're both part of the Order; we should be working together, Zach. We could end all of this, restore the Order as a team.'

'You're even more stupid than I thought. What would be the point of all our work and centuries of waiting, just to fall at the final hurdle? You've led me right to where I needed to be.'

'But you can get into the Reflectory any time. The judge knows–'

'Do you think the judge would share such powerful knowledge with just anybody? It has to be protected.'

'You mean he doesn't trust you.'

'That's not true.'

'You father's right. The judge is using you and when he gets what he wants he'll get rid of you. If he's so powerful, why doesn't he kill me himself? Why does he have to get you to do his dirty work?'

'Shut up!' Zach shouted as he slapped Ebony hard across the face. 'I'm sick of listening to you. Now, let's go.'

Zach gripped Ebony's arm and yanked her hard towards the door. A strange howl came from Winston as Ebony stumbled. In a flash, the rat launched himself into the air, teeth bared, hissing and snapping, determined to make contact with Zach's skin. Foam frothed at the corners of Winston's mouth – he looked as wild as Mulligan. Zach swatted the rat out of his way.

'Stupid rat!' he said. 'I should have cut your throat, not your tail.'

That was the final straw.

Ebony threw herself at Zach, but he shoved her hard and she fell backwards. Zach caught her by the scruff of her neck and pulled her up. Ebony kicked and scratched, fighting to get away. When Zach lost his grip, she ran to the window, as far from Zach as she could get. Zach followed, blind with fury. He grabbed her throat and pushed the top half of her body out of the window so she was leaning out into the night air, her hair tangling in the wind. She screamed and held fast onto each side of the window pane to stop herself falling out.

'Are you ready to come with me, yet?' cried Zach.

Zach's grip was tight around her throat and she felt herself losing consciousness. Then he shifted position, accidentally freeing up one of her legs. She kicked his shin as hard as she could and he reeled back with a high-pitched yowl, losing his balance and sprawling on the floor. This gave Ebony a few precious seconds to pull herself back in through the window. But Zach was on his feet again.

Struggling hard to hide her fear, Ebony's voice quivered as she tried to reason with him. 'Don't do this, Zach!'

There was a loud rattling as someone tried to get into the room. Her scream must have alerted whoever was in the house that they were there, but the door was locked. Zach glanced towards the noise, watched the door handle jiggle for a moment, then shook his head.

'I have to – even if I changed my mind, the judge would kill me if I stopped helping him now. I've gone too far to turn back, I know too much. This is the only way!'

'Don't you see? You don't have to work for the judge – things don't have to be this way. Your father, my aunt, they'll help you.'

'You heard my father in the museum – elimination. He intends to do away with the opposition so you can help the

Order – that means me! We're so close – I can't wait until my next incarnation to help my mum. By then it'll be way too late.'

'It's your last life too?' asked Ebony, suddenly understanding why Zach was so desperate to succeed. When he didn't reply, Ebony tried reasoning with him.

'He won't hurt you if you come with me and tell them you've seen the error of your ways, that you want to put things right. Tell them that you know you've done bad things but that you did them all out of love.'

The rattling stopped, replaced by a succession of loud slams as someone threw their weight against the door. It looked for a moment like Zach was struggling with his conscience, but then crazed desire gleamed in his eyes. 'If I kill you, I can bring my mother back. Like I said, it's nothing personal. If I didn't need you dead, I'd probably quite like you. But it's time to get this over with.' He gestured to the door that led to the attic. 'We'll go over the roof. You first.'

Ebony's gut flooded with an immense feeling of failure. After all the help she'd received from her aunt, Uncle Cornelius, Icarus Bean and her past selves, she'd still messed up and, unless she came up with a plan, her imminent death would condemn everyone else as well. She couldn't let that happen.

As Zach pressed the gun into Ebony's back, she spun round and made a grab for the weapon – if she could transport him to somewhere else, it would save her life. Hand in hand they wrestled, staggering around the room as Ebony tried to yank the gun from Zach's grip. Suddenly Winston leaped from out of nowhere and clamped his teeth down on Zach's hand. Ebony felt Zach's grip loosen and managed to snatch the gun away. But then Zach switched tactics. Rather than try to retrieve the gun, he held her hands tightly so she couldn't use it and used his superior strength to push her backwards. No matter how hard she struggled, Ebony could not break free.

She gave one last tug with all her strength and managed to break Zach's grip. But she hadn't realised how close she was to the open window. With the sudden release, Ebony fell backwards and slipped over the window ledge, falling out into the night sky, the gun tumbling from her grip. As she hurtled towards the ground – exactly the same spot that she had died in a previous life – her heart flooded with fear, disappointment and guilt all at once. She – Ebony Smart – thought she had been *so* close to figuring it all out and avoiding death, but she'd failed. Only this time there'd be no more reincarnation. Her last life was about to be taken from her.

All of a sudden, her clothes loosened and billowed and her fall began to slow; as she gasped, her hand caught the amulet around her throat. A warm wind brushed her body and tickled her ears, scented like *Ebonius Tobinius* roses. A glimmering grey mist surrounded her as the girl from the mirror in the black dress appeared, her arms outstretched as she floated. Certain she must be close to hitting the ground, Ebony readied herself for pain and the crunch of broken bones, as all her mistakes flashed through her mind. But when she reached where the ground should be, there was no sound and no pain. Instead, face to face with her past self, she passed through into the earth and sank down into its dampness. The girl in black smiled.

Suddenly, more identical faces appeared, each with pale skin and wild black curls. There were eight in total – all of her past selves had gathered to help her. Each of the Ebony Smarts joined hands around her and together they started to sing a melancholy tune, their voices lifting and falling like the crest of a wave. As their voices combined, the glittering mist shone so brightly it was as if her birth moon had climbed out of the sky to greet her. The ghostly face of her grandpa appeared in the brightness; Ebony reached out to touch it but the familiar wrinkles exploded into myriad images dancing in the mist: seahorses, butterflies, bluebirds. Ebony's skin warmed and the girls moved closer, their presence comforting, like sunshine on a crisp autumn day. An overwhelming sense of calm enveloped Ebony and, surrounded by her other selves, she began to rise.

Suddenly, she was standing on the pavement outside 23 Mercury Lane, completely alone. The mist evaporated and she felt a cold slap of wind across her face. She hadn't died; she was still here! And on the ground next to her lay the gun.

Looking up, Ebony saw Zach's face peering over the edge of the windowsill. He looked relieved to see her still alive, but fear was also etched on his face – the judge would not be happy. A clunk sounded from the doorway and Ebony instinctively snatched up the gun and pointed it towards the noise. The front door to her aunt's home opened wide and Icarus rushed out. Zach cried out angrily when he saw his father. 'This isn't finished. We're coming after you, Ebony Smart.'

Then his head disappeared from view.

'Quick, Ebony, inside!' said Icarus, beckoning wildly.

Ebony did as she was told. As soon as she was safe in the hallway, Icarus spun on his heels and ran up the stairs two at a time – but he was too late. Ebony could hear a clatter of footsteps running the length of the roof as Zach fled the scene.

36

Later, when everyone had returned home, they gathered in the living room, looking bruised and broken as they each mulled over recent events. The fire was left to smoulder away to ashes as the moon sank outside. Uncle Cornelius was quiet and brooding, and Aunt Ruby's face was so badly beaten that she was barely recognisable. They were both exhausted from the events of the day and their long drive home. Ebony felt shaky and mentally exhausted and even Winston was unusually still on Ebony's shoulder. No one had the energy or will to speak, until a cough sounded in the hallway. Ebony sat upright and alert, her gun poised.

'Who's there?'

The door creaked open and in walked Icarus. He headed straight for Ebony. She shrank back, gun still in hand, expecting him to be angry. Instead, Icarus reached out and shook her hand.

'You did an excellent job, Ebony. Well done.'

Confused, Ebony pocketed her gun and ran her fingers through her hair.

'I don't understand. I found the Reflectory, but I've failed you. I uncovered Grandpa's murderer far too late and I don't know who I'm meant to tell. I let other people into the Reflectory behind me and Zach got away.'

'We have the gateway secured,' said Icarus. 'Old Joe has the land cordoned off – people think there is a risk of falling trees so it buys us some time to figure out how to close it. And I still have some supporters who will make sure that no one uses it to enter the Reflectory if they shouldn't.'

Winston leaped down onto Ebony's lap and waved his paws around.

'Winston's right,' continued Icarus. 'You've revealed the truth to us, Ebony. Now that we have the evidence against Ambrose we needed, as well as access to the Reflectory, we can continue our work to restore the Order.'

Aunt Ruby smiled, even though she struggled to speak. 'The judge is too powerful to overthrow just yet. And if we take over the Order forcibly, we're just as bad as he is. We want to restore things to the old ways and earn the people's support. However, there aren't enough of us – we have to find a way to release those poor souls you found trapped in the Reflectory first. You didn't fail – you helped us in many ways. If I was you, I'd check *The Book of Learning*.'

Doing as she was told, Ebony checked the inside cover. Everything looked the same, but then something caught her eye.

'The final year – 2015 – it's disappeared!'

Aunt Ruby's face relaxed then brightened with a huge smile.

'You mean … I've done it? I'm not going to die?'

Aunt Ruby nodded. 'You've broken the cycle. The future of the Order of Nine Lives is in your hands, Ebony.'

Uncle Cornelius gave a small howl of appreciation, and Winston did a little flip. But Ebony was filled with guilt. Her aunt had done all this to protect her even though she had done her best to alienate her.

'I'm sorry, Aunt Ruby. It was because of me that Zach hurt you so badly. *The Book of Learning* showed me him hitting you and even then I thought he was protecting me. I'm such an idiot.'

'I understand why you didn't trust us, Ebony. You were hurt and scared and Icarus didn't exactly help.' She glared at her brother. 'I can see how you thought Zach was your friend. He always was a charming boy, and none of us realised just how deeply involved he had become with the judge's schemes. No one blames you for being taken in by him.'

Her aunt's words didn't ease Ebony's guilt. 'What about poor Mulligan? I think I killed him – a large rock fell on his head when I blasted the cave to escape.'

'Oh, you don't need to worry about Mulligan; he's a hardy creature – there's hardly a scratch on him. He was a bit dazed is all. He's back in Oddley Cove, helping Old Joe and the others guard the gateway.'

Stunned, but thankful, Ebony didn't know what to say. She couldn't believe how wrong she'd been about Mulligan – and all of her Nine Lives family.

'I still don't understand how I got back here,' she said, searching out Icarus's eyes. 'Or you. I saw you – disappear.'

'The Reflectory,' said Aunt Ruby, 'is a sacred place. It regenerates life – it does not allow death. So when the gun went off, the Reflectory simply expelled the person that was hit by the bullet back to the normal world. It must have sent Icarus back to somewhere familiar, but you …?'

'I was touching Zach when the gun went off by accident. He wouldn't have dared use it after Icarus disappeared. It must have expelled us both.'

'It's a good job it did,' said Aunt Ruby. 'If the gun had been functioning properly you'd have been a goner.'

Ebony swallowed hard, pausing for a moment to try to find the right words. In the end, she blurted out what she wanted to say as best as she could. 'I'm sorry I put everyone in so much danger.'

Icarus gave her a forgiving smile. 'You've brought us closer in our mission than we've ever been before, Ebony,' he said. 'We have to close the gateway to the Reflectory for its own protection, but you can get us back in.'

'I can't. My rose … it turned bronze.' As Ebony took the rose out of her pocket to show everyone, Aunt Ruby gasped.

'It's better than I could ever have imagined,' she said, eyeing it carefully.

'But it's useless,' said Ebony.

'Useless? It's perfect. This means the sky world recognises you as the guardian – it's turned your rose permanent as a gift.

It will be easier for you to get into the Reflectory now, which is good because I suspect our work has only just begun.'

'Because I let Zach escape?' asked Ebony.

Winston ran up Ebony's arm and snuggled into her curls to comfort her. She laughed as his tail tickled her ear.

'No,' said Aunt Ruby. 'Because the judge still has friends and power – Zach is just one of his supporters. The judge needs to know that we will no longer stand for this. He needs to know that we're back in action – no more hiding.'

'Even if we had captured Zach, we'd still be at war,' added Icarus.

'War?' A chill ran down Ebony's spine. 'I thought we were going to make things better.'

'And so we will,' said Aunt Ruby. 'But things will have to get worse before they can improve. We have to figure out a way to return those souls to earth and increase our numbers so we can defeat our enemy. The judge – and Zach – won't let it happen without a fight. Your powers will grow as you get older, but having witnessed their determination, I doubt Zach or the judge will give up trying to swap souls that easily.'

'Then all of this was for nothing? It could still happen? I thought it would be fine now, that the Order would be saved.'

'It's not that simple, but now we have the tools to save it. Will you help us?'

Ebony didn't need to think twice.

'Yes. And I won't stop until we succeed.'

'Spoken like a true Smart,' said Icarus. 'Your grandpa would be very proud of you.'

Feeling her heart lighten, Ebony checked the gun in her pocket and headed to the window. Her hand splayed against the cool glass, she gazed out into the breaking dawn, certain she could hear the melancholy song of eight lost girls fading with the night.

Acknowledgements

With thanks to Mary Feehan and all at Mercier Press for seeing the potential in this trilogy, and to my lovely editors, Wendy Logue and Emma Dunne, for making *The Book of Learning* shelf-worthy. The beautiful cover is all down to Sarah O'Flaherty – isn't she wonderful?

Huge thanks go out to my agent, Sallyanne Sweeney, for being such a joy to work with and so full of grit – and to Vanessa O'Loughlin who paired us up in the first place and has remained a constant source of inspiration.

To all my writer friends who listened and understood, and all my non-writer friends who listened and nodded in the right places – you helped keep me sane and motivated. For that, I'll always be grateful.

But the biggest thanks of all go to my very supportive, very understanding husband, who has made more cups of tea than any person should ever have to make – and without whom none of this would be possible. Mick, you're awesome.

Follow E. R. Murray on
Twitter and Facebook at:

 @ermurray

 www.facebook.com/
ERMurray.Author

or check out her website:

www.ermurray.com